Cocktails and Cowardice

A Peridale Cafe MYSTERY

AGATHA FROST

Published by Pink Tree Publishing Limited in 2020

All characters and events in this publication, other than those clearly in the public domain, are fictitious and any resemblance to real persons, living or dead, is purely coincidental.

Copyright © Pink Tree Publishing Limited.

The moral right of the author has been asserted.

All rights reserved. This book or any portion thereof may not be reproduced or used in any manner whatsoever without the express written permission of the publisher except for the use of brief quotations in a book review.

For questions and comments about this book, please contact pinktreepublishing@gmail.com

www.pinktreepublishing.com
www.agathafrost.com

About This Book

Released: *April 28th 2020*
Words: *73,000*
Series: *Book 20 - Peridale Cozy Café Mystery Series*
Standalone: *Yes*
Cliff-hanger: *No*

Julia's memories of her great-aunt Minnie Harlow are vague at best. Despite annual birthday and Christmas cards throughout her childhood, Julia has never actually met the glamorous former model and actress, so she was more than a little surprised to find out her great-aunt was alive and well and living in the south of Spain.

Her surprise only grew when her gran, Dot, informed her that Minnie's boutique hotel, La Casa, which she ran with her daughter, Lisa, would be the stunning location of their much anticipated joint honeymoon along with Barker and Percy. Halfway through her pregnancy, Julia was looking forward to the sun, sea, alcohol-free sangria, and hopefully no sleuthing, and she also couldn't wait to get to know her distant relatives.

But their reunion and honeymoon quickly take a turn for the worse when they arrive in the gorgeous town of Savega nestled in the tree covered mountains. Savega has secrets, and Julia can smell them. Why is Minnie terrified of leaving her hotel? Why is Lisa pressuring her mother to sell? A ransom note, a stabbing, and suspected gang activity set Julia, and her private investigator husband, Barker, on their hardest and most personal case yet. Will they ever get to have the honeymoon they deserve?

WANT TO BE KEPT UP TO DATE WITH AGATHA FROST RELEASES? *SIGN UP THE FREE NEWSLETTER!*

www.AgathaFrost.com

You can also follow **Agatha Frost** across social media. Search 'Agatha Frost' on:

Facebook
Twitter
Goodreads
Instagram

ALSO BY AGATHA FROST

Claire's Candles
1. Vanilla Bean Vengeance
2. Black Cherry Betrayal
3. Coconut Milk Casualty

Peridale Cafe
1. Pancakes and Corpses
2. Lemonade and Lies
3. Doughnuts and Deception
4. Chocolate Cake and Chaos
5. Shortbread and Sorrow
6. Espresso and Evil
7. Macarons and Mayhem
8. Fruit Cake and Fear
9. Birthday Cake and Bodies
10. Gingerbread and Ghosts
11. Cupcakes and Casualties
12. Blueberry Muffins and Misfortune
13. Ice Cream and Incidents
14. Champagne and Catastrophes

15. Wedding Cake and Woes

16. Red Velvet and Revenge

17. Vegetables and Vengeance

18. Cheesecake and Confusion

19. Brownies and Bloodshed

20. Cocktails and Cowardice

1

JULIA

No matter the condition, the weather always provided an endless source of conversation amongst the regulars in Julia's café, and today had been no exception. Thanks to the morning news forecast of heavy rain before the end of the evening, no one had talked of anything else.

"It simply *cannot* rain!" Amy Clark, the church organist, had cried earlier that afternoon while fanning herself with one of Julia's laminated menus. "We're having the most *glorious* summer in years!"

"Decades," amended Shilpa Patil, the owner of the post office. "I blame global warming."

"*Thank* global warming!" Amy fired back. "I've never seen us all with such lovely tans."

"The tea leaves predicted the forecast would be incorrect," said Evelyn Wood, the mystic owner of the local B&B, "although, I'd quite like a *touch* of rain for my garden's sake. My poor flowers have never looked so dry."

And so the conversation had continued throughout the day. Some were adamant it couldn't possibly rain, while the rest begged for some relief from the heat.

While Julia most enjoyed her village during the summer months, this August had been one of the hottest on record. The heat wasn't as pleasant as usual while being twenty-one weeks pregnant. She wasn't sure how many more nights of waking up soaked in sweat she could take.

The fan balanced on the pile of books on Julia's coffee table swivelled past her face again. The breeze licked at her dampened chocolatey curls, threatening to send them springing out from behind her ears. Warm air poured through the open sitting room windows, dancing the net curtains enough to reveal the perfectly clear sky. Streaks of pink and orange already stained the horizon, but there wasn't a cloud in the sky to be seen. How could the day still be so hot this close to sunset?

Of course, in twelve hours, Julia would be on an aeroplane heading to Spain's southern coast, where the current temperature was somehow five degrees hotter than Peridale's sizzling thirty-one degrees celcius. If it weren't for Spain being more equipped to deal with the heat than the usually chilly island of Great Britain, she might have suggested they go somewhere cooler for their honeymoon. Thankfully, the boutique hotel they'd booked into had air conditioning throughout.

The fan shuddered around, teetering on the pile of hardbacks she'd pulled from Barker's collection of vintage mystery books. Though the placement had been meant to ensure the cooler air would hit her face with each pass, the top-heavy fan had tilted its face down until only her chin, the ends of her hair, and the old shoebox of cards and photographs on her lap felt it.

Too exhausted to move and tilt it back up, she slouched further into her favourite armchair by the fireplace, which hadn't been lit for months, and back into the stream of the fan's air. With her chin resting on her chest and her baby bump jutting upwards through one of the few vintage dresses that still fit twenty-one weeks into her pregnancy, she could only imagine how ridiculous she looked. The fan provided only minimal relief, but it was enough to justify her poor posture.

Turning her attention back to the shoebox, she plucked out another card. The front of the card, with a log cabin nestled in fluffy snow felt vaguely familiar and was enough to indicate it had been sent at Christmas, but nothing more concrete formed in her memories. The message inside was almost identical to the others: *To Julia. Merry Christmas. From your great-aunt Minnie.* There were no kisses or personalised messages in any of the tatty old cards, just the same generic phrases written in the same perfect swirly handwriting.

Julia hadn't thought about her great-aunt Minnie in years. She'd been an enigma throughout Julia's childhood – a glamorous model and actress who sent Christmas and birthday cards every year until Julia's mid-teens. Each came with a cheque for ten pounds, and more bizarrely, a modelling headshot.

They had never met in person, and yet Julia had a collection of at least two dozen signed headshots of the woman. She hadn't remembered their existence until her gran recently unearthed the box from a dusty corner of her attic where it had lived for the best part of three decades.

"You *must* remember your great-aunt Minnie!" Dot had said when she'd handed over the shoebox. "She's your grandfather's younger sister."

In Julia's defence, Grandfather Albert died in 1974, five years before her birth. According to Dot, Minnie left the village almost immediately after to pursue her dreams of becoming a star, and she hadn't been back since. The vague cards and gloriously 1980s photographs were all Julia had to work on.

After the surprise of remembering her great-aunt's existence had worn off, Julia was doubly surprised to learn Minnie was now living in the south of Spain, where she owned a small boutique hotel with her daughter, Lisa – yet another relative Julia hadn't known existed.

The surprise only grew when Julia learned that this

boutique hotel owned by mysterious relatives was where she and Barker were going to be spending their honeymoon. Not that they were going alone; Dot and her new husband, Percy, were joining them.

Dot had insisted on sorting out every detail of the two-week honeymoon. Even though her initial plan, which included a five-star resort in the Canary Islands, had changed when Minnie reached out after so many years, the alteration didn't trouble Julia. She'd looked up Minnie's hotel, La Casa, online, and it seemed like the perfect place for a relaxing holiday.

"Wow, is that her?" asked Jessie, Julia's nineteen-year-old adopted daughter, when she finally came in from sunbathing in the back garden. "What's wrong with her hair? She looks like she sucked her finger and shoved it in a socket."

"It was the 80s." Julia chuckled, turning the photograph over, where the handwritten date confirmed it was taken in 1984. "The makeup was loud, and the hair louder still."

Jessie collapsed onto the sofa and took the stack of glossy signed pictures from Julia. She flicked through them, her eyes popping out of her face as though she had never seen anything so outrageous. Jessie's personal style had once comprised of only black hoodies, baggy jeans, and Doc Martens. However, the older she got, the more it evolved. Recently, she'd cut her long, dark hair even shorter, to just above her jaw, and dyed the tips ice blonde. She now wore less black in favour of paler shades. Her usually milky complexion had a warm, olive glow, bringing out faint freckles across her nose and cheeks, thanks to the weather.

"Absolutely ridiculous," Jessie said, tossing the pictures onto the coffee table and narrowly missing the stack of books holding up the fan. "I guess she's sorta kinda my great-great-aunt?"

"Sorta kinda."

"Isn't it going to be weird meeting her for the first time *and* staying in her hotel?" Jessie asked, stretching out and yawning. "She must be properly ancient."

"I think she's in her early seventies."

"Like I said, properly ancient."

"Well, I'm looking forward to it." Julia placed the shoebox on the side table and picked up her leftover peppermint tea. "Not only am I looking forward to having a break from the village—"

"Who are you, and what have you done with my mother?" Jessie cut in, arching a brow. "You were only saying this afternoon how much you were going to miss the café."

"And I will." Julia rested her hand on her bump and gave it a soft rub. "But I'm also aware that I'm now halfway through this little one growing inside me, and he or she will be here before I know it. People have been warning me for weeks to 'enjoy the calm while I can', so I intend to. Besides, you've looked after the place on your own enough times now. I trust you with the café."

"Can I get that in writing?"

"Very funny." Julia pulled the cushion from underneath her back and tossed it at Jessie. "But yes, I'm looking forward to the holiday, and I'm looking forward to getting to know Minnie properly. And Lisa, for that matter. She's around my age. According to the internet, she's my first cousin once removed, and before you ask, I have no idea what that means, but they're family. That's all that matters."

"Get them to like you, and we can have free holidays for life." Jessie leaned into the fan and tilted it until the cold air hit both of them; since Jessie slouched all the time naturally, Julia remained as she was. "Where's that husband of yours, anyway? I'm starving. He went to pick up Chinese food nearly an hour ago."

"Good point." Julia reached for her phone, which had been facedown on the side table and no doubt set to silent. "Oh, three missed calls and a text message. 'Sorry, had to rush off to do one last thing for Mrs Morton. She's paying me triple time. Promise it's the last thing for the next two weeks. Will be back tonight.' Oh."

"So, no Chinese?"

"I guess not." Julia quickly replied and let him know there was no problem. "I haven't been shopping since we won't be here, but there's frozen pizza in the freezer?"

"Life's too short for frozen pizza, Mum." Jessie pulled her phone from her pocket. "Leave it with me."

Forty minutes later, a fresh pizza arrived as the last of the light faded from the sky. The sun slipping over the horizon took some heat with it, but the air left behind was still thick and humid.

They ate pizza while watching an old repeat of *Who Wants to Be a Millionaire?* By the time the last contestant, fifty-seven-year-old Steve from Wiltshire, walked home with only £8,000 because he didn't know that 'Funny Spice' wasn't a member of the Spice Girls, Jessie was yawning every couple of minutes and clearly ready for bed.

"Don't get up," Jessie said, taking the last slice of pizza as she stood. "I can't bear those groaning sounds you make every time you get out of a chair these days."

"My middle doesn't move like it used to." Julia pulled herself upright from her slouch, resisting the urge to grunt or groan. "You try having a belly this big."

"I'm alright, thanks." Jessie leaned in and kissed her on the cheek. "Have a nice honeymoon and all that. Send a postcard, if those are still a thing. And don't worry about anything here. For the next two weeks, Peridale doesn't exist for you. I've got it all covered. The café, Mowgli, your plants. It'll all be here in one piece when you get back."

"I have complete faith in you."

"I'm glad one of us does." Jessie winked. "Kidding, of course."

Jessie tossed her denim backpack over her shoulder and headed for the door with one final wave. Julia thought she was going to leave without following through with her usual routine, but Jessie stopped and popped her head into the guest room, as usual. It hadn't been Jessie's bedroom since she moved into the small flat above the post office next to the café five months earlier, but she still looked in every time she stopped by. Not much had changed, except the addition of boxes of flatpack nursery furniture Barker had been promising he'd put up for weeks. Julia had also thrown paint samples on the wall. They had yet to decide on a shade of yellow.

For the next few hours, Julia pottered around the cottage packing up the last of her holiday things, one eye always on her watch. She'd grown used to Barker's late-night investigations since the start of his private investigation business earlier in the summer. He'd already had a handful of small local cases, although Mrs Morton had been the most demanding of them. She also happened to be the wealthiest, and it seemed she'd pay any price to prove her suspicions of her husband's infidelity.

Julia tried to force herself to stay awake for Barker. Still, when the hands slipped past midnight, she drifted off in the armchair with another *Millionaire?* repeat playing in the background.

A little after one in the morning, a key slotting into the front door stirred her from her light sleep.

"Don't get up," Barker whispered, kissing her on top of the head, a bunch of red roses in his hand. "I'm so sorry I'm this late. Mr Morton has had quite a night of it."

"It's alright." Julia rubbed her eyes and sat up as much as she could. "Have you proved Mrs Morton's theory?"

"Not quite." He handed over the flowers. "But I think he might have a serious gambling addiction. Followed him to two different casinos in the city, and it looked like he was kicked out of both. You go back to sleep, and I'll quickly pack my case."

Julia placed the flowers on the coffee table and followed Barker into their bedroom. Both their cases were open at the bottom of the bed, already neatly packed. Mowgli, their grey Maine Coon, was fast asleep in a tight ball inside Barker's fully packed case.

"You didn't have to." Barker pulled her into a hug. "Have I told you I love you lately?"

"I was happy to do it." She yawned, resting her head against his shirt and tie. "One of us has to be organised."

"Well, from this moment on," Barker said, tugging his tie away from his collar, "Barker Brown, PI is clocking off, and Barker Brown, Husband Extraordinaire is clocking in. No more work. We're going to have the best honeymoon anyone has—"

Barker's phone rang and vibrated between them. He smiled apologetically and pulled away. Neither seemed surprised to see 'Mrs Morton' on the screen.

"Right after this phone call," Barker said, closing one eye, his finger hovering over the green answer button. "Do you mind?"

"Of course not."

Barker hurried into the hallway, and while he attempted to appease Mrs Morton, Julia changed into her pyjamas. She climbed into bed, her alarm already set to 5 A.M. for their 6 A.M. taxi pick-up. Mowgli curled himself up against her belly, and as she drifted off for a second time that night, she heard the promised rain finally pattering softly against the bedroom window.

2

DOT

As it had been years since Dot last flew, she hadn't expected to be so fascinated by aviation. She had barely taken her eyes away from the small window for most of the flight.

"This is wholly unnatural," she whispered to her husband, Percy, sitting next to her in the middle seat of the row of three. "We shouldn't be this high up, and yet here we are."

"Marvellous invention, don't you think, my dear?"

"Quite."

After leaving an England encased in clouds thanks to the sudden influx of rain, they flew over the tip of France, a stretch of uninterrupted ocean, and finally, over mainland Spain. Some of the views were blocked by white fluffy clouds, but when those clouds broke, Dot could see right down to the land below. The view terrified and captivated her in equal measures. As much as she loved her husband, she was glad he hadn't put up a fight for the window seat.

Dot's eardrums told her they had been descending ever since they broke away from the southern coast of Spain to head back over the ocean. The water below was calm and apparently never-ending, the deep navy blue dotted with defined patches so vibrant they glowed turquoise.

"Tray tables up, please," the smiley stewardess said as she walked backwards down the narrow aisle collecting any last rubbish in a large bag.

Dot passed down the small bottle of wine they'd shared from little plastic cups. Quite uncivilised, she had thought when the cabin crew handed them over, especially since she'd upgraded to premium economy. Of course, she'd soon learned 'premium' meant only a little extra space for her feet and nothing more.

"Shame we never got to finish our game," Percy said as she gathered up the cards from their abandoned poker match. "I was sure I had a winning hand this time."

Dot wasn't. She'd been trying to teach Percy how to play poker for weeks, but he had yet to win a single game. Much to her shock, she was actually growing bored of always winning – but not *quite* tired enough to tell him about the subtle earlobe-tugging tell every time he attempted to bluff.

"I glanced at your cards when you went to the bathroom," Dot said as she fastened the tray against the seat in front of her. "A decent hand, but mine was better."

"You're so good at everything, my dear." Percy sighed, also tucking up his table. "I fear I may never be a worthy opponent."

"We've got two weeks of practice ahead of us."

"That is true."

"I'll make a poker player of you yet." Dot winked and patted his exposed knee; he'd changed into his tropical floral shorts at the airport. "Maybe we can get Minnie in on the action and up the stakes a little? I'm tired of playing for chocolate buttons and toothpicks."

"Did you used to play poker with her?"

"Oh, yes." Dot reached into the carry-on bag tucked under the seat in front of her and pulled out the small, leather photo album she'd recently spent a lot of time poring over. "We had quite the little routine."

Dot flicked through the faded photographs of parties, birthdays, and Christmases, mostly covering the early seventies up until her dear Albert's tragic passing halfway through the decade. Back then, she'd always had a camera in her hand. She'd been as fascinated with capturing every moment as the younger generation seemed to be with taking pictures on their phones. However, she'd never felt the urge to snap a photo of her dinner before eating it.

"Those were the days," she said wistfully. "I suppose Albert and I were around forty. Brian had grown up and left the house, and life was settling into a nice rhythm."

"And Minnie was a decade younger?"

Dot nodded. "While her husband, Bernard Harlow, was a decade older than Albert and me, so you can imagine the scandal *that* caused in the village. They seemed happy enough."

"And Bernard is the husband who died recently?" Percy asked, fiddling with his glasses as he examined a photograph of the four of them playing poker around the same dining room table that still took pride of place in her cottage today. "The television director?"

"Minnie divorced Bernard not long after my Albert passed," Dot reminded him, having already told the story several times. She could hardly blame him; Minnie's love life was complicated. "She kept his name, though. Minnie Harlow had more of an actress flair than Minnie South, or whatever her later married names were. She had four husbands, but the most recent was the one she'd settled down with."

"Still time to find a fifth." Percy chuckled. "We've proven that."

"Bernard promised he'd get me a walk-on part as an extra on *Coronation Street*." Dot flicked to another page, showing the four of them on the set of the soap. "All fell through when they broke up. Poor fella. Minnie kept his name and took him to the cleaners in the divorce, but I supposed that's how she could afford to jet around the world for her modelling and acting jobs. He died not long after from a heart attack. He did like his steaks and red wine."

"Oh, dear."

"Isn't Minnie fabulous?" Dot landed on one of the early 80s headshots that had come in Minnie's annual Christmas cards, all autographed, of course. "I have absolutely no idea what she looks like now. I should have asked her to send a recent photograph. What if I don't recognise her at the airport?"

"Perhaps she'll look the same, as you do, dear?" Percy patted her hand. "As beautiful now as you were then."

Dot smiled and pushed up her curls at the back. Her personal style hadn't changed much. Her hair was still short and neatly curled, and she still favoured simple white blouses tucked into high-waisted pleated skirts.

Over the years, this had become what Dot liked to call an all-weather outfit. On its own, it was the perfect uniform for spring and summer. An added cardigan and a pair of thick tights, and it was ready for autumn and winter. All that, and comfortable enough to wear in a tiny aeroplane seat.

"Well, I doubt Minnie is still sporting the giant backcombed hair." Dot flicked to another picture showing Minnie with bright pink blush and heavily mascaraed lashes that made her crystal blue eyes pop. Albert's eyes had been the same. "It's a shame we lost contact for so long. A forgotten Christmas card here, a missed phone call there, and next thing you know, you've all lost touch."

"We're here now." Percy gave her arm a subtle nudge. "Two weeks is plenty of time to get caught up."

"But is it enough to turn you into a decent poker player?"

Percy laughed as Dot glanced back two rows. Julia and Barker were on the other side of the plane, still buried in the books they'd been reading for most of the two-and-a-half-hour flight. She'd tried to have them all sat next to each other, but there had only been two premium economy seats left when they checked in, and they hadn't seemed too bothered about the upgrade. Perhaps they'd known the extra twenty pounds for a little more foot room wasn't worth it.

The plane banked hard left, sending Percy into Dot's side. When they finally levelled out again, the view was no longer the sprawling ocean. They were heading back to the coast they'd just left, flying the lowest they'd been since take off.

In fact, Dot was sure they were far too close to the ground, but she kept her concerns to herself. The cabin crew didn't seem panicked, so she didn't intend to make a fool of herself

They continued descending towards the coastline. Dot saw people sunbathing on the beach below. Beyond them, clusters of white buildings with terracotta roofs were sprinkled amongst the trees of Andalusia. According to Minnie's letters, Andalusia was a region of hills, rivers, and farmland bordering Spain's southern coast. She'd promised it was the most beautiful region of Spain, and even from up above, Dot couldn't disagree. She hadn't expected so much greenery, but it was everywhere.

They whizzed over the beach, and just when Dot was sure they would crash into one of the hills and go up in a giant fireball, the traditional buildings became much more modern and corporate-looking. A runway appeared in front of them, easing Dot's worries.

"Hold on tight, Dorothy." Percy looped his fingers through hers. "This bit's always bumpy."

They hovered over the runway for an impossible amount of time before the wheels finally bounced onto the tarmac. Then they zoomed ahead, forcing Dot back into her chair. She glanced back at Barker and Julia again. They were holding hands and laughing, just like she and Percy. A couple of people started clapping, but Dot wouldn't be partaking in that. She didn't applaud when a bus arrived on time, so she wasn't about to start for a plane.

Premium economy was right at the front of the aircraft, so they were amongst the first off. They thanked the pilot and disembarked, waiting at the top of the tunnel for Julia and Barker to appear.

"Everything okay?" Dot asked, nodding down at

Julia's stomach as they walked up the tunnel towards the terminal.

"I think so," she replied, resting her hand on the pretty little bump. "Didn't notice anything, actually, and the seatbelt fit perfectly. I think I was more comfortable than Barker."

Barker rubbed at his side. "Guy next to me seemed to think my ribs were the perfect place for his elbow."

In Dot's opinion – obviously, the only one that mattered – Julia and Barker were perfect for each other. Not only were they age-appropriate, but they also seemed to want the same things out of life. If Julia had never fallen pregnant, it wouldn't have ruined her life. Still, Dot knew how desperately her eldest granddaughter had always wanted to have a baby of her own one day.

Although, thinking back to the photo album, Julia was almost at the age she and Albert had been, and she couldn't imagine starting over with a new baby at that age. It would have made Albert's passing far more complicated. The mid-to-late 1970s were still a blur.

A quick flash of their burgundy British passports was enough for border control to wave them through. Dot had always thought she was too old for the jet-set life, but the flight had been so easy and smooth, she could get used to the idea of annual, or maybe even more frequent, holidays abroad.

Unlike the semi-rural and natural view that had

greeted them on their descent to the runway, the airport looked as though it could have belonged to any country. The ceilings were high, the floors tiled, and the air crisp and conditioned.

"What are the odds!" Percy cried as they walked to the carousel. "Our cases are already circling around!"

Barker retrieved all four and loaded them onto a trolley as Dot pulled Minnie's final letter from her handbag. She'd instructed them to wait in front of the airport, where she'd pick them up and drive them to the small town of Savega, and her hotel.

After quickly using the bathroom facilities, the four of them made their way to the clearly marked exit. The front doors slid open, and the heat hit Dot like a slap in the face. She'd grown used to the recent heatwave gripping Peridale. Still, even that hadn't prepared her for the reality of the Spanish summer.

"Heaven's above!" Percy cried, pulling a handkerchief from his pocket and running it over his glistening bald head. "I think someone's left the heating on."

"Certainly toasty." Julia fanned at her bright pink face with her passport. "Have any idea what Minnie's car looks like?"

Dot scanned the letter. "She simply said she'd be here when we landed. I gave her all our flight information, and we're right on time, so I suspect she'll be here any minute."

Any minute now turned into five, and then ten. By

the fifteenth, Barker and Julia retreated into the terminal to partake of the cooler air. By the twentieth, Percy had sat down on his case – and promptly fell asleep leaning against a post, his canvas hat covering his face. After a full half-hour, Dot began to wonder if the whole thing had been an elaborate prank played by someone who knew about her connection to Minnie.

"I don't believe it," Dot whispered, squinting as a slightly rundown car pulled up in front of the airport. "That's impossible."

"Huh?" Percy jolted awake. "What is it, dear?"

Dot pulled the photo album from her handbag and turned pages until she landed on a photograph of Minnie, pre-modelling, with curlier and less backcombed brunette hair. Her gaze flicked between the picture and the woman behind the wheel of the car. They looked identical – as if no time had passed at all.

"Dorothy South?" the woman called, shielding her eyes from the sun as she climbed out of the car.

"*Minnie!*" Dot couldn't help but laugh. "Look at you! You haven't aged a—"

"Oh!" The woman laughed, shaking her head as she slammed the car door. "I'm Lisa. Minnie's daughter."

The closer Lisa got, the more foolish Dot felt. Clearly no older than forty-five, this woman could never be mistaken for someone in her seventies. Still, the resemblance was striking, almost eerie.

"People always tell me I look just like my mum from

her younger days." Lisa pulled Dot into a hug immediately. "It's so nice to finally meet you, Auntie Dorothy. Mum's told me so much about you. You look as exactly as I imagined you would." She let go and extended a hand to Percy, who'd pushed himself up from the suitcase. "And this must be Percival. It's a pleasure to meet you."

"Percy's just fine." He took her hand and gave it a hearty shake. "Dot's right, you're the spitting image of your mother! Uncanny."

"Where is she?" Dot asked, looking towards the car.

"Back at the hotel," Lisa explained. "She's not up to driving much these days. Doesn't like the steep roads. So I offered to come and get you. Sorry for the delay. Someone's chickens got loose and were blocking the road out of town."

"Spain has chickens?" Percy tapped a finger against his chin. "How interesting!"

The airport doors slid open and Julia and Barker rejoined them. After another round of introductions, Barker and Lisa loaded the cases into the car's large boot, and they set off.

With all four windows rolled down, they whizzed away from the airport. On the ground, things were even greener than they'd looked from the sky. Perhaps these roads were like the roads anywhere else in the world, but the crystal blue sky and lush trees made everything look so exotic. If the motorways back home looked like this, Dot might not have minded venturing out of the village more often, if only to enjoy the view.

"Not much farther," Lisa explained as she pulled off the main road and onto a narrower, more rural looking one. "Savega is in the foot of the Sierra de Almijara mountain range. The view is about to get really interesting."

The flat, straight roads became steep and twisting, and Dot was more than aware of how high up they were actually driving. The lanes wrapped around the hills and breaks in the trees showed small settlements here and there. When things eventually levelled out again, Percy tapped her and nodded through the window on the other side.

"Wow," Dot gasped, looking down the slope of white buildings amongst the trees, which seemed to go all the way down to the sea. "Minnie wasn't lying about this place."

They vanished into the trees again, and when they came out, they entered a small town, which Dot assumed was Savega. The roads narrowed until they were almost alleyways, twisting every which way. They drove through a crowded backstreet market filled with clothes and food stalls, coming out into a large square with a central water fountain.

"This is the main plaza," Lisa explained as they crawled along at a snail's pace to avoid the hundreds of people milling around. "You're going to find a good mix of locals and tourists here. The hotel is all-inclusive, but if you fancy a bite to eat out one night, I can recommend some great restaurants and cafés."

They entered another system of tight alleyways, the white-painted buildings tall on either side as they twisted deeper into the town. There were balconies with clothes hanging over them, and some people high up were even sitting out in the sun. After a couple of minutes, the car slid to a halt and Lisa finally yanked up the handbrake. Dot ducked to see where they were, wondering how the hotel from the pictures could be tucked away down such a shady back alley.

"Don't worry," Lisa said, smiling through the rear-view mirror at Dot as though she could sense her reservations. "Don't let the entrance fool you."

Promising she'd bring their cases in later, Lisa motioned for them to enter ahead of her. The hotel entrance, which looked a little more basic than the stylish boutique hotel she'd expected, was down four terracotta-tiled steps. They passed tall palm tree plants, as well as an extensive menu for what appeared to be a public restaurant within the hotel.

Julia and Barker entered first, with Percy and Dot following. The softly air-conditioned air hit Dot's warm face and her misgivings melted away instantly. Lisa had been right, the entrance was deceptive.

"Look at that view, Dorothy!" Percy gasped, his hand slipping around hers. "Can you believe it?"

Dot couldn't. While Julia and Barker lingered by the reception desk, Dot let the view pull her in. She walked through a large dining room and then a sunroom before emerging onto the large terrace. Though she registered the generously sized pool and even a hot tub, neither interested her just then. She walked right up to the black railing, the only thing separating her from the miles and miles of greenery ahead. A valley dipped down away from the railing, sloping up to a tree-covered mountain. There were the odd clusters of white buildings poking out here and there, but the landscape had remained mostly untouched. They were right on the edge of one of the most beautiful views Dot had seen with her two eyes. The plaza and tight streets felt like they belonged to a different place entirely.

"As I live and breathe!" a voice called from behind her. "Is that Dorothy South I see before me?"

Dot tore her gaze away from the view as the familiar voice called to her through the decades. Her ears knew precisely who it belonged to, although when she turned, her eyes didn't find Minnie amongst the faces of the few people lounging in the sun on the terrace beds.

"*Dorothy!*" An elderly woman with a short and wide constitution similar to Percy's rose from a sunbed. She had a mop of thick grey hair, a round face, and deeply tanned skin. She wore a leopard-print kaftan, sandals, and thick bangles on either wrist, and she looked absolutely nothing like the image of Minnie Dot had in her mind, even though the voice was the same. "Would you look at that! Somehow you avoided the middle-age spread. You look fantastic!"

"And you look . . ." Dot's voice trailed off as the short woman pulled her into a tight hug. "You look so different!"

Minnie pulled away and held Dot at arm's length. Up close, there was some resemblance buried somewhere in her plump and aged features. Still, the eyes were the biggest giveaway. While paler than the photographs in the album showed, they were still the same crystal blue eyes she had shared with her brother.

"Minnie," Dot said finally, relaxing a little. "It really is you. How many years has it been?"

"Far too many, my dear sister-in-law." Minnie looked her up and down again. "Welcome to La Casa! It translates as 'home', and I want you to take that as literally as possible while you're here." She looped her arm through Dot's and led her back into the sunroom. "I think it's time for a cocktail and a nice catchup, don't you?"

Dot glanced back at the view and nodded for Percy to follow. There was no other place, with any other people, she'd rather be at that moment.

3

JULIA

*A*fter a generously laid out three-course dinner, they spent the rest of the evening on the terrace listening to Dot and Minnie reminisce about old times while the sun set over the gorgeous valley. The sangria flowed late into the night, although in Julia's case, she'd settled for an equally delicious mocktail version, which suited her fine.

Not only was Lisa the one to cook and serve the whole meal, but she also made and served their drinks all night, only briefly lingering to listen to her mother regale tales of her modelling and acting days. Julia had been under the impression that the hotel belonged to her great-aunt, but it seemed Lisa was the one running the day-to-day business. Julia didn't get to talk with Lisa much, but that was mainly because Minnie was fantastic at holding court.

Splayed out on a chaise lounge in her leopard-print kaftan with a never-empty glass of sangria in hand, Minnie told stories of skiing with Paul McCartney in the Alps, dinner in France with Rick Astley, shopping with Joan and Jackie Collins in Italy, helicopter rides with Meatloaf over the Grand Canyon, and even lunch with Princess Diana in London. They were wild and fantastical tales, all with more twists and turns than most Hollywood movies.

Whether they were incredibly genuine or wholly made up, Julia didn't care. Dot had promised that Minnie was always a lot of fun, and it seemed the years hadn't dimmed her shine in the slightest – even if she no longer resembled the glamour-puss from the photographs.

When Julia and Barker fell into bed in the early hours of the morning, she fell asleep instantly, with a smile on her face. She didn't set the alarm, and she awoke still smiling the next morning. Julia had no idea how many hours she'd slept, but it felt like the best night's sleep of her life.

Stretching out, she rolled over to wrap herself around her husband on the first morning of their honeymoon. Her arm hit fresh – and very empty – air. She sat up, and a vision of her wild, matted hair greeted her in the dressing table mirror at the foot of the bed.

She scanned the room and spotted Barker out on the

small balcony. He was slouched on one plastic chair with his feet up on another in nothing more than his underwear and reading glasses. With a book in his lap and against the backdrop of the valley, he looked like he'd been ripped from the pages of a travel brochure.

"How long have you been up?" Julia asked when she joined him. "I slept like a baby."

"Me too." Barker left his book and stood behind her as she took in the view, his hands naturally drifting down to the bump. "I think I have that holiday feeling people always talk about. I don't know what it is, but I don't think I ever want to it leave."

"I think it's called *relaxation*."

"Never heard of it." He laughed. "Mrs Morton started calling me from six this morning, so I turned my phone off. Who knew you could just . . . do that?"

"Be careful, Barker Brown." She turned to face him with a playful smile. "Your sparkling reputation as the village's hottest new PI might sour."

"Let it." He winked. "Fancy going down for breakfast? You woke up just in time."

After a quick shower, Julia threw her hair up into a damp ponytail, put on her two-piece swimming costume, and tossed a floor length maxi dress over the top. Loose and flowy, it was nothing like her vintage dresses back home, but maxi-dresses were all she'd brought outside of some t-shirts and shorts. It would never have crossed her mind to buy them, but her more fashion-conscious sister, Sue, had insisted they were a 'must' for a stylish holiday. She'd claimed they transitioned seamlessly from day to night depending on how she 'styled' them. While Julia didn't quite know what that meant, she liked how she looked in the blue tie-dyed number she'd chosen for the day. The burst of dye fanned out from her belly button, creating an optical illusion that made her bump look almost invisible from the front. A quick turn to the side confirmed that it was still there, bigger every time she looked in a mirror.

Strangely, she'd never liked her body more.

"Here they are!" Minnie announced when they walked into the dining room. "Come! Sit! Have some breakfast!"

Dot and Percy were already there. They had glasses of orange juice and cups of tea, and they were working their way through a stack of wholemeal toast and half a dozen different pots of jam. Dot wore her usual uniform, but Percy had opted for a bright cotton shirt the same shade of red as his round spectacles, which he'd paired with loose cream trousers. A straw fedora adorned his bald head, a pair of silver aviators hung from his left breast pocket, and a yellow pocket square poked out from the other. He was the personification of a holiday.

"How did you both sleep?" Minnie asked, ushering them into seats on the other side of the large round table. "Was everything to your liking?"

"It was all perfect," Julia replied, sitting. "Thank you."

"I'm glad to hear it." Minnie slathered a glob of soft butter onto a slice of toast. "Breakfast is all self-service. Continental style, I think they call it, but I've lived on the continent for so long, I can scarcely remember how anywhere else does it. Help yourselves, and if there's nothing to your liking, I'm sure Lisa wouldn't mind whipping something up."

Having only just sat down, they stood again and walked over to the buffet table. There was a selection of mini boxed cereals, several different types of bread for toasting, and a large selection of small pots of jam for spreading. There were also croissants, a cold meat and cheese platter, a large bowl of fruit salad, pots for making tea, a filter coffee pot, jugs of orange juice, and even a varied offering of individually wrapped teabags. Julia was pleased to find peppermint was one of the options.

For the first day, at least, Julia kept things simple and opted for a croissant and a small bowl of corn flakes. Barker, on the other hand, piled up his plate with a little of everything. She almost pointed out that they had nearly a fortnight ahead of them to sample the lot, but she held her tongue. They were on holiday, after all, and if Barker wanted to eat everything in sight for two weeks, so be it.

"We were just talking about how we're going to

spend the day," Dot said when they returned with their breakfast. "Minnie thinks we should all stay in the hotel and relax, but Percy and I think it would be a good idea to get our bearings and explore the town."

"Why do you want to go out *there?*" Minnie laughed, tossing her arms out. "The view is in *here!* Relax, Dorothy. You never could sit still."

"Says the woman who's travelled the globe twice over," Dot pointed out.

"For work." Minnie wafted her hand before taking another bite of her buttery toast. "Everything you could possibly want is right here, and if it's not, Lisa will happily go out and get it for you."

Julia looked around for Lisa, surprised to find she wasn't eating breakfast with them. She spotted her out on the terrace, skimming leaves from the surface of the pool. Did she do everything on her own? Julia had yet to see any other staff.

"I would like to explore a little," Dot said, a little more firmly this time. "Get the holiday shopping out the way early, as it were. There's plenty of people to buy for back home, and I saw quite a few shops on the way in."

"Fine." Minnie huffed. "But be careful, will you? We've had some . . . trouble, as of late."

Julia and Barker glanced at each other, and so did Dot and Percy.

"Trouble?" Barker asked.

"Yes, trouble." Minnie squirmed in her seat, her finger circling the rim of her glass of orange juice. "It's nothing to worry about. Things have just gone a little strange lately, but hasn't the whole world?" She scratched at her mop of grey hair before looking around. "Where's that daughter of mine got to? *Lisa?*"

Lisa abandoned her pool cleaning, walking through the sunroom and into the dining room. She didn't rush, but she also didn't push forward a smile until her mother could see her.

"Yes, Mother?"

"Be a dear and get me some more toast, would you?" Minnie handed over her plate. "Some of that new wholemeal. It's rather lovely."

Lisa took the plate and walked to the buffet without question. Julia and Barker glanced at each other with the same perplexed look they'd shared only moments earlier. Julia could tell they were thinking the same thing: was there something wrong with Minnie's legs?

Lisa returned with the toast before getting back to work on the terrace, and the conversation drifted to Minnie's memories of Peridale, which didn't sound like it had changed all that much since she left. Minnie announced she was full after a couple of bites and pushed the plate away before glugging down more orange juice. The conversation shifted from Peridale back to Minnie's adventures as a model, this time featuring her escapades around Paris in the summer of 1988.

By the time Julia finished her breakfast, she was starting to understand precisely what made Minnie the type of woman who would send her distant relative twice-annual autographed headshots.

"Right." Dot slapped her knees and stood when Minnie paused for breath. "Time to go exploring, don't you think, Percy?"

"Right you are, dear." Percy wiped the crumbs from his lips and joined Dot in standing. "Are you two tagging along?"

Julia and Barker shared yet another glance, and once again, she was sure she could read her husband's mind.

"I think we're going to have a lazy day by the pool," Julia said, offering an apologetic smile. "Get some reading in, have a little dip, enjoy the view."

"That's the spirit!" Minnie clapped her hands together and looked around again. "Where's that daughter of mine? I'll get her to pop up a parasol so you can have some shade, considering your current condition. *Lisa?*"

"Suit yourselves." Dot pursed her lips as she checked her watch. "Shan't be long. Should be back before lunch. C'mon, Percy. Let's make ourselves useful."

"Right you are, dear."

Dot pecked Julia on the cheek as she left, and Percy tipped his straw hat. Minnie rushed off to find Lisa – no doubt to give her more tasks – proving her legs did, in fact, work perfectly fine. When they were alone, Barker held Julia's hand under the table.

"Would it be greedy of me to have a second go around the breakfast buffet?" Barker asked, his eyes already fixed on the food. "I should be full, but there are croissants, and croissants are . . . well, they are *croissants,* which means they must be eaten."

"You're on holiday."

"It would be rude not to, wouldn't it?" Barker let go of her hand and stood. "Want anything?"

"I'm eating for two," she said, shaking her head, "not two hundred."

While Barker filled his plate for the second time, Julia watched Lisa drag a parasol from the sunroom onto the terrace by the pool. At the same time, Minnie stood and admired the view. When it was set up, Minnie marched back into the dining room, her kaftan billowing out behind her.

"I'll get Lisa in here to clear this lot away," Minnie said, almost to herself. "*Lisa?*"

"It's alright." Julia started gathering the plates. "I don't mind. I run a café back in the—"

"No." Minnie pulled the plates from Julia and put them back onto the table before craning her neck to look out of the open doors into the sunroom. "You're on holiday. *Lisa?* Would you come in here and get this table cleared away?"

Minnie turned around to smile at Julia as though she'd just done a great thing. While it wasn't Julia's place to judge their relationship and how they ran the hotel, she couldn't imagine being half so demanding of Jessie. Even when the café was packed to capacity, she never asked Jessie to do something she couldn't or wouldn't do herself, if she could.

"Ah!" Minnie clapped her hands together, looking towards the reception area. "*Rodger!* How long have you been stood there?" She tapped Julia's shoulder and nodded for her to follow. "Come, Julia. You *must* meet Rodger. He's a fellow ex-pat. He's been running the hotel next door for the past few years."

Minnie scooped her hand around Julia's and dragged her through to the reception foyer, where a short and slender man with combed-over hair and large glasses was waiting with a crate of what appeared to be straw. He wore a neatly pressed beige linen suit, which fit him like a glove.

"*Rodger!*" Minnie air-kissed both his cheeks. "Are those the eggs I ordered?"

"The full dozen, and freshly laid," he said in one of the poshest accents Julia had ever heard. He tilted the box to show the brown eggs hidden in the straw. "Frittatas again tonight?"

"You know I love them." Minnie placed Julia in front of Rodger. "I'd like you to meet my great-niece, Julia. She and her husband, and my former sister-in-law, and *her* new husband are staying for the fortnight."

"Almost a full house?" he said, smiling ear to ear at Julia. "It's a pleasure to meet you. How are you finding our little town?"

"So far, so good."

"Best kept secret in all of Spain," he said in a lower voice, flashing a wink over his glasses as he put the box on the counter. "Although, between us, I think the word may have slipped out. It's absolute pandemonium out there! Could barely get through the plaza when I picked up my paper this morning."

"Oh, dear." Minnie sighed and leaned against the reception desk. "You know I like to stay inside. I can't be dealing with all of that."

"It's good for business though, Minnie," he said like it was something he'd been reminding her of for some time. "I've not had room to spare all season. It's marvellous."

"Hmmm." Minnie glanced over her shoulder into the almost empty dining room. "I was never a fan of the full vacancy weeks. How are the chickens?"

"Splendid as usual."

"Rodger keeps chickens," Minnie explained to Julia. "Wouldn't buy our eggs from anywhere else. The ones from the supermarket just don't compare."

"You can't beat fresh, Minnie." Rodger pulled back the sleeve of his jacket to check his watch before offering his hand to Julia. "Must dash! I've already been gone for too long." He shook Julia's hand, resting the other on top before offering the same to Minnie. "A pleasure as always, Minnie. You let me know if you need any more eggs. They're always laying."

"That's because you treat them like queens." Minnie again kissed the air to either side of his face. "He's given them all names, haven't you?"

"Happy hens lay more eggs," he said with a laugh. "Right, must be off! Enjoy your day, the both of you."

When he left, Julia re-joined Barker. He had already finished his second helping of breakfast and was now sunbathing on the terrace in his swimming trunks.

"Who was that?" he asked, squinting through one eye at Julia as she sat next to him on a bed in the shade of a parasol. "Sounded posher than The Queen."

"Next-door neighbour." Julia settled into the chair and pulled her phone from her pocket. She snapped a picture of the view. "I think Minnie has a crush on him."

"How cute."

Julia sent the picture to Jessie, who replied almost instantly with a one-word text: *JEALOUS!!!!!* She also included a yellow face blowing steam through its nostrils, a black heart (Jessie only ever sent the black ones), and a laughing crying face. Julia didn't really understand the coded string of emojis, so she sent back a pink love heart and tucked her phone away.

After admiring the view for a little while longer, she

pulled her book from her bag: an old Danielle Steele paperback she'd bought at the local charity shop for 50p. She settled into the chair and picked up where she'd left off on the plane.

"This is the life," she whispered to herself. "This is *the* life."

4
DOT

"You continue to impress me, my dear!" Percy said as they emerged into the busy town plaza. "Your impeccable sense of direction never fails you."

"I've always been good at finding my way," Dot replied, fluffing up her curls, which were already fighting the rising humidity. "Now, where do we start?"

If Peridale had been built in a warmer climate, Dot imagined the central village green would look something like Savega's plaza. It was similar in size, and the buildings seemed as old, if not older. Yet, the plaza couldn't have been more different than the village green she knew so well.

The greenery was confined to hanging baskets and the distant views of the mountains. Terracotta tiles in a traditional herringbone pattern covered the ground. The surrounding buildings weren't made of golden Cotswold stone bricks. Instead, they were smooth and white, no doubt covered in a couple of centuries' worth of layered paint.

A three-tier water fountain with shooting streams commanded attention in the centre of the plaza, an obvious gathering point. A sizeable three-storey restaurant filled one corner, its outdoor seating taking up a good chunk of the space. Smaller bars and cafés were dotted around, all of them full. She noticed a good many clothes shops and a few places selling souvenirs.

Still, the shopping seemed to be confined to the narrow alleyways that snaked away from the plaza in every direction. Quite a few of them appeared to have turned themselves into crowded makeshift markets.

Like the hotel, the side of the plaza opposite the restaurant had a railing, although instead of looking up to the mountain, it looked down to the coast. Once again, Dot was drawn to the view. A flight of blue and white tiled steps sloped downwards, with more shops, hotels, cafés, and bars sprinkled along the way.

Although Dot couldn't see where the steps ended, she imagined if they walked down them for long enough, they'd eventually reach the beach. Of course, for the sake of Percy's knees, she wasn't likely to find out.

"This is *exactly* how I pictured it," Dot said with a contented sigh, spinning back to face the crowded plaza.

"When Minnie said 'small, gorgeous town in on the Spanish south coast', *this* is what I saw."

"It's quite something."

"And the air." Dot inhaled a lungful. "I know we have good air in Peridale, but it feels fresher, almost. Like that feeling you get after you've just brushed your teeth and you drink something cold, but in a nice way. And hot."

"I know exactly what you mean, dear." Percy inhaled too. "I wonder what Minnie was talking about when she referred to the trouble?"

"Poor dear's probably losing her marbles."

"Oh, no."

"But she's still great fun!" Dot nudged her husband. "I *told* you she was fun. Shall we start with the grandchildren and the great-grandchildren? I think they'll be the easiest to buy for."

"Right you are, my dear."

They went into the nearest clothes shop, and to Dot's surprise, the offering wasn't what she would have expected for something so off the beaten track. She wasn't a fashion expert by any means. In fact, she tried her best to avoid such matters, but the clothes seemed rather trendy. And the prices were reasonable too. She left the first shop with t-shirts and hats for her grandson Vinnie, and her twin great-granddaughters, Pearl and Dottie, all with a hefty seven-euro discount off the overall price thanks to her haggling skills.

"They're going to love these," Dot said, inspecting her loot as they left their first shop. "Where to next?"

"Perhaps a spot of tea somewhere?" he suggested, his voice low and strange. "Let's pop into that café over there, dear."

Percy linked arms and practically dragged her into the small café next door. Rather than sitting outside, he took them into the two-storey café and all the way up the spiralling staircase to a second floor looking out over the first.

"Not to alarm you," he started, lifting the menu to hide his face, "and don't look now, but I think we're being followed."

"By whom?" Dot cried, immediately looking over the balcony to the café below. "Don't be so silly, Percival!"

"I said, *don't* look." He popped open a second menu and handed it to her. "Play it cool. There's a man with silver aviator sunglasses who followed us around that entire shop, and he didn't take his eyes off us."

"I didn't see a man!"

"That's because you were doing a wonderful job of shopping and bartering, my love," he said, offering her a smile over the menu. "But remember what Minnie said about trouble? Paranoid or not, she could have been talking about pick-pocketers."

"Oh." Dot's heart sank. She could feel the weight of the purse in her handbag without needing to check it was still there. "I think I may have done something unwise. I've brought all our spending money out at once."

"Not to panic."

"I didn't think."

"How much is currently in your purse?"

"Around five hundred euros," she said, her heart sinking. "Give or take. I know we're planning to eat in the hotel most meals, but I wanted to treat everyone to at least one nice meal out at the end of the holiday."

"That's very kind of you, my love."

"We might not get there now." Dot went to look over the menu, but Percy gave her knee a quick squeeze. "What if we're being silly?"

"We probably are." He laughed. "Better to be safe than sorry, isn't it? It was only the other week we watched that documentary about the pick-pocketers in London. I know we're not in London, but I doubt there's any honour amongst thieves anywhere in the world. Remember the targets they prefer?"

"The elderly."

"Exactly." Percy turned a page in the menu, doing an excellent job of appearing calm. "They think we're all slow and gullible. Well, I might be a little slow, but you're still the sharpest knife in the box. What do *you* suggest we do?"

Dot thought for a second, but she was more panicked than she wanted to let on. They'd known each other for less than a year and been married only a couple of months. While she felt she could be the most authentic version of herself with Percy, prickly edges and all, she knew he idolised her. Whether he didn't see her flaws, chose not to, or simply didn't care, she didn't know, but she loved the pedestal he'd put her on.

Well, she loved it right up until she actually had to be as brilliant and quick as he thought she was. Dot had a hard time accepting her age most days because she still felt like that woman in her forties from the photo album in her bag, but denial didn't stop her brain being eighty-five years old and slowing each year. Just slightly, mind.

Thank goodness it hadn't slowed entirely because a little spark of an idea flickered. For that split second, she felt as brilliant and wonderful as Percy thought she was. Without saying a word, she knocked one of the forks off the table, and in one swift action, leaned over to pick it up. Her eyes glanced over the balcony for only a moment, and she saw a man matching the description Percy had given.

"He's there," she said, placing the fork neatly back. "Man with the silver aviators and black leather jacket?"

"That's the fella."

"He's sat outside, watching us." Dot felt the heat rise up in her chest. "Oh, he's picked the wrong pair of OAPs to rob today. Do you know what we're going to do, Percy?"

"No, dear."

"We're going to outsmart him." Dot slapped the

menu shut and caught the attention of a white-shirted waitress downstairs by the counter. "But first, a nice calming cup of tea is in order, don't you think?"

And that's precisely what they did. The waitress brought them a pot of tea to share with two small cups, and they took their time, drinking several helpings each. When it felt natural, Dot glanced over the balcony to look casually outside, as one would – and each time, her heart skipped a little beat when she saw the silver aviators staring up at her.

"Marks for persistence," Dot said, pulling a five euro note, enough for the tea and a tip, from her purse. "Now, you stay here and make yourself look useful, and I'm going to pop to the ladies' room. When I come back, we walk out the front door, and we blend into the crowd."

"Then what?"

"We get the hell back to the hotel and apologise to Minnie for not believing her." Dot snapped her purse shut and dropped it back into her handbag. "Come down when you see me leave the bathroom, but not before. If he comes in and comes up here, you scream."

"Scream?"

"Yes." Dot kissed him on the cheek. "Fake a heart attack, or something. Scare the little bugger silly. Shan't be long."

Without giving their watcher the satisfaction of letting him know they were onto him, Dot walked as quickly and casually as she could to the bathroom downstairs. Once inside, she locked the door, glad it was a single room with one way in and one way out instead of a row of cubicles.

Once alone, her hands immediately started shaking. She felt reckless for what she was about to do. Still, it had been one of the tips in the documentary. For the sake of not losing five hundred euros, she wasn't prudish enough not to use the one place most men wouldn't think to look for money.

She pulled the thick stack of colourful euros from her purse, split them in two, unbuttoned the middle of her blouse, and slipped a pile under the wire of each side of her bra. Dot gave herself a little wiggle, and when no money fell out, she refastened her blouse and looked in the mirror.

"Genius," she said, turning from side to side to make sure the colours didn't shine through. "You've still got it, Dorothy South."

Dot dropped her empty purse into her handbag and caught sight of the leather photo album in her bag. If a mugger wanted to rob her of her saved pension money, there was a good chance he would snatch the whole bag. She pulled it out and flicked through. It contained too many happy memories to lose. She'd rather hand over every penny she had than lose these pictures of Albert.

The years before his death had, ironically, been some of their happiest. The album was the only tangible thing she had left to trigger the memories of those blissful times, and she didn't have duplicates for most of them.

Using her brains once again, she looked around the bathroom. There weren't many places to hide something so substantial, but there was a bin. Sighing, Dot wrapped the book in toilet paper and gently placed it inside.

Dot always carried a pen and paper around with her, a necessity the younger generations seemed to have abandoned entirely. After scribbling a note, she retrieved an orange fifty euro note from her hiding place and wrapped it around the letter. She dropped the pen and pad back in her bag, content to lose the rest of its trivial contents. She took one last look in the mirror, fluffed up her curls, adjusted her brooch, straightened the creases in her blouse, and nodded that she was ready.

"Thank you so much," she said to the waitress after leaving the bathroom. "The tea was lovely."

Dot shook the girl's hand – Maria, according to her name badge – and planted the fifty euro bill concealing the note into her palm. The young woman's features dropped when she realised the amount of the second tip. Unravelling the bill, Maria revealed the note. Dot widened her smile, and the girl seemed to catch what she was throwing.

Maria smiled back, slotted the money and note into her pocket, and nodded at Dot. All the while, the man who appeared to be the manager hadn't looked up from the paper he was reading at the end of the bar.

"All set?" Percy asked when he joined her at the bottom of the stairs.

"All set."

Hand in hand, they walked straight out of the café, past the man with the aviators, and into the crowd. Dot glanced over her shoulder immediately, and their tail was already following them.

"This way," Dot said with as much calm as she could muster. "Just down here."

They slipped down an alleyway and through a market Dot didn't remember coming through. Another peek over her shoulder confirmed the man was hot on their heels.

"Not far now," she said, turning down another, less-busy alley. "Just a little farther."

Another glance.

He was still following them.

"Dorothy?" Percy squeezed her hand tightly when they reached a four-way junction. "Are we a little lost?"

"A little."

The further away from the plaza they ventured, the more danger they'd be in. She closed her eyes for a split second, and without thinking too hard about it, hurried in the direction she thought she heard the most people.

They came out into another market street, this one even busier than the last. She looked over her shoulder as they squeezed through the shoppers, and found that the man was so close he'd be able to touch them if he reached out.

"This is like that film with that Austrian man," said Dot.

"Hitler?"

Dot shot him a sharp sideways glance. "When did Hitler make films?"

"War films, dear."

"Not Hitler." Dot looked around. "Arnold Schwarzenegger."

"Oh, I quite like him." Percy chuckled as they took another turn down another market street. "*Kindergarten Cop?*"

"No, the one where he's a robot."

"*Twins?*"

"A robot," Dot repeated. "From the future, with molten skin."

"*Total Recall?*"

"How do you know so many Arnold Schwarzenegger films *except* the one I'm thinking of?"

"How do you even know any?"

"Because Jessie made me watch it!" Dot looked back, and he was closer still. "It doesn't matter! In here."

Without thinking too hard about it, Dot pulled Percy into a clothes shop deep in the market that seemed to sell trendy clothes identical to the ones she was carrying in the bag. Knowing their options were limited, Dot chose honesty.

"Hello, there," Dot said, letting go of Percy's hand to hold it out for the bearded shopkeeper to shake. "Erm . . . parlez vous Anglaise?"

"I am afraid I do not speak the French," he replied with a dry laugh, "but English, yes. Can I help you?"

"You can." Dot glanced over her shoulder. The man was stood in the shop doorway, staring at them without expression – was he a robot after all? "That man right there is following us. I think he's trying to rob us. Would you please help us?"

"Of course," the shopkeeper said, looking over their shoulder at the man. "We have had problems with this man before. Follow me, please."

The shopkeeper took them through to a back room, which looked like an office-come-staff area. The dark wallpaper was peeling, the sofa looked like it didn't have a spring left in it, and the television currently broadcasting a football game probably should have been thrown out in the last century.

"Make yourself comfortable," he said, motioning to the desk with two chairs. "I shall call the authorities, but I will need to use my neighbour's phone. Mine, you see, is broken."

Dot collapsed into a chair, adrenaline rushing through her system like it never had before. Sweat was also pouring down her face like it never had before, and for once, she didn't care about her curls. She could feel they were drenched and plastered to her neck.

Percy sat in the chair next to her, every limb visibly shaking. She let out a laugh, and he joined in, although she knew it was more from shock and confusion than anything.

"*Terminator,*" Percy said, breaking the silence. "You were thinking of *Terminator.*"

"That's the one."

Out of curiosity, Dot picked up the old-fashioned rotary telephone on the desk. As old as it was, a distinct dial tone waited for her to input a telephone number. Before she could swivel the numbers, or even wonder why the man had said it didn't work, a door opened, and it wasn't the one in front of them.

Unlike the bathroom in the café, the dark room behind the shop had more than one entrance and exit. She turned in time to see the shopkeeper, with the man in the aviators by his side. Before she could ask what in heavens was going on, someone crammed a black sack over her head and dragged her hands forcefully behind her back.

5

JULIA

"I can't see a thing," Julia said, squinting through Barker's fingers. "Where are you taking me?"

"You'll see," he whispered, guiding her around a corner. "Just a couple more steps. Keep your eyes closed."

Barker lifted one hand away and opened a door in front of her – or that's what it sounded like – but she did as she was told and kept her eyes closed. He covered them again before guiding her forward. This time when he let go, he closed the door behind them. From the familiar scent and her vague understanding of the hotel's layout, she guessed they were in their bedroom.

"Okay," he said, his voice coming from further ahead now, "you can open them."

Julia opened her eyes and blinked hard – not that she needed to. The candles dotted around the room weren't bright, but they provided enough light to show the rose petals all over the floor and the bed. Out on the balcony, the plastic table had a red cloth over it. It was set for two, with a vase of roses in the middle. Barker had even changed from his t-shirt into a pale-blue cotton shirt, slightly open at the collar.

"You did all of this?" Julia walked into the room, fingers grazing the petals on the bed. "Barker Brown, I have no words."

"Good husband points?"

"All the points."

"I had a little help from Lisa," he admitted, scratching the back of his head, "but the idea was all mine. I wanted to do something special for us, something romantic. When you fell asleep outside, it felt like the perfect opportunity. Do you like it?"

She tiptoed to kiss him. "I love it."

Out on the balcony, they looked out over the valley. The moon cast an icy glow over the trees, and yellowy lights from buildings here and there caught her attention. It was like a fairy-tale.

"I can see the stars," she whispered, leaning back into Barker's chest. "I can't remember the last time I looked up and saw the stars."

"Let's just stay here." He wrapped his arms around

her and looped his fingers through hers. "We don't need to go home. Jessie can keep the café, and we can just live on holiday forever."

"Is a holiday a holiday if it's permanent?"

"Minnie's life seems to be one long holiday." He kissed her on the top of the head. "And if not forever, a holiday home then? There's not much left on the cottage's mortgage, and I still have a good chunk of the book money left. Enough for a deposit."

Julia pulled away and turned to face him. "Are you being serious?"

He shrugged. "Why not?"

Julia couldn't think of a reason why not. She glanced at the valley again, and even in the dark, it was the most relaxing place she had ever been. She loved the comforts of home, but she now understood the appeal of being a fish out of water, especially somewhere so beautiful. Before they could talk about it further, there was a knock at the door.

"That'll be the starters," Barker said. "Lisa said she'd serve us dinner up here tonight."

He opened the door, and it was Lisa, but she didn't have any food with her. She did have a worried look on her face, and one thumbnail crammed in her mouth.

"Everything okay?" Julia asked, joining Barker by the door.

"Yes," she replied. "Actually, no. I'm not sure."

"What's happened?" Barker asked.

"Nothing's happened, as such." She glanced up and down the corridor before exhaling. "Have you seen Dot and Percy?"

"Not since breakfast," Julia replied. "Surely they should be back by now?"

Lisa shook her head.

Julia squeezed past Lisa. She walked down to the corridor to the room she knew her gran and Percy were staying in. She knocked and knocked, but nobody answered. No light poured through the small gap under the door.

"Barker?" Julia stared at her husband, unsure of what to say.

"Let's not panic," he said, fanning his hands. "They probably got caught up somewhere. You know what your gran is like. Maybe she found herself a nice café somewhere, and she's getting plugged into the local gossip channels and having a good chat with the locals?"

Julia checked her watch. "It's half past eight at night. They should be back."

"I think you should come downstairs," Lisa said, already walking to the lift at the end of the hallway. "My mother is going out of her mind. She sent me up to here to fetch you."

They took the lift down to the ground floor and found Minnie pacing back and forth in the softly lit sunroom with the pool and valley serving as her backdrop. Two couples were eating dinner, the only noise the scraping of cutlery on plates and barely audible Spanish guitar music playing from some concealed speakers somewhere. Aside from them, the hotel was empty.

"They haven't seen her," Lisa explained before Minnie could ask, "and they're still not in their rooms."

"Oh, sweet Julia!" Minnie cried, hand on her forehead as she continued to pace, her kaftan blowing dramatically around her. "I *told* them. I *said* there'd be trouble! If they'd only stayed in the hotel, this never would have happened."

"We don't know if anything's happened," Barker said, his voice carrying all the calm authority left from his detective inspector days. "Has anyone looked for them? It's only a small town. They can't have gone far."

"And vanish like they did?" Minnie shook her head, eyes trained on her feet at she paced. "No, thank you."

"Mum..."

"*Don't!*" Minnie stopped pacing to extend a finger at her daughter. "Don't you say it. Don't you tell me I'm paranoid. I'm not crazy, Lisa. I can see what's going on around here. The troubles. It's not the same, and you know it. Everything has changed."

"When you say 'the troubles', what do you mean?" Julia asked, guiding her great-aunt to a wicker chair out of view of the curious diners. "You mentioned it this morning, too."

"Oh, you know." She waved her hand vaguely.

"I really don't."

"Things aren't the same," she repeated, hands clutching fistfuls of her grey hair. "Everything has changed."

Julia glanced at Barker, but he looked as confused as she felt. Despite Minnie's rebuttal of paranoia, she was doing an excellent job of coming across as paranoid. Lisa handed her mother a glass of sangria. Minnie took a big gulp before relaxing into the chair. Knowing she wouldn't get much out of Minnie in this state, Julia decided to change tactics. She nodded for Lisa to follow her out onto the terrace.

"Could you perhaps clarify a little?" Julia whispered, looking back at Minnie as she fanned at herself with a magazine. "How have things changed?"

"She never used to be like this," Lisa explained, desperation in her voice. "Things haven't been the same since Bill died three years ago."

"Bill?"

"Her fourth husband," she said, glancing at her mother. "The only one that stuck. They opened this hotel together twenty years ago. I only came out to help her get settled into a new routine after the funeral, but how can I leave her when she's like this? She's pushed everyone out. The chef, the cleaners? All fired. I know she says she's not paranoid, but I think she's been having a slow-wave breakdown ever since the day of Bill's funeral."

"And the town?" Julia pushed. "The trouble? Is there any truth in it?"

"Maybe." Lisa shifted her head from side to side, although Julia could sense some reluctance. "Quite a few of the old hotels and cafés have packed up and left, but it's not like new people haven't taken them over. I think that since Bill's death, she's just terrified of change. I don't know what to do with her. I've been trying to get her to sell up for months, but she won't entertain the idea."

Julia couldn't focus on a solution to the problems Lisa was having with her mother. Family or not, she didn't know them well enough yet. She did, however, know her gran and Percy, and she was no closer to accounting for their whereabouts.

"I'm going to go out and look for them," Barker said when he joined them on the terrace. "Like I said, it's not a big town. They *have* to be somewhere."

"I'll come with you."

"No." He rested a hand on Julia's shoulder. "Not in your—"

"Condition?" She shrugged his hand away. "Barker, my grandmother and her husband are missing. I'm going out to look for them whether you like it or not." She turned to Lisa. "You know this town better than we do. Would you say it was safe?"

"I don't . . ." Her voice trailed off as her eyes drifted back into the hotel.

Julia spun around, hoping to see her gran and Percy so they could laugh about how silly they'd all been. It was only Rodger, the posh neighbour she had met that morning.

"I'll get rid of him," Lisa said, almost to herself. "Most nights, he comes around to drink wine with my mother, and they listen to music and dance the night away. Tonight's not the night."

Rodger crossed the dining room with confident steps, his earlier beige linen suit swapped out for a darker brown one. He had a bottle of red wine cradled in his arm and an envelope in his hand.

"My dearest Minnie!" he exclaimed when he found her half-collapsed in the sunroom clutching her sangria. "Whatever has happened?"

"It's *my* turn, Rodger!" she cried, trying to stand but barely able to steady herself from the nerves. "I can feel it. It's *my* turn."

"Calm yourself," he said, easing her back into the chair. "No good will come of getting yourself worked into a state." He motioned for Lisa to fetch him some glasses for the wine. "Now, let's sit down and talk about what's troubling you."

Minnie gulped down more sangria and settled into the wicker chair while Lisa hurried in with two wine glasses.

"This was on the doormat," Rodger said, handing the envelope to Lisa. "It's addressed simply to 'La Casa', so I thought I'd best bring it in. Looks to have been hand-delivered."

Lisa took the letter to the reception area, leaving Julia and Barker lingering in the doorway between the sunroom and terrace.

"If we're going," Barker said, checking his watch, "we should leave now."

Julia nodded, and they set off towards the front door. She still wore the blue tie dyed dress and two-piece swimming costume from earlier. She thought about going up to the room to change or grab a jacket to fend off the slightly chillier night air, but the knot in her stomach stopped her.

Something wasn't right.

"Oh, God!" Lisa cried, a hand over her mouth, the letter clenched in the other. "No, no, no, no."

"What is it?" Barker asked, stepping back from the front door he'd just opened.

Lisa didn't say anything. She put the note on the reception desk and turned it to face them before picking up the phone. She spoke quickly and quietly in what sounded like perfect Spanish. Julia's Spanish skills were basic at best, but even she could figure out what 'policía' meant.

Julia snatched up the letter. The top half was written

in Spanish, with what appeared to be an English translation of the same text below it.

La Casa,

We have taken two of your guests. If you do not wish any harm to come to them, you will pay a ransom of one hundred thousand euros. You will pay this in cash in an unmarked duffle bag.

When you are ready to pay, advertise a tractor for sale in the window of the post office in Savega Plaza and await further instructions.

We do not wish to commit murder. We only want the money. Follow our instructions, and your guests will be released within twenty-four hours of delivery.

Co-operate, and no harm will come to your guests. You have exactly one week. Any delay will be taken as a failure to pay.

See picture on the reverse for confirmation of authenticity.

Julia turned the paper over, and the image confirmed her worst nightmares. With black sacks over their heads, Dot and Percy were sat side by side on an old sofa, wearing the outfits they'd left in that morning. Their hands were bound with rope, but they were holding hands the best they could.

"We'll find them," Barker said. "I promise we'll find them."

His hands tightened on Julia's shoulders. She let the note slip from her hands, and everything went black.

6

DOT

The van drove over what felt like another rock, jerking Dot to the side. With her hands still bound in her lap, she could do little to steady herself, although the seatbelt stopped her from slipping into the footwell. At least they had taken the sack off her head.

"Are you still okay, dear?" she asked Percy, who was staring through the blacked-out windows like he could see something she couldn't.

"Quite alright." He offered a meek smile. "Yourself, my love?"

"Fine."

"I think we're going up into the mountains."

"I think you're right." Dot sighed, scratching at the itchy rope around her wrists. "They could have done these a little looser, don't you think?"

"That they could."

Dot decided not to continue the conversation. For obvious reasons, Percy seemed reluctant to have an in-depth discussion on the matter. The front of the van was blocked off by cardboard taped over the back of the front headrests. She guessed the man with the aviators and the shopkeeper were the ones driving them wherever they were going. At least one of them was wearing a strong aftershave that had been tickling Dot's throat since they set off from the market, although she'd been resisting the urge to cough.

As much as she wanted to cough, scream, shout, and kick the backs of the chairs in front of her, she remained stoic –more for Percy's sake than anything. He'd shut down as soon as the sacks had gone over their heads. He was too gentle a man for such hardship. They'd only been close while they'd posed for a photograph, and he'd been shaking like a poor little leaf.

It wasn't that Dot wasn't scared. She was more terrified than she'd ever been in her life, but she couldn't let those emotions take control. She knew better than anyone how razor-sharp and cold her tongue could be, especially when she was on the back foot. The last thing they needed was for her icy words to add to the problem.

No, she needed to remain calm and collected.

With no indication of light or dark beyond the blacked-out windows, Dot had no way to know what time it was, but it felt late. They'd been kept in the back office of the shop, guarded by two men with guns, for the entire length of the football game on the television, and then another, and another.

She yawned, wondering if she'd get to sleep anytime soon or even wake to see another sunrise. If not, at least she got to see the sunrise over the valley that morning. Small mercies, she thought, and she smiled at the memory. Like most people did, she'd hoped her final moments of life would be in bed at home, but at least this way she might go out in style in a beautiful part of the world. That would have to do.

After at least an hour of driving upwards, the terrain finally levelled out. The winding became more erratic and the roads bumpier. When Dot thought her old bones couldn't take another jolt from the rocks in the road, they ground to a halt, and she heard the handbrake yank up. The two men spoke in hushed tones before jumping out.

Doors on either side of the van slid open. Percy jolted awake. Dot hadn't even realised he'd fallen asleep. She'd wanted to, but she'd forced herself to stay awake if only to avoid the confusion that usually accompanied napping in unfamiliar places.

"Out," the shopkeeper instructed after unclipping Dot's seatbelt. "Now."

She shuffled to the edge and jumped out, glad to move her legs at last. From the thinness of the air, they had to be high up, but as the only light came from the headlights of the van, she could see nothing else.

Everything was as dark as nature intended it, making her wonder how anyone had survived before the invention of streetlamps.

"If this is the end, Percy," Dot called out, having no idea where he was, "I want you to know I'm glad I met you."

"Likewise, my Dorothy," he called back from the other side of the van. "Likewise."

The bearded shopkeeper grabbed Dot by the wrists and pulled her away from the van. His grip was firm, but he didn't yank hard enough to hurt her, so she followed without argument. Were they about to be forced to their knees with guns placed to the back of their heads for defying the men's pick-pocketing plan? Extreme, she thought, but perhaps this was how criminals did things this far south.

Instead, the man dragged her to a small, white, single-storey villa nestled in a clearing of tall trees. It looked like most of the buildings she'd seen since landing in the country, except this one had bars on the windows.

After unlocking the door, he pushed Dot inside. Before she could worry about what was going to happen to Percy, the man in the aviator sunglasses pushed him inside to join her. The man flicked on some lights, cut off their ropes, and shut the door, locking them in with what sounded like multiple padlocks and a deadbolt.

Dot looked around, rubbing at her tender wrists.

They were in a pleasantly decorated, open-plan villa. It was small but still large enough to house a family. There was a kitchen area along one wall, a dining table with four mismatched chairs, and two sofas. The floors were tiled – some cracked, most not. The walls were painted cream, and there were even framed pictures hanging on the walls. An old television sat on a wheeled stand in the corner, and porcelain flamenco dancer ornaments sashayed across the top of it.

"What do you suppose is happening?" Percy asked, glued to her side.

"Perhaps we've been upgraded?" She licked her thumb and wiped a dark smudge off his cheek. "I don't know, dear, but we're alive."

"For now."

"For now." She nodded. "But at our age, that's all we have, isn't it? Getting through the winters in one piece is a challenge in itself."

"I suppose it is." He took a small step away from her and looked around the room. "I wonder why we're here."

"Maybe we're going to be trafficked?" She turned the TV on, glad to see that it worked. "Remember that documentary we watched? They might be getting ready to sell us on the black market and shipping us off to the highest bidder."

"Weren't those all young women?"

"What are you trying to say?" She shot him a sharp look over her shoulder as she fiddled with the dials on the old set. "But perhaps you're right. I'm sure time will tell."

To Dot's dismay, all of the channels were Spanish, and without a remote control, there was no way to put subtitles on. She'd hoped to come across the BBC somewhere in the mix, but it cycled back to the beginning again with no luck. She turned up the volume to hear some voices but quickly turned it down again when the locks began opening. Re-joining Percy in the middle of the room, she clutched his hand.

"Be brave," she whispered to him.

"You too, dear."

The door opened. The man in the aviators walked in, carrying a tray with plates of cold meats, cheeses, olives, bread, and even butter. He also had a large plastic bag dangling from one arm, which he let slide down to the floor by the door once he'd closed it behind himself. He placed the tray on the dining room table before striding over to yank the curtains shut over the sink.

"Water," he said, showing them the bottles in the fridge. "Do not drink from the tap. It is only clean for washing." He pushed open one of the doors to show them a bathroom, and another to show a bedroom. "I will come in the morning with your breakfast."

"Thank you," Dot found herself saying. "If you don't mind me asking, why are we here?"

The man pulled off his sunglasses, and to Dot's surprise, he was much younger than she'd initially thought. Not much older than Jessie, she guessed, and he had lovely hazel eyes with thick lashes. Bonny, or handsome even, but nowhere near as menacing as he'd looked when stalking them through the plaza and the markets.

"It is better to not ask questions," he said, pushing the sunglasses into the inside pocket of his leather jacket, revealing a gun holster clipped to his belt. "Behave, and you will be fine."

He left, securing all the locks behind him. When the deadbolt slid across, Dot got the impression they'd be left alone until the morning, which steadied her nerves.

"Do you suppose it's poisoned?" Percy asked, biting into his lip as he hovered by the food. "I am rather hungry."

"I don't think so," Dot said as she checked the bag he'd left by the door. "He's given us changes of clothes. I don't think he's trying to kill us."

"Why would he bring us here then?"

"I don't know," she admitted, "but don't you get the feeling we're dealing with the monkey and not the angle grinder?"

"Do you mean 'organ grinder', dear?"

"I'm sure it's angle grinder."

"Right you are."

Percy folded thinly sliced ham and crammed it into his mouth while he buttered slices of bread. Hoping he'd butter her a few slices to make a sandwich, Dot checked the bedroom.

It had two single beds like they had at their cottage in Peridale and some furniture for storing clothes. The curtains had already been closed but peeking through offered nothing but more darkness.

"Shame," she whispered, "I bet the view is spectacular from up here."

Deciding she'd take the bed farthest from the door, which was the one she had at home in Peridale, she tested the mattress. Firm, just how she liked it. She checked the bedside drawer, surprised to see two items. One was a Bible, which wasn't much use to them now. The other, a sealed pack of cards, made her smile.

"Surprisingly," she mused, shuffling the cards as she returned to the main area, "I've stayed in worse places."

"As have I." Percy handed her a plate with two ham and cheese sandwiches. "But it's not exactly the honeymoon we wanted, is it?"

Dot pulled out a chair at the table and sat down with her food. Before tucking in, she finished shuffling the cards and dealt their hands.

"While not the honeymoon we envisioned, it's the honeymoon we've got." She nodded for Percy to join her at the table. "What do you say about a quick game of poker before bed, Percival?"

"Dorothy," he said through a yawn as he took the seat across from her, "I'd like that very much."

7

JULIA

Soon after the police arrived, the local doctor showed up. Barker had caught Julia before she hit the ground and, according to him, she'd been unconscious for only ten seconds at the most.

Still, for the sake of the baby, everyone agreed it was best to have the doctor check her over. The tests were quick. The doctor concluded that the shock of the news must have triggered a drop in blood pressure, which could cause anyone to faint but was more common in pregnant women. Since Julia had no pain, he gave her something to help her sleep and left almost as quickly as he'd come.

After talking with the local police officers and answering their confusing and repetitive questions until close to midnight, Julia and Barker finally went up to bed. Neither said much. With the help of her phone, she translated the box the doctor had given her. They were standard sleeping pills like those she could buy over the counter anywhere back home. More importantly, they were safe for pregnant women to take within the recommended doses. She tossed back two and let them drag her off to sleep.

The next morning, she woke with the sun. Like the day before, she rolled over the cuddle up to Barker but found only fresh air and cold sheets. She sat up in bed, hair matted and wild, and looked around. Barker sat on the balcony, his mobile phone pressed to his ear. She didn't remember what had happened until she heard his side of the phone call.

"*Dammit!*" Barker cried after slamming his phone down on the table, still set for the romantic dinner they never had. The word echoed back from the valley. He rushed in as soon as he noticed that she was awake. "How are you feeling?"

"Fine," she replied, rubbing at her tired eyes, a far cry from how rested she'd felt only the day before. "Groggy. Any news?"

"None." Barker dug through his suitcase and pulled a fresh t-shirt from the selection Julia had packed for him. "I called DI Christie back in Peridale, but until it gets escalated to Interpol, it's a job for the Spanish police, and the Spanish police only. His hands are tied.

Which, of course, I knew. I just hoped . . ." Barker grimaced. "He told me to behave myself and do what they tell me. Can you believe that?"

Julia bolted upright as Barker's words sank in. She jumped out of bed and dressed quickly before digging in her bag for her phone.

"I haven't told the family," she said, scrolling through her contacts, wondering who to call first. "If Christie knows, it will be all over the village before everyone's finished their breakfast. They can't find out like that."

The night before, the police had told them to keep the information quiet so as not to startle the kidnappers into overreacting. They suggested that the kidnappers would most likely have eyes on the hotel. From now on, they said, they would send plainclothes officers to deal with the case. While the ransom note hadn't told them not to contact the police, the authorities were always cautious when it came to situations like this one.

First, Julia called her father. Dot's only son needed to know what was going on. After he got over the shock and asked all the questions she didn't have the answers to, she called Sue and repeated the process. Finally, she called Jessie.

"Kidnapped?" Jessie started laughing. "Nice one, Mum. How's the holiday going?"

Jessie's laughter stopped when Julia didn't join in. Once again, she was inundated with the same unanswerable questions. Jessie insisted on coming over to help, but Julia told her to stay where she was and carry on as normally as she could. By the time the café opened, likely everyone in the village would know, and they'd need somewhere to congregate to theorise and bask in the shock. With or without her, there was no better place for that than Julia's café.

They took the lift to the ground floor, and like yesterday, found Minnie seated for breakfast. Today, instead of Dot and Percy slathering jam and butter on toast, she sat with two men Julia hadn't seen before. One had a full head of greying hair, a square jaw, and a sharp suit. He brought a slightly aged James Bond to mind, and Julia assumed he must be the inspector the police had promised would arrive for more questioning. The other was younger, somewhere in his thirties, with dark hair and tanned skin.

"Thank you, Mrs Harlow," the older man said, his accent surprisingly British. "I think you've given me a lot to work with. I'll see myself out."

"Inspector?" Julia rushed over before he could leave the dining room. She held out her hand. "My name is Julia. I'm Dot's granddaughter. Is there any news?"

The inspector quickly looked her up and down, his eyes landing on the bump under her green maxi dress. For some reason, this detail seemed to irritate him, and he hesitated before accepting her handshake.

"Inspector George Hillard," he replied, giving her a

tight smile. "This is Sub-Inspector Lorenzo Castro." The younger man offered her the same tight smile. "I'm afraid there's nothing as of yet, but I assure you, we're working on the case as best we can. Ransom cases aren't straightforward, as I'm sure you can appreciate." He tried to step around her, but Julia matched him move for move. "If you'll excuse me, I really must get on."

"Don't you want to question us?" she asked. "To find out more?"

"That's not necessary." He stepped again, and she followed like they were engaged in a very unpleasant dance. "I suggest you try to enjoy your holiday. We will do everything we can to return your grandparents safe and sound."

His suggestion shocked her so much she didn't move along with him the next time he tried to step around her. Without a second look, the two inspectors left the hotel, hopped up the steps, and jumped into a car.

"What did you tell him, Minnie?" Julia asked, taking the seat next to her great-aunt. "Do you know anything?"

"He asked so many questions," Minnie replied, her brows scrunched up as though she didn't want to talk about it a moment longer. "Why does he think *I* know anything? I'm not responsible for this."

"No one is saying you are." Julia ducked to meet Minnie's gaze, but it didn't stay still long enough. "What questions did he ask you?"

"This and that." She wafted her hand. "You know."

"Minnie." Julia lunged forward and clutched her great-aunt's round face between her palms, forcing her to meet her eyes. "We don't know each other all that well, and you haven't seen my gran for forty years, but she's one of the most important people in my life. I need you to tell me what you told the inspector."

With her cheeks squashed between Julia's hands, Minnie nodded, her eyes wide and focused. Content that she wouldn't flee, Julia let go and sat back in her seat. Firm as they'd been, Julia couldn't feel any remorse for the actions she'd taken to snap Minnie out of her delirious daze.

"He wanted to know if I had any enemies," she started, frowning. "Silly, don't you think? Me? Enemies? The only person I ever considered an enemy was Jessica Lange, and that's only because we were both up for the *King Kong* role and she knew it should have been mine."

"Is Jessica Lange currently in Savega?"

"I suspect not." Minnie thought about it for a moment. "I suppose she's in a nice big mansion in the Hollywood Hills, just where I'd be if she hadn't stolen my role. And let me tell you another—"

"Minnie," Julia interrupted resolutely. "Focus. What did you tell him? Do you think anyone you know could have done this?"

Minnie traced her finger around the edge of her plate, mopping up the toast crumbs scattered there. Julia didn't know how she could eat since she didn't feel hungry in the slightest.

"I could only think of Arlo Garcia."

"Who's Arlo Garcia?" Barker asked, taking the seat opposite Julia.

"He used to work here," Lisa explained as she emerged from the kitchen and began clearing the table. Evidently, the inspectors had also helped themselves to the breakfast buffet. "He was the chef here for nearly a decade. Mum fired him last month."

"And I was well within my rights!" Minnie cried, banging her fist on the table. "He was stealing from me. Caught red-handed! Things are tight enough as it is without a thief in our midst." She inhaled deeply. "And it all worked out for the best, didn't it, Lisa? We don't need him. You're just as good a cook as he was. Your paella might not be up to Arlo's standard, but you'll get there."

Julia pinched the bridge of her nose and exhaled. If Lisa was bothered by her mother's put-down, she didn't show it, vanishing with the dirty plates as quickly as she'd arrived.

"Where might we speak to this Arlo?" Barker asked, leaning across the table to take Julia's hands in his. "Is he local?"

Minnie nodded. "He lives right here in Savega. He works in Chocolatería Valor, in the plaza. It's one of the few old places that has survived in Savega since before I moved here. I warned Danilo not to hire him."

Julia couldn't listen to any more of the chattering. She stood, almost knocking her chair over in the process. Barker rose, taking her arm to steady her before she could flee.

"Breakfast first," he pleaded, squeezing her shoulder. "Making yourself ill is the last thing your gran would want, all things considered."

Julia's hand fluttered over her rounded belly, and she didn't need to be told twice. Some of the tension left her, and she sank down into her chair again. She'd been so careful to do everything textbook-correct during her pregnancy, but she hadn't given her condition a second thought since the letter arrived. Resting her hand on her bump, Julia offered the baby a mental apology. Barker was right. Her gran wouldn't want her to rush out on an empty stomach. And she certainly wouldn't want Julia forgetting to nourish her great-grandchild.

Minnie slipped away, leaving them to eat their breakfast in peace. Barker opted for fruit salad with his black coffee, but Julia went for the meat and cheese platter. She needed something substantial after missing dinner because of last night's chaos.

She washed her breakfast down with a small cup of peppermint tea and felt instantly better with food in her belly.

"We should have gone with them yesterday," Julia said, guilt colouring her voice. "If we had, this wouldn't have happened."

"You can't blame yourself." Barker wiped a tear from her cheek; she hadn't realised she was crying. "I spent the morning trying to figure out if we could somehow afford the ransom. Even with my savings and your savings, it's barely a quarter of the way there, which means we need to focus on other tactics." He stood. "C'mon, let's check out the fired chef. It's as good a place as any to get a start."

Finding Chocolatería Valor in the plaza wasn't difficult, though the streets looked different on foot. She hardly noticed anything else around them, zeroing in on the shop's sign. Right now, she only cared about finding Arlo Garcia, their only lead.

"Do you want me to take this one?" Barker asked.

Julia was about to dismiss her husband's suggestion, but she looked down at her bump. She nodded. Her internal panicking might be wholly warranted, but she didn't want the 'hysterical pregnant woman' stereotype to prevent them from getting useful information.

On any other day, stepping into Chocolatería Valor would have been like stepping into a dream. It was a chocolate shop-café-bar hybrid, with more mouth-watering chocolate creations in the counter display cases than Julia could count. If – *when* – this all blew over, she would return and taste everything.

"Arlo Garcia?" Barker asked the young woman behind the counter.

She nodded her chin up to the quiet second floor

where a man in his mid-to-late thirties was clearing a table. They climbed the spiralling staircase, and Julia was glad to see they were alone.

"Arlo?" Barker asked, surprising Julia by pulling one of his recently printed business cards from his wallet. "Barker Brown. I'm a private investigator looking into a recent kidnapping and ransom situation. Is this something you've heard about?"

"Yes?" he replied, arching a brow at the thick, black card with embossed gold lettering. Julia had suggested something subtler, but she'd been overruled. "Everyone is talking about this. Two old people, right?"

Proof there were gossips everywhere, Julia thought, and not just in Peridale.

"That's correct." Barker motioned for Arlo to sit down. "I understand you used to work at La Casa hotel not too from here?"

"That is correct," he replied, sitting.

"The people who were taken were guests of—"

"Minnie Harlow," he cut in. "Yes, I know. I know why you're here also. Minnie says I 'stole' from her, and this is why she fired me. But you have been putting two and two together and getting five." Arlo looked down at the card and tossed it onto the table. "I am sorry, Mr Brown, I cannot help you. I do not know anything about this."

"When you say 'stole'," Barker said, copying Arlo's air quotes, "I assume you refute the allegations?"

"Yes, I do." He arched a brow, clearly growing

irritated. "I was . . . how do you say? Stitched up? Framed? Minnie wanted a reason to cut costs, so she did this. There is no proof, but she fired me anyway. For ten years I work as a chef for that woman, and now I am waiting the tables and scrubbing floors."

"So, Minnie has been having money troubles?" Barker asked before glancing up at Julia, who was too nervous to sit. "Do you have any proof of *that*?"

Arlo shook his head. He stood and continued gathering plates and cups.

"You want proof, you must talk to Gabriel Caron," he said, picking up the tray. "He runs the Eiffel restaurant. It is in this plaza. He gave Minnie money to keep her hotel running and she does not pay him back."

"What does Gabriel look like?" Barker asked, jotting the name down on his phone.

"You will know him," Arlo replied with a roll of his eyes. "He is French."

Arlo descended the spiralling staircase, leaving them alone upstairs. Julia wasn't surprised to hear about the money issues after what Lisa had said, but she hadn't considered them in this context.

"Let's go," Julia said. "Arlo said Gabriel works in a restaurant in the plaza. There's no time like the present."

Barker didn't argue. He seemed to be following a similar train of thought. It was nice to be on the same page regarding an investigation for once. DI Barker Brown wouldn't have played so loose, but Barker

Brown, PI didn't have superiors to answer to. Julia liked that.

They left Chocolatería Valor and found Eiffel immediately. Three-storeys tall and obviously French-themed, it stuck out like a sore thumb in the traditionally Spanish plaza. This seemed to work in the restaurant's favour since it was the busiest restaurant in view.

Before they reached the restaurant, a man stormed out who fit Arlo's brief and condescending description of Gabriel. In a sea of Spaniards and tourists, the man in his fifties with shaggy dark hair and matching goatee stuck out just as much as his restaurant did. A cigarette dangled from his lips, and his tight-fitting outfit was effortlessly stylish.

Cigarette still in his mouth, he jumped into a red, vintage, convertible sports car, stuck on a pair of black sunglasses, and pulled into the plaza, his decorative silk scarf fluttering behind him. He honked his horn and shouted in French at slow tourists until he cleared a path out. Right before the red car vanished from view, Julia noticed his licence plate: CARoN1.

"Barker, how serious are you about helping find my gran and Percy?" Julia asked, unable to take her eyes away from where the car had just been.

"Very."

"Good." Julia looked around the plaza, her stomach turning. "Then from this moment on, I'm hiring you as a private investigator. Something is going on here. It doesn't feel right."

"I feel it too." He wrapped his hand around hers. "C'mon, let's get back to the hotel. We need to talk to Minnie about the seriousness of her money troubles."

8

DOT

*D*ot fanned herself with her playing cards. Percy could have seen her hand if he'd looked over, but he didn't. The pitiful amount of air did very little to cool her, but she continued anyway.

"I'll never complain about the British summer again," she said, wiping away more sweat as it dribbled from her hairline. "Couldn't they have chosen to hold us captive somewhere with air conditioning?"

"That would have been ideal, Dorothy." Percy's tongue poked out the corner of his mouth as he stared at his cards. He tugged at his left ear lobe. "I think I'm all in for this one. What about you?"

"All in." Dot pushed her remaining toothpicks into the pile without a second thought. "You don't suppose we've just been left here, do you?"

Percy glanced up at her, but his gaze didn't linger.

"It had crossed my mind." Percy turned over his cards to reveal his hand. "Now, how did I do?"

Dot slapped her cards onto the table and claimed the pile of toothpicks for the fourth time that morning.

"I was *sure* I had it that time," he said, scratching the side of his head. "Ah, well! Maybe next time? Fancy another game while we wait for our breakfast to turn up?"

"I can't play another game of cards." She let out an exasperated sigh and folded her arms. "I feel like they've left us to cook to death in this heat! And according to my watch, it's already noon! He said he'd be here for breakfast."

"Right you are, my dear." He scratched the side of his head. "It's just . . . are you sure it's noon? It doesn't quite feel that late."

"Noon!" She bent her wrist to show her watch. "Couple of minutes to, but noon all the same."

"Did you change the time on your watch?" Percy asked as he gathered the cards. "We're two hours ahead here, remember."

"I know that." Dot pursed her lips, but she couldn't remember changing the time. Under the table, she twisted the dial back two hours. "Okay, for argument's sake, let's say it's only *ten* in the morning. If we were at home, we'd have eaten by now."

"But we're not home, are we?" Percy reached across to pet her hand. "Now, how about I make us another nice cup of tea while you see if you can get any of these windows open to let some fresh air in?"

Dot nodded, once again grateful her husband had awoken in a better mood than she. She'd fallen asleep with the resolve that she'd stay as positive as she could until they knew what was going on, but in practice, it hadn't been so easy. She'd always enjoyed firm mattresses, but according to the dull ache across her entire back, there was such a thing as too firm.

Even with the rock-solid bed, she might have slept if not for the heat. Minnie's air conditioning had done an excellent job of masking just how hot things could get. The blatant lack of so much of a piece of paper to waft the air about meant she endured a restless night of tossing and turning.

Percy, on the other hand, slept all the way through, going as far as to remark on how well-rested he felt when he sprang out of bed that morning.

As much as Dot didn't want to do anything other than sit around and not think about how boiling hot she was, no doubt the relief of a little fresh air would take the edge off.

While Percy got to work making tea with the box of teabags they'd found in the cupboard while searching for food, she walked into the sitting room part of the villa. She flicked on the television and it landed on what she imagined must be a Spanish soap opera, based on the dramatic costumes. Without subtitles, she had no idea what was going on. She considered switching to another channel, but if last night had taught her anything, she'd be in the same boat no matter what channel she chose.

The glamorous actors on the screen swanned about in a large manor house that vaguely reminded her of Peridale Manor back in the village, which was enough to keep it on.

Home had never felt so far away.

She knelt on the sofa to try opening the biggest window in the room. While she fiddled with the latch through the bars, she looked out at the clearing in front of the house. The van that had brought them was gone, and aside from the birds flitting around, there were no other signs of life.

Across the clearing, nestled on the edge of the trees, was a small white outbuilding with a single window and door. Was their captor in there? Were they being watched? Or had they really been left to die up in the mountains?

"It's painted shut," she said, giving the window a whack for good measure. "They thought of everything."

"Don't give up, dear."

Dot had never so distinctly wanted to give up. She plonked herself in the middle of the sofa and stared at the television. The quickly moving pictures kept her attention, and it only took her a couple of minutes to feel like she was following along with the gist of things.

A lady with bouncy, blow-dried curls slapped a tall, handsome man. He grabbed her, and seconds later, they were kissing in a fashion Dot found most dramatic, especially since their lips were barely touching.

"Anything good on?" Percy set the tea on the coffee table in front of them.

"I couldn't tell you," Dot replied, already reaching for her tea, eyes still on the screen. "I think that lady in the white top is having an affair with the man in the blue top, but he's married to the one with the large mole on her chin. Oh, and the gardener is involved, but don't ask how because I haven't figured that part out yet."

"Maybe we'll come out of this learning Spanish."

"Maybe."

Percy chuckled. "They do talk rather quickly."

Dot blew on the hot surface of her tea before taking a sip. The beverage didn't calm her like it usually would, merely adding to her overheated state. She put it back on the table. The soap opera cut to the advertisement break, which was just as confusing and fast-paced as the programme.

As she gazed away from the telly, disinterested, movement through the open bedroom door caught her attention. A bird flew back and forth across the window a couple of times before darting into the trees, holding Dot's gaze long enough for her to notice something.

"Won't be a second," she said, using Percy's knee and

the armrest to push herself upright. "Keep my seat . . . I was going to say 'warm', but I won't ask for more of that."

She walked through the open door and up to the bedroom window. The trees blocked out most of the natural light, casting the whole room in dim shadow. Despite the lack of direct daylight, her eyes hadn't mistaken her.

"I think it's coming back on," Percy called.

"Two seconds."

Dot perched on the bed and stared at the window. She hadn't noticed last night, but the bedroom window was different from the others.

There were bars on the inside.

There were no bars on the outside.

Dot tugged at the metal, and to her delight, the screws attaching it to the wall pulled back slightly, bringing out brick dust with them.

"*Dorothy!*" Percy cried. "Dorothy, come quick!"

Dot gave the bars another tug, and the screws came out even further. The bottom left-hand corner screw fell out onto the tiles in a shower of more brick dust. She grinned from ear to ear.

"Dorothy!"

"I'm not *that* invested in the programme, dear!"

"It cut to the news first," he called, beckoning her. "C'mon, dear! Don't dilly-dally."

Dot exhaled and crammed the screw back into the wall. She reluctantly left the bedroom, but she didn't quite make it to the sofa. A car pulling into the clearing outside caught her eye through the sealed-shut window.

"There's a car out there," she said. "Come look!"

"*You* come look!" Percy tugged her down onto the sofa. "We're on the *news!*"

Dot's eyes immediately snapped onto the television, just in time to see a recent picture of them, taken while out on a family picnic in Peridale only a couple of weeks ago, flash onto the screen. Dot hadn't seen the picture before, but she had a vague recollection of it being taken.

"We're on *television,* Dorothy!" Percy exclaimed. "This is almost exciting, don't you think?"

Dot attempted to purse her lips, but she couldn't help but smile a little. As a girl, she'd dreamed of being a famous actress, and aside from a brief turn in the Peridale Amateur Dramatics Society's annual Christmas nativity two years earlier, this was the closest she'd ever been to fame.

"They could have chosen a more flattering picture," Dot said, pushing up her deflated curls. "You can't tell how slender I am slouched down in the grass like that. I look like a bridge troll."

"You could never."

"What do you suppose she's saying?"

"I have no idea." Percy tapped her knee excitedly. "I'm *certain* Julia took that picture on her mobile telephone, so they must be looking for us!"

Dot's excitement vanished. The thought of her granddaughter tracking her down didn't fill her with joy like it should have.

"Dorothy?" Percy ducked to meet her eye line. "What is it?"

"It's nothing," she lied, pushing forward a smile.

"This is *good* news!"

"I know."

"It would be worse if they hadn't noticed."

"I know," she repeated. "It's just . . . it's Julia."

"What about her, dear?"

"She's good at this."

"Exactly!" Percy clapped his hands together. "I've seen her brilliance up close. She's a super sleuth, and I don't think the girl gives herself enough credit for it. She'd give any detective a run for their money with that mind of hers."

"Which is why I'm worried about her." Dot stood up and took two steps, her hand on her forehead and her back to Percy. "She's probably already halfway to tracking us down, and I don't know if you recall, my love, but she's twenty-one weeks pregnant with my third great-grandchild."

"Ah, yes. That does complicate things, rather."

Dot turned and looked through the window again. There were now three men on the opposite side of the clearing. Two wore garish clothes similar to the ones in the untouched plastic bag by the door, but the third wore jeans, a white t-shirt, and silver aviator glasses. Even from this distance, Dot recognised the man who'd chased them through the market and who'd promised to bring them breakfast.

"You saw the man's gun last night, I assume?" Dot asked.

"I did." Percy gulped. "Didn't want to bring it up in case you hadn't. Didn't want to scare you, my dear."

"That's very sweet of you," she said, pausing to smile, "but I've been terrified this entire time."

"Then you do a great job of hiding it," he said, tapping the sofa next to him. "Now sit down and tell me your plan. You have that look in your eyes."

"What look?" Dot shot back, quite sure her poker face was too good to show any kind of 'look'.

"It's the 'I think I have a plan' look," Percy replied with a soft smile. "Some people call it the 'Julia look', but to me, it's the 'Dorothy look'. Julia might be brilliant, but where do you think she got her brains from?"

"Certainly not from her father."

"Precisely." Percy winked. "She got them from her gran. Her brilliance is *your* brilliance. So, tell me your plan."

Dot was continuously surprised, surprised and truly touched, by how highly Percy thought of her. People had often remarked on her unshakeable confidence. While she had a steelier determination than most, she had never thought of herself as a 'brilliant' woman. But to look in Percy's eyes at that moment, she knew he must have been looking at someone special – or, at the very least, special in his eyes. That single look cleared away the last vestiges of her earlier melancholy and near-defeat.

"I could tell you," she started, nodding at the bedroom door, "*or* I could show you."

Keys jangled on the other side of the front door, and they froze. Lock by lock shifted and clicked until the deadbolt finally slid back and the door opened. They watched silently as the young man in the aviators walked in with another tray and a plastic bag. While the soap opera's dramatic music swelled in the background, he dumped the bag by the door and put the food on the kitchen table.

He looked as though he meant to head straight through the door again, but Dot stepped forward and smiled, hands clasped in front of her.

"Excuse me," she began, her voice as soft as she could muster. "I was wondering if you had any updates about our business here?"

"I told you." He stopped in his tracks and sighed, one hand on the door handle. "It is better to ask no questions."

"I have money," she said, remembering the stash of euros she'd taken from her bra and put in the bedside drawer; ironic, since she'd been so keen on protecting in only a day earlier. "Five hundred euros, give or take. You can have it all."

"I do not want your money," he replied flatly. "Eat breakfast. Later, I will bring dinner."

"Thank you," she said, scrambling for something. "What about requests?"

He sighed, let go of the handle, and waved to one of the men outside, giving the impression he had been instructed to drop off the food and nothing more. Blocking the exit, he pulled off his sunglasses and turned to Dot. His gaze darted uneasily around the room before finally landing on Dot's shoes.

"Requests?" he echoed, nodding for her to speak.

"Medication," Dot said, her sharper edges still intentionally softened. "You've probably noticed we're not the youngest, and between us, we take enough pills to keep a small pharmacy in business. Without them, I'm afraid we won't last much longer."

Dot saw the worry flash across his face as clear as day, so she fluttered her eyelids and rested her hand on her forehead, as though she could faint at any moment. It wasn't her finest work, but he seemed to buy it.

"Medication?" he repeated, looking between the two of them. "What kinds of this medication?"

Dot tapped her head and let her finger flutter away. "Brain isn't what it was. I think I'd be more confident writing them down. Names come easier that way. Uses a different part of the brain, you see. Have you got a pen and paper?"

The man patted down his pocket and pulled out his mobile phone. He tapped the screen a couple of times before handing it to Dot. It appeared to be a digital checklist, or even a shopping list, blank and waiting to be filled in. She'd never actually used a mobile phone in this way. She had a tablet for the few internet activities (shopping, watching old movies, and listening to old music) she could handle, so it wasn't completely foreign to her.

After spending an embarrassingly long time staring at the screen, she realised the squashed-up letters and numbers at the bottom were a condensed version of the wider keyboard she was more used to. Taking a seat at the table and remembering what Jessie had told her about 'tapping not pressing', she started writing down the names of all the medications her limited medical knowledge could provide. After writing down something she was sure was used as a stool softener, she froze. Her hands started shaking when she realised what she held.

"You done?" he called, his tone desperate. "Hurry."

"Old fingers," she replied, continuing her tapping. "Won't be a moment."

The urge to somehow use the phone to call for help left her mind as quickly as it entered. She had no idea how to use the thing beyond what she could see in front of her, and had no concrete idea who to call even if she did. She didn't even know the Spanish number for the police.

"Thank you so much," Dot said as she handed the phone back. "I think I got them all."

"Okay." He checked the list before pushing the phone into his pocket. "At dinner I will come—"

"One more thing," Dot called, another idea springing to mind. "It's hot in here. Very hot."

As though only just noticing the sweltering heat in the villa, he reached up to his bronzed forehead and wiped away beads of sweat with the back of his hand.

"A fan?" Dot suggested, smiling and nodding. "Please?"

The man looked between them and sighed. He slid his glasses on again and left, locking them in. She checked the new bag, which contained towels and toiletries.

"Now then, Dorothy," Percy called from the sofa, one brow arched, "what was all that about?"

"A test." She walked back to the window and watched as the two men, definitely older, chastised the sunglasses-wearer. "I wanted to find out two things."

"The first?"

One of the men in garish clothes slapped Aviator Sunglasses around the head. He flinched before the hand even struck, but he didn't duck. He was used to the abuse, Dot could tell that much. Once again, she was taken aback by his youth. Though he was working a man's job, those eyes belonged to a boy.

"I wanted to see how easily he would bend." Dot frowned as the young man retreated to the outbuilding while the two men sat in the plastic deck chairs in the shade. "I think you saw for yourself how that went."

"Young lad seemed to be quite compliant," Percy agreed. "How did you know he would be?"

"A feeling." Dot sighed and sat back next to Percy on the sofa. "You get to our age, and people assume you get simple and slow. Nobody wants to say no when a sweet old lady asks something of them, gun on his hip or not."

"And the second thing you wanted to find out?"

"That's not as trivial," she said, pausing to gulp. "The suggestion that we might die without our medication seemed to scare him so much that he handed over his mobile phone."

"You don't take any medication."

"I wrote down the name of your blood pressure pills," she said, "and that one you take to stop you getting up to use the lavatory in the middle of the night."

"I hadn't even thought about them."

"Good job one of us is on the ball." Dot smiled. "The rest, I pulled from thin air. I think I might even have made some of them up, but that's not the point. We'll see how hard he works to find as many as he can."

"To send him on a fun little wild goose chase?"

"To see how much the boy values our lives," Dot

replied darkly, nodding for Percy to follow her into the bedroom. "I think my theory that he's only a worker bee has been confirmed, at least."

"So, who's the queen, then?"

"Hardly matters, does it?" Dot closed the bedroom door behind them and walked over to the window. "Look, no bars on the other side. It's sealed shut like the others, but it won't take much to smash that glass, and I reckon we'd both fit through there quite easily."

"What are you suggesting, Dorothy?" Percy perched on the edge of the bed, his hands shaking until he clasped them tightly. "That we make a run for it?"

"Not right now." She turned the loose screw around and around. "It's nice to have the option, but I don't think we'd get very far. Not with those three out there. They're probably all carrying guns. We need to be smarter than that."

"How?"

The keys started jangling again. Wordlessly agreeing that they shouldn't be caught doing anything other than sitting around being old and sweet, they hurried back into the sitting room. Dot sat on the sofa seconds before the deadbolt slid back. The door cracked open, and a fist held out a plastic white desk fan.

It shook, and Dot realised the hand wanted one of them to take it. She hurried over, glad to see the boy again.

"Thank you . . ." She paused, waiting for him to fill in his name.

"Rafa," he replied, smiling a little. "Behave, okay?"

The door closed and he began locking it again, but his smile had told her she had him.

"Dorothy, how will we outsmart them?"

"I don't know yet," she admitted, plugging the fan into a socket near the dining table. "If I'm as brilliant as you claim I am, I'm sure I'll come up with something soon."

Dot sat down in front of the fan and switched it on. The first cool breeze brushing across her face made her smile more than she had since first seeing the view from Minnie's hotel terrace – a memory that already felt fuzzy. She pulled off her brooch and unbuttoned the top of her blouse, and the crisp air felt delicious on her skin.

"Is the fan part of your plan, dear?" Percy asked.

"No, this is because it's bloody boiling." She pulled up a second chair and moved over so her husband could fit in the fan's stream. "Now, come sit down and enjoy the air while I let my brilliant brain come up with the next bit."

9

JULIA

*J*ulia drummed her fingers against the reception desk, her wide eyes fixated on the printer. It fired out sheet after sheet, and yet there still wouldn't be enough to cover the whole of Savega in missing posters. They were already on their third batch of the afternoon. If not for Lisa's help – she'd translated everything into Spanish for them – they'd have had nothing at all to hand out.

If the police were doing anything to help, Julia certainly couldn't see the evidence. She glanced into the dining room, where Barker and Inspector Hillard were still exchanging words, and Sub-Inspector Castro picked listlessly at the breakfast leftovers. Barker and Hillard had their hands on their hips and their chests puffed out, but at least the shouting had stopped. Private investigator or not, it was hard taking Barker, in his denim shorts and sleeveless vest, seriously – especially when contrasted with Inspector Hillard's sharp suit.

The printer spat out its final pamphlet. Julia stared at the picture of Dot and Percy she had taken on a picnic only weeks ago. Everything had been so normal then. Their honeymoon was supposed to be normal, too, but things couldn't have felt more surreal. Even staring at the picture of her gran and Percy surrounded by English and Spanish words pleading for help and information, Julia couldn't quite comprehend what was going on.

Everything had moved so fast. Even now, she half-expected them to walk through the door with a funny explanation for their absence. Remembering the ransom note brought her right back down to earth.

Before her mind could wander to dark places, Lisa pushed through the door behind the desk marked 'PRIVATE', wearing the apologetic smile Julia had dreaded but expected. Once again, Minnie was conspicuously absent.

"She still won't come down," Lisa said with an exasperated sigh. "She's having one of her manic episodes. She's hysterical."

"I *need* to talk to her." The desperation in Julia's voice came through loud and clear. "I know there's more to this than she's letting on." She shook her head. "I know there's more to this than *both* of you are letting on. My gran means everything to me. I just want to find her."

"I appreciate that," Lisa said as she slapped down the fresh pile of posters on the counter, "but when my mother gets in these moods, there's no talking to her. I'm telling you, nothing on this planet could get her out of bed and downstairs right now. And quite frankly, you wouldn't want to be around her. She won't see – or talk – sense."

Julia had never felt so helpless. Neither getting down on her knees and begging or vaulting over the reception desk and breaking into the hotel's private quarters to find Minnie would bring back her gran. She didn't doubt Lisa. From what she'd already seen, Minnie could be a . . . very difficult woman.

"Thank you for these," Julia said, resting her hands on the stack of posters and making sure that Lisa could see her smile. "I do appreciate what you've done."

"And there's plenty more where they came from. The suppliers had a great deal on office supplies a few years ago, and I bought enough ink and paper to last us a lifetime." Lisa rested her hand on the stack of posters, the tips of her fingers touching Julia's. "They'll turn up. After all the stories Mum told me, I'm really looking forward to getting to know her." Lisa offered a smile in return. "I'm sure wherever your gran is, she's giving someone hell."

"I bet she is," Julia said, allowing herself a small laugh; it felt good. "Are you *sure* there is nothing I need to know? Anything at all?"

For a moment, Lisa looked like she might say something. By the shadowed look in her eyes, it was serious.

And then the phone behind the reception desk rang before her lips parted. Lisa's hand hovered over the receiver for three chimes before picking it up. Julia had an idea who it was before the phone even reached Lisa's ear.

"Yes, Mother," Lisa said, pinching the bridge of her nose and closing her eyes. "Mmhmm. Yes, I'm bringing it up. I was just talking to Julia. Yes, I know, I won't make it too hot. No, I won't make it too cold either. I do know what I'm doing, Mother. Yes, I understand. I'll be right up."

Lisa flashed Julia another apologetic smile before scurrying back through the door she'd just come through. As different as mother and daughter were, right now, their reluctance to speak was something they had in common.

Perhaps it was asking too much, but Julia could hardly believe they weren't out searching the streets of Savega right alongside her and Barker. If they'd been visiting Peridale and the shoe had been on the other foot, Julia wouldn't have hesitated to do everything in her power to help. As helpful as the posters were, she and Barker could only do so much – especially as they didn't speak the language and knew virtually nothing about the locals and the area.

Inspector Hillard stormed past Julia, the wind stirred by his passing fluttering the top few posters. The front doors slammed behind him, rattling the wooden flip sign in the window. Sub-Inspector Castro followed after him, smiling frustrating and ultimately unhelpful apologies, just like Lisa. In the dining room, Barker let out an exasperated and sustained grunt deep in his throat, both hands clenching fistfuls of his dark hair.

"That man is an *idiot!*" Barker cried as he marched up to Julia. "No wonder he doesn't work in the UK anymore. No police force in the country would promote a man like that to the rank of inspector. It's an *insult* to the profession!"

"The profession you are no longer a part of," Julia reminded him gently. "But I agree, he doesn't seem like the sharpest tool in the box. It's like he's trying to do the bare minimum while also making things more difficult for us."

"*Exactly!*" Barker huffed and leaned against the desk, hands covering his face. "He couldn't even explain why he blasted that picture of Dot and Percy all over the news. If I'd known what he'd intended, I would never have suggested that you give it to him. What kind of inspector pastes the faces of two people being held for ransom all over the television the day after they're taken? It's like he's *trying* to spook the captors! He's treating it like a missing persons case, not a ransom. The two need to be handled differently."

Sharp claws clenched around Julia's heart, squeezing the life from her. Barker's words were honest and frank, and as much as they shocked her, as much as she wanted to deny them, she knew they were true.

"I'm sorry, love." Barker pulled her against his chest, his vest smelling of coconut-scented sun cream. "The inspector might have had a point somewhere in there, though. The kidnappers didn't specify that we shouldn't call the police, which is unusual. I haven't seen many ransom notes first-hand, but I know part of the deal is usually that the police aren't to be involved."

"Why do you think they'd leave that out?"

"Inspector Good-For-Nothing seems to think it's because everyone always calls the police anyway, so why bother pretending we won't?" Barker pulled away from the hug, already rolling his eyes. "I'm not sure if that's the dumbest thing I've ever heard, but it ranks pretty high. He refused to tell me what they were actively doing to investigate the case. If things carry on like this, I'm marching myself down to the station and demanding to speak to his superior."

"Let's get this fresh round of posters out before we start antagonising the local authorities." Julia picked up the thick stack and divided it in two. "You know if we split up, we could—"

"Cover more ground?" Barker interjected with a half-smile, wrapping his arm around Julia as they headed to the door. "Nice try, love, but I'm not letting you out of my sight. I've seen the films."

Once again, they returned to the plaza. By this point, they had been back and forth so many times that it seemed like an eternity had passed since they'd interviewed Arlo at the café. Julia had to remind herself that they'd spoken to Arlo just that morning. On each trip back to the hotel to get more posters, Julia had tried and failed to talk with Minnie. She had also been keeping her eye out for the Gabriel, the mysterious Frenchman Minnie apparently owed money to, but he and his red car had yet to reappear.

Over Barker's protests, they separated at the fountain, each taking a side of the plaza, desperate to reach more people before the place emptied out for the day. The daytime shops and cafés were already starting to close up, and as the light in the sky shifted toward twilight, the restaurants and bars began to fill up.

Feeling Barker's eyes trained firmly on her, she handed out poster after poster. Few people accepted them, and even fewer wanted to listen to her. She only wanted to know if anyone had seen Dot or Percy in the hours before the ransom note appeared at the hotel, and yet nobody seemed willing to speak. Buying souvenirs and drinking coffee was apparently far more important than helping Julia find her gran. Once again, she couldn't help but compare this town unfavourably to Peridale.

She missed home much more than she'd expected to only two days into her honeymoon.

"*Miss?*" came a timid voice from behind Julia, accompanied by a rustle of paper. "Excuse me? Miss?"

Julia turned to see a pretty young woman in a café uniform, a poster clutched in her hands. Despite her youth, worry lines furrowed her forehead, exaggerated by her scrunched brows as she stared at the pamphlet.

"Miss," she said again, holding out the poster, "I saw them. Yesterday I saw them."

"You did?" Julia grabbed the woman's shoulders, and the waitress blinked, obviously startled by Julia's ferocity. "When? What happened?"

Barker joined them, gently prying Julia's fingers from the girl's shoulders.

"She saw them, Barker," Julia said, eyes frantically darting around the plaza. "She said she saw them yesterday."

"Before the lunchtime," the waitress said as she reached into her apron. She pulled out a small, folded-up piece of paper. When she unfolded it, Julia instantly recognised her gran's unique, curly handwriting. "The lady, she gives me this."

Julia's eyes scanned the short note a handful of times before any of the words even registered. Closing her eyes, she forced herself to calm down. When she opened them a moment later, she was ready to read her gran's words properly.

I've hidden something very dear to me in the bathroom bin for reasons I can't explain now. I know this is a strange request, but please can you keep it safe for me? I'll be back later to collect it. Thank you in advance.

"'Collect it'?" Julia echoed. "Collect what?"

The young woman, whose tag identified her as Maria, ushered them into the nearest café. The café had an exposed upstairs balcony like Chocolatería Valor, but it was nowhere near as uniquely decorated. Football played on several televisions, and an older, slightly overweight man propped up the counter, eyes darting between the sports pages of the newspaper and the screens. The few customers seemed more interested in the televisions than the newcomers.

Maria joined the portly man behind the counter and pulled something out of a plastic carrier bag. Toilet roll encased the mystery item, but the second Julia noticed the leather, she knew exactly what it was.

"My gran left this here?" Julia picked up the album and flicked through it. "She would never do that. These pictures mean too much to her."

"Did you see anything strange when they were

here?" Barker asked, squeezing Julia's shoulder reassuringly.

Maria shook her head. "I did not notice them," she said, glancing up to the balcony, hinting that was where they'd sat. "Not until this lady, she gives me fifty euros and this note. I wait for her to come back, but she does not. I keep the book here, for when she comes. The, how do you say, this look in her eyes, like she was..."

"Like she was what?" Julia pushed.

"Scared." Maria gazed at Julia with wide eyes. "Very scared."

The words sank like lead balloons, followed by the hollow echo of cheers from the TV as someone scored a goal. Never had a sound seemed more out of place. The man behind the counter gave a silent cheer, clenching his fist in victory, before returning to the newspaper.

Julia wished she hadn't asked. She didn't want to know what could possibly make her indomitable gran look *very scared*.

"These cameras?" Barker asked, looking around the room and nodding the domes in the corners. "Are they real?"

She nodded. "After all the troubles, Papa insists."

"Troubles?" Julia asked, her ears pricking up.

"Break-ins," she said, glancing down the bar at the man reading the paper. "We are not the only ones. It is the whole plaza. Things, they have not been the same since..."

The man at the end of the bar coughed, rustling his paper as he did. The look he gave his daughter told Julia all she needed to know: this was something they didn't speak of.

"Can we look at the footage?" Barker asked, pulling a business card from his pocket. "Please?"

The move was so seamless Julia didn't notice the twenty euro note hidden underneath the black card until she spotted the blue poke out in Maria's palm. She looked down at the money and immediately tucked it into her apron, nodding for them to follow her deeper into the café.

"What are you thinking?" Julia asked in a hushed tone as they followed the woman to a door at the back.

"If your gran left a precious photo album in a bin, wrapped in toilet roll, she must have had an inkling that something was about to happen," he said. "Maybe she didn't know she was about to be kidnapped for ransom money since she planned on coming back for the book last night, but something must have spooked her. If we can figure out where she was and what she did between leaving the hotel and the ransom note turning up, we'll have a better chance of pinning down her last known whereabouts – and a better chance of finding whoever took her."

Julia clutched Barker's hand, grateful to have her husband by her side. Whether it was the bizarreness of the situation, the personal interest, the pregnancy hormones, the heat, or some mixture of it all, she couldn't quieten the noise in her mind long enough to let her usual logic take the lead.

The room at the back of the café was a small, windowless office with a wraparound desk, a couple of filing cabinets, some stacked cardboard boxes, and two screens displaying a live feed of the security cameras. Maria bent over and used the mouse to navigate through the screens.

After a couple of minutes, Dot and Percy appeared on the screen, rushing into the café from six different angles. They went straight upstairs, where they did a terrible job of hiding behind menus and trying to look inconspicuous.

"Something had them agitated," Barker said, glancing at Julia, clearly pleased his hunch was right. To Maria, he asked, "Did you notice anyone following them in?"

Maria shrugged and waved her hand, the visit clearly not etched in her mind enough to recall anything other than the money and the note. Without those, Julia knew her gran and Percy would just be two more tourists in an ever-changing sea of them.

"What do they keep looking at?" Julia mused aloud, squinting at the screen. "See? They keep peering over the balcony and doing a terrible job of pretending they're not. Do you have a camera focused on the door, perhaps?"

"Why the door?" Barker asked.

Maria clicked a couple of buttons, and the camera feeds changed, this time to two separate angles of the outside seating area. Barker made an impressed sound, but Julia couldn't bask in it.

One man immediately stuck out like a sore thumb. He was the only one alone, the only one not looking at the menu, the only one without an order on his table, and the only one staring intently into the restaurant. Even with his eyes hidden behind his reflective glasses, the angle of his head made it obvious where he was looking.

"Fast forward to when they leave, please," Julia requested, moving closer to the screens. "I want to see what he does."

After a few clicks, the video sped up. Maria hit play when Dot and Percy appeared at the bottom of the frame. They hurried past the man, and without missing a beat, he jumped up and followed them.

"Do you know this man?" Barker asked firmly. "Is he a regular here?"

The woman stared at the seat where the man had sat, but eventually, shrugged and shook her head at the same time.

"Who are you?" Julia asked under her breath. "Why did it have to be my gran and Percy?"

"That doesn't matter right now," Barker said, giving Julia shoulders another reassuring squeeze. "We have a solid lead. I know it's not much to work with, but it's something." He turned to the woman. "Can I use my phone to film a copy of this to show to the police?"

"Of course," she said, rewinding the video to Dot and Percy leaving, and stepping aside so Barker would have an unimpeded view.

After dropping a pile of posters on the counter for Maria to give out, they left, armed with yet another lead that meant nothing without context.

"There's something more to all of this," Julia said, looking around the quickly emptying plaza. "The way her father cut her off when she mentioned the break-ins, for one thing. My gran's not the only one who was scared. They're scared. Minnie is scared. Something is going on here, Barker, and I have a feeling that if we don't find out, we'll never stand a chance of finding them."

"Don't say—"

"It's true." She gazed blankly into the distance, her eyes going all the way out to sea without taking in any of the beauty in front of her. "Minnie and Lisa are playing games, and the inspector isn't on our side. We need to figure this out, and quickly. I don't want to find out what happens when that timer runs out."

Hand in hand, they took the weaving network of back streets and alleyways to La Casa. They arrived at the entrance at the same time as a taxi coming from the opposite direction. Julia recognised the passenger before the taxi even stopped. Impossible as it was, she knew her eyes weren't failing her.

"*Jessie?*" Julia and Barker cried at the same time, in an identically shocked tone.

Jessie climbed out of the taxi and passed something to the driver through the window. She wore cutoff denim shorts and a black vest, and she carried a heavy-looking backpack. She ran, the bag bouncing behind her, and crashed into them with open arms.

"What are you doing here?" Julia asked, clinging tightly to her daughter.

"Did you think I was going to sit at home and play café while this was going on?" Jessie pulled away from the hug and tucked Julia's loose curls behind her ears. "Not a chance, Mum. Everyone is losing their minds back home, seriously. It's all people in the café are talking about, and even the choir are trying to do a benefit concert to raise the ransom money, although I doubt they'll be able to raise the full amount. I couldn't just sit at home and do nothing. Everyone else feels the same."

"Who's watching the café?"

"Katie. She's also feeding Mowgli." Jessie repositioned the bulky backpack on her shoulders, eyes on her beat-up black and white Converse shoes. "Are you mad at me?"

Julia pulled Jessie into a hug, this time on her own, and whispered, "I've never been gladder to see your face."

10

DOT

The setting sun pushed through the dense trees and into the bedroom. The bars on the window broke the warm light into uniform strips, illuminating the specks of dust in the air. The sunset was probably gorgeous, but Dot could only imagine it since none of the windows provided a view of anything beyond the clearing and the tall trees surrounding it.

She flicked on the naked bulb in the ceiling and continued her search for something tasteful amongst the garish clothes they had been given. There were several items for each of them, but none of it resembled any clothing she had ever worn or would ever wear.

The patterns were busy, the colours loud, and the materials artificial. Still, despite her horror, she needed to wear something. Tightening the towel around her chest, she glanced at her usual clothes, laid out on her bed. After two days of wear in the Spanish heat, she couldn't bear the idea of climbing back into them.

Defeated, she plucked a matching tracksuit from the pile. Both top and bottom were covered in the same graffiti pattern, which included every colour of the rainbow amongst the mess. They were hideous, and yet somehow the least awful option.

"Oh, dear," she whispered at her reflection after dressing. "Dorothy South, you have never looked more ridiculous."

She turned to get a look at the back, but it was just as bad as the front. In any other situation, she would have pulled them right off, but choice was a luxury she didn't have. People often referred to her as a control freak, a title she never felt fit her. Now that all control had been taken away, she was beginning to understand they might have had a point. She picked up her brooch from the bedside table and attached it to the front pocket of the tracksuit. It wasn't much, but at least it was familiar, and it was hers.

"You coming out any time soon, dear?" Percy called through the door, accompanied by a gentle knock.

Dot pulled herself away from the mirror and reluctantly opened the bedroom door. Percy looked her up and down, tapping his finger against his chin as he assessed her outfit with a level of care the ugly print didn't deserve.

"It shows off your figure tremendously!"

"Not every cloud has a silver lining, my dear." She pinched her husband's cheek. "But I appreciate the effort all the same."

Percy laughed, and she couldn't help but join in. Despite the direness of their situation, it felt good to laugh, even if it was at her expense.

"My turn," Percy said as he plucked the damp towel from the door hook where Dot had hung it. "How's the water pressure?"

"Abysmal."

"As I suspected."

After Percy undressed for his first shower in captivity, Dot collected his clothes and added them to her own pile. She took everything through to the kitchen and filled up the sink. In the absence of washing powder, the bar of hand soap would have to do. At least they could wear their own outfits by morning. If they were still alive, of course.

While she scrubbed at the armpits of her blouse, Percy's off-key impression of Frank Sinatra floated through the villa, accompanied by the sound of running water. She was used to his shower concerts by now. His pitch issues and habit of making up his own words to the classics usually made her purse her lips and roll her eyes, but tonight, it brought a smile to her face. Still scrubbing the blouse, she closed her eyes, and just for a second, she was back in Peridale.

The jangling of keys on the other side of the front

door brought her back down to reality. Once again, the locks opened one by one, with the deadbolt last of all. She saw Rafa's reflection in the dark kitchen window without needing to turn around. As he carried in their dinner, she finished scrubbing the armpit of her blouse and dried her hands on a tea towel.

"It is much cooler in here now," he remarked. This time, he did not seem to be in a rush to leave again.

"I know you're not talking about my jazzy new outfit," she said, pulling at the hem of the zip-up tracksuit top. "But yes, it is. I don't think I could have coped today without the fan. Thank you again. We really do appreciate it."

Dot cast her eyes over the food on the tray. More of the same, but with one subtle difference: two small pots of strawberry yoghurt were nestled next to the bread, cheese, meat, and olives. Though the desert was modest, Dot took it as a sign that she had managed to soften the boy's edges. He'd even come in without his sunglasses, although he still couldn't look her directly in the eyes. Not a bad thing, she thought, wondering if he was nervous or ashamed.

"I found some of these medications," he said, reaching into the inside of his leather jacket. "Not all. I did the best I could."

Rafa handed over a white pharmacy bag. Dot opened it and cast her eyes over the boxes, glad to see Percy's blood pressure tablets amongst them. She had no idea how he'd managed to source so much medication without prescriptions . . . and she wasn't sure she wanted to find out. Rafa had passed her test. For now, at least, he wasn't ready to see them die. As dangerous as she knew it was, Dot felt hope.

"Thank you, Rafa." Dot made sure to look him in the eyes when she said his name. "One day you'll get to be my age and know what it feels like to have to toss back pills just to get through the day."

Dot never thought she'd be in a situation where she'd openly lie about her health. A lifetime of eating well and keeping active, along with good genetics had, for the most part, kept her in the small minority of people her age who didn't need to depend on daily tablets. And yet, this little lie played into the half-baked plan she'd come up with during her brainstorming session in front of the fan.

"Why don't you join me for a cup of tea?" Dot asked, already reaching for the kettle. "I know you're probably not supposed to, but I couldn't help but notice that those men left a couple of hours ago."

Rafa scratched at the back of his head, staring at the door he'd left open. As tempting as it was, making a run for it wasn't on the agenda quite yet. She wouldn't get very far, for one thing, and she would never leave Percy behind.

"I think I should not," he said.

Dot couldn't help but smile as she stood at the kettle,

her back to him. That he didn't flat-out refuse was enough of a thread to pull.

"Oh, go on," she whispered over her shoulder, sending him a wink. "Don't refuse an old lady a little company. My dear husband likes to take long showers."

Rafa said nothing, but he closed the door and locked it from the inside. Perched on the edge of the sunken sofa, he leaned against his knees and looked around the room as if he'd never really seen it before.

The kettle pinged. Dot quickly filled two cups to the brim before he could change his mind, adding milk and sugar without asking. In her experience, most non-British folk never seemed to know how to make a good cup of tea, so she made it exactly how she liked it.

"There's nothing a cuppa can't fix," Dot said she set the two cups on the coffee table next to the recently abandoned game of poker. "How old are you, Rafa? Eighteen? Nineteen? Twenty, at a push? You look about my great-granddaughter Jessie's age."

She could tell Rafa didn't want to answer the question, but she didn't stop. Getting him talking was part of her plan, and she'd do it one way or another.

"I have three great-grandchildren," she continued, "and another one on the way. My granddaughter, Julia, is pregnant. She's here. Well, not *here*, as such, but she's in Spain. We were all here for our joint honeymoon. You might think it's silly at our age, but Percy and I are only recently married. It's coming up on our two-month anniversary next week. We were going to celebrate it with a meal out in Savega."

Trying not to stare, Dot assessed his reaction to her rambling about her family. He looked uncomfortable, which was exactly what she'd hoped for. She didn't want to tell her kidnapper all about her family – but she needed to.

"Nineteen," he said. "Last month I am nineteen."

"Ah!" Dot sipped her tea. "So you're a Cancer. Very giving people."

Dot believed in horoscopes about as much as she believed in extra-terrestrials, but she'd heard enough about it all from Evelyn, Peridale's local mystic, to sound convincing.

"I know this isn't your fault," she said, offering him a smile as he reached out for the tea. "I might be old, and sometimes foolish, but I can see in your eyes that you don't want to do this any more than I want to be here."

Rafa's tanned cheeks darkened subtly.

"I-I should go," he said, already standing.

"Please," Dot said, reaching out and grabbing the sleeve of his leather jacket. "At least finish your tea. I can't bear to see things go to waste. I'm sure your grandmother is the same way."

He sat down. Percy's enthusiastic singing picked up again from the bathroom. Again Dot smiled.

"You're not much of a talker, Rafa." She sipped her tea. "Is Rafa a nickname?"

He nodded.

"Everyone calls me Dot, but it's short for Dorothy." His lack of response was becoming unbearable. "And my husband, he's Percy, which is short for Percival."

"Rafael," he said, eyes on the tiled floor. "But only my abuela calls me this."

"Abuela?"

"My grandmother," he explained. "She raised me."

"And I bet she only calls you Rafael when you're in trouble," Dot said as playfully as she could. "Where are your parents, if you don't mind me asking?"

"Dead," he said flatly. "When I was a boy."

Dot hadn't expected to feel sorry for him, but she did. She'd hoped he'd reveal something personal she could use to her advantage, but knowing he was an orphan made her plan to manipulate him feel wrong, suddenly. Ironic, she thought, considering what he had done to them so far. Still, she'd spent enough time around wayward teenagers over the years to know their actions weren't always thought out. Heck, even she made mistakes at that age – although at least she could say she'd achieved the ripe old age of eighty-five without participating in the kidnapping of two pensioners.

"I'm sorry to hear that," Dot said, and she meant it. "The great-granddaughter I told you about, Jessie? Her parents died too. My granddaughter, Julia, the pregnant one, took her in a few years ago. Jessie was on a bad path. She was a homeless thief, but she turned her life right around. Does your grandmother know what you're doing now?"

Dot expected Rafa to shake his head, but he threw a spanner in the works and nodded. It wasn't exactly the family relationship Dot had expected.

"She's involved?" Dot pushed, her sweet voice dropping.

"This is not her fault," he replied, frowning at the tea. "It is her husband."

"Your grandfather?"

"He is *not* my grandfather," Rafa stated firmly. "He's – I-I need to go." He quickly drained the rest of the tea. "I am sorry, Mrs Dorothy."

Dot gripped his leather jacket again, this time with so much force that his right hand went for the gun. She let go and held her palms up, her hands shaking for real and not for effect.

"My family," she said as her heart pounded in her chest. "I'd very much like to see them again."

He stared at her blankly and the apology in his eyes scared her more than anything else over the past two days had done. Before she could push any more, he left, locking the doors quicker than ever. It wasn't likely she would catch him so off his guard again.

Hugging her tea and staring silently at the blank television, Dot was unable to think of anything but her family. She had avoided focusing too much on them, trying, instead, to live in the moment, but after talking about them out loud, she couldn't get their faces out of her mind. She didn't realise tears were streaming down her cheeks until the shower cut off in the bathroom and she reflexively wiped them away.

"Dinner's here!" Percy remarked as he walked out of the bathroom. "Butter us some bread while I get dressed, my dear, and then we can see what's on the telly."

Dot rinsed the cups in the sink before Percy could notice anything amiss. She wouldn't tell him about her conversation with their captor. She wouldn't tell him about the look she'd seen in the boy's eyes.

The glimmer of hope she had felt earlier was now nothing more than a burnt-down candle, but Percy's hope would burn bright for as long as she could nurture it. The truth would scare him more than it scared her. If they were going to get out of this situation alive, Dot needed her jolly Percy by her side.

If only she had some concrete idea about just how they were going to pull off such a feat.

11

JULIA

The next morning, Julia, Barker, and Jessie woke early to continue plastering as many missing posters around Savega as they could.

Jessie had insisted that she'd go out on her own to look for them as soon as she arrived, clearly eager to get started after her flight. Missing the previous night's sleep thanks to the early flight time had Jessie asleep in a deck chair on the terrace before sunset. If it weren't for the baby, Julia would have thrown a blanket over Jessie and gone out with Barker to continue their mission. As it was, she was wise enough to know that an early start after a decent night's sleep was the better option.

In the end, her sleep was far from decent. She tossed and turned all night, able to think only about her gran. Alone in the dark, with Barker softly snoring beside her, Julia's imagination ran away with her.

She imagined her gran and Percy locked up somewhere, starving, possibly bruised, and most likely terrified for their lives. The worst part was not knowing if her imagination was being cruel or honest. She had seen enough films involving kidnapping to understand they weren't being put up in a five-star resort somewhere.

Behind the reception desk the next morning, they watched silently as the printer rapid-fired more posters of Dot and Percy's faces. They had set early alarms, but they still weren't down before the start of breakfast – and Lisa and Minnie were nowhere to be seen.

The other guests, not one of whom had said so much as two words to Julia despite everything going on, were also down, but they weren't waiting for breakfast. They sat in the sunroom, fully clothed, cases at their sides, checking their watches every couple of minutes while they waited for the transfer to pick them up and take them home.

"Here she comes again," said Jessie, rolling her eyes in the direction of the plump, sunburnt woman who had already tried to check out with them once. "We already told you, we don't work here, so buzz off!"

The woman scowled and huffed, but turned on her heel and returned to the sunroom. She whispered something to her party, and they all glared in the direction of the desk. If Jessie cared, nothing showed on her face.

"I wonder why they haven't come down yet?" Julia glanced at the clock on the wall. "Do you think they're avoiding us?"

"I heard arguing last night," Jessie said in a low voice. "I know I haven't met this Minnie chick yet, but I'm sure I recognised Lisa's voice."

"What were they arguing about?" Barker asked.

"No idea." Jessie shrugged and picked up the stack of posters as soon as the printer spat out the final sheet. "I thought we could hit the beach if you haven't already been down there. I saw it when I flew in, and it's not that far away."

"That's a good idea, kid." Barker attempted to ruffle her hair, but she ducked before his hand made contact. "Minnie said a lot of tourists travel into town. Someone who might have been up here the morning Dot and Percy went missing could be anywhere – and the beach is as good a place as any to try and catch them."

"Would explain why this place is so quiet," Jessie said, glancing into the empty dining room, where nobody had even turned the lights on. "Remember when we were looking at all of those glowing reviews for this place, Mum? Well, I could barely find them under the mountain of one-star reviews that have poured in over the last few weeks. People were ripping this place to shreds."

"What were they saying?" Barker asked, arms folded, clearly intrigued.

"It's what they weren't saying," Jessie replied, splitting the pile into three and handing them out. "I was expecting to turn up to a bug-riddled hostel run by lunatics, and while I can't attest to the latter, it's certainly not as bad as people were making out."

Another member of the waiting party walked towards the desk – this time a plump, sunburnt man, looking even more irritated than the woman before him.

"What's the big idea then?" He folded his thick arms across his chest, and he might have looked menacing if he weren't a generous inch or two above five foot. "First you won't let us check out, and then you insult my wife? Our transfer will be here in ten minutes."

"Like I told your missus," Jessie snapped, slapping the pile of posters down on the desk, "we don't bloody work here, mate."

"Then what are you doing behind the desk, *mate?*"

"This is my great-aunt's hotel," Julia explained, smiling to make up for Jesse's abruptness; she had never been a morning person. "We're guests too."

"And if you hadn't noticed, mate, we're trying to find two missing old folks." Jessie held up a poster and shook in his face. "Or haven't you been paying attention to what's been going on around here? You're about to go home and tell everyone what a lovely holiday you had, including how you *clearly* forgot to put on any sunblock while you were here. And when you get off the plane and go home and hug your family, who I assume are as awful as you and your wife, we will still be here, searching the streets, desperately trying to find these two."

As harsh as Jessie's words were, the man didn't bite back. He shifted his weight from foot to foot and readjusted his arms, exhaling through his nostrils.

"Look," he said, his voice softer this time, "I'm sorry for what you're going through, but we just want to pay our room service bill before the transfer picks us up."

Leaving the posters on the desk, Julia sat down at the computer. She moved the mouse, and the screen came to life, displaying a complicated system she didn't recognise. She let her eyes drift across the screen, but she couldn't make heads or tails of what needed to be done so the man could pay his bill.

"Jessie?" Julia glanced over her shoulder at her more technologically savvy daughter. "Any ideas?"

But before Jessie could take Julia's place at the desk, footsteps creaked slowly down the stairway behind them. Minnie shuffled through the door to the private quarters, wearing a leopard-print silk dressing gown, a pair of large sunglasses that covered her eyes, and a scarf concealing her hair – which, by the looks of it, had yet to see a brush.

"Where's Lisa?" Minnie croaked, last night's sangria still hot on her breath.

"I don't know," Julia said, gesturing toward the

waiting man, "but the other guests are checking out, and I don't know how to use the system."

Minnie stared blankly first at Julia and then at the computer. "Neither do I. Lisa does all that."

"But Lisa hasn't always been here," Julia pointed out.

"My husband took care of everything." Minnie shuffled forward in her slippers, but she didn't quite reach the reception desk. "We had a book, but Lisa insisted we get the computer system."

"I just want to pay my room service bill," the man repeated, clearly losing what little patience he still had left. "The service here has left a lot to be desired, but this is a new low."

"Whatever," Minnie said, wafting her hand through the air as she set off to the dining room. "No charge. Room service is on me. Won't make a difference at this point." She flipped on the lights and stared at the empty buffet table. "Where's Lisa?"

"Is she senile?" Jessie whispered, hooking a thumb at Minnie. "Let's just go. Sooner we're out of here, sooner we can find them."

The man lingered by the reception desk for a moment before cursing under his breath and heading back to the sunroom. Like his wife before him, he whispered something, and the whole party glared in their direction.

"You two go on without me," Julia said, her eyes firmly on Minnie, who was now wandering out onto the terrace and ignoring her few remaining guests. "I need to get some answers, and I don't know how many chances I'll get if she keeps locking herself away."

"Are you sure you don't want me to stay?" Barker asked, resting a hand on the small of her back.

Julia shook her head. "Like Jessie said, the sooner you get out there, the higher our chances of finding them. I'll see what I can do here, and if she gives me nothing, I'll get a taxi down to the beach to find you."

After a quick kiss and hug, and with a promise to keep safe, Barker and Jessie headed for the beach. As soon as they left, a minibus squeezed down the narrow street in front of the hotel. The driver jumped out, clipboard in hand. Fearing he, like the others, would expect her to help, Julia left the computer and the reception desk. The party rose to their feet, one even giving her slow, sarcastic applause.

"Aren't you going to help with our cases?" another barked at Julia, looking down at her bump with disinterest.

"You heard my daughter," she said, walking right through them. "I don't work here."

More grumbling followed, and she could practically feel their eyes glaring at the back of her head, but she didn't give them the satisfaction of sticking around. While they struggled to get the cases out of the hotel, she joined Minnie on the terrace.

"This is because we argued last night," Minnie

muttered, hands clenched against the railing as she stared out into the valley. "She's punishing me. She does this. Her father was the same way. Argumentative to the core. Spiteful."

Julia joined her at the railing and looked out at the valley. The view was as gorgeous as ever, but she couldn't help wondering where in that expansive view her gran was being kept. Julia considered mentioning that Jessie had heard arguing but decided against it. The last thing she wanted was for Minnie to think they were eavesdropping on her, especially if she did have something to hide.

"I hope it was nothing serious," Julia said.

"Same old, same old."

"Which is?" Julia prodded gently, trying not to spook her.

Minnie waved vaguely, but once again, Julia had no idea what the gesture was supposed to mean.

"Money," Minnie said with a heavy sigh, pulling off her sunglasses to reveal tired eyes. "It's always about money with her. Once again, just like her father. Counting every single penny. It was like living with an accountant. And she wonders why I divorced him."

"You said you had money troubles?"

"Who doesn't these days?" Minnie pushed her sunglasses onto her head. "I'm what they call land rich, cash poor. I'm sitting on money with this hotel, and ironically, it's barely making any. I once had dinner with

Alan Sugar on a skiing trip in the Alps, and he told me then I didn't have a brain for business. He was right."

"Is that why you borrowed money from Gabriel Caron?"

"How did you know about that?" she snapped, turning to Julia with a frown. "Did Lisa tell you? She swore she wouldn't. It's supposed to be private."

"Arlo told me," Julia confessed, deciding honesty might increase the chances of getting the same in return. "He also thinks he was fired to cut costs, and that he was framed for stealing."

"*Framed?*" Minnie scoffed. "Lisa caught him red-handed, dipping into the takings. I don't care how long he worked here – nobody is above being fired for stealing."

"I thought you said you caught him?"

"No," she replied sharply. "Lisa did. But it was my job to fire him, and I did so. Gladly." She dragged her sunglasses back down to her eyes and returned her gaze to the valley. "And yes, I borrowed money from that bloody Frenchman. I thought we were friends, but apparently, friendship means nothing around here anymore. I was desperate, the bills needed paying, and I heard he worked as a loan shark in an unofficial capacity."

"And you haven't been able to pay back the loan?"

"A little." Minnie bobbed her head from side to side. "But when the money's not there, the money's not there.

I can't magic it out of thin air, and the bookings just aren't coming in." She sighed. "Ever since my husband died, everything has gone to pot. He made running this place look easy. We were always fully booked. Maybe Lisa isn't up to the job, but it's not like we can afford anyone else. She never complained. Not to me, anyway. Not until last night. She's always been a people pleaser, and I admit, I take advantage of that sometimes."

"Lisa mentioned that she wanted you to sell the hotel."

"I *cannot* sell this place," Minnie said she ran her hands along the railing. "I won't! It's all I have left of Bill. La Casa was our pride and joy. I know it sounds silly coming from an old woman like me after living the life I've lived, but this hotel was the first time I ever felt settled." She shook her head. "Don't get me wrong, I loved the jet-set life. But that's a young girl's game. I'm too old to start again. Too old to get used to a new life. I've only just got used to being a widow, for goodness' sakes." She sighed. "I know it's never too late to find someone else – just look at your gran – but after four marriages, three divorces, and that final devastating death, quite frankly, my dear, I haven't the energy."

Though it hurt to hear the pain in Minnie's voice, Julia still couldn't see how these troubles could connect to Dot and Percy's disappearance.

"Minnie?" a familiar voice echoed around the dining room. "There you are, neighbour."

Rodger, dressed in another linen suit with another box of eggs in hand, was already headed towards them. Julia wanted to scream, to tell him to go away until she had learned something of importance from her elusive great-aunt. Instead, she bit her tongue for the sake of keeping the peace.

"My dear Rodger." Minnie met him on the other side of the pool, both hands already outstretched. "I can always rely on you to put a smile on my face. Are those eggs for me?"

"The chickens have been laying well." He handed over the box. "What has so troubled you that I need to put a smile on your face?"

"I'm so stressed, Rodger." She placed the eggs on a side table and dramatically collapsed into one of the deckchairs. "Lisa and I are at each other's throats, and things aren't looking any better in the booking department."

Julia couldn't fathom how Dot and Percy being held for ransom somehow didn't even make the list of things troubling her. She gritted her teeth and slowly counted to ten in her head.

"Still not looking up?"

"I couldn't tell you which way was up right now if I tried." She sighed and pulled off the glasses again. "You're lucky you never had children, Rodger. You try to do everything right, and still they grow up and resent you. I tried my best, you know. My very best."

"I don't doubt you have." Rodger pulled up a chair and took Minnie's hands in his. "Is that why you were unavailable last night? I stopped by, but Lisa said you weren't to be disturbed."

"As much as I appreciate your visits – and I do, Rodger – it was probably for the best that Lisa turned you away." Minnie patted his hand and looked out over the valley. "I haven't been at my best recently. A woman can only deal with so much stress. I was just telling sweet Julia all about my money woes. Maybe it's time I accepted one of those offers?"

"Are you sure you want to give up like that?" he asked, edging closer to her. "Your hotel has the best view in Savega, and everyone knows it. Nobody else is so happily situated. Your vistas of the valley are second to none."

"I'm not sure I have much choice," she said, staring blankly at the calm surface of the pool. "Lisa says the offers keep coming. I daresay it's The Buyer. It's my time. I've been marked. I can feel it."

"Not this nonsense about The Buyer again," Rodger said, stroking her hand steadily. "I thought you knew better than to believe in those silly conspiracy theories."

"The Buyer?" Julia asked, stepping forward.

"A local myth," he said. "People will believe anything around here."

"But maybe it's *true*." Minnie pulled her hand away and returned to the railing. "Look what has happened to this place. So many people have left, scared away." She glanced sideways at Julia. "Nobody knows what's going on. When people refuse these offers, they come back even bigger – for a time. But if you refuse those . . . well, bad things happen."

"You sound like the rest of them now, my dear," Rodger said, joining her at the balcony and wrapping his arm around her shoulders. "The Buyer is a bogeyman people have invented because they're so desperate to connect dots that aren't there. And not all change is bad. Why, if nothing ever changed, we wouldn't have become neighbours. I haven't been here as long as you, have I?"

"Well, no," Minnie said, smiling for the first time that morning. "But you must admit how strange it is, Rodger. The fires. The burglaries."

Julia wished for her trusty notepad as she tried to keep up with these details. This was precisely the kind of information she had been trying to extract from Minnie from the moment it became apparent her great-aunt was scared.

"Why didn't you mention The Buyer before?" Julia asked firmly, eyes trained on the terracotta-tiled floor as she tried to organise her thoughts.

"I didn't think it mattered." Minnie wafted her hand again. Julia wanted nothing more than to smack it out of the air "Like Rodger said, it's just a rumour. Nothing's been proven."

"But you've had offers?"

"Well, yes." She frowned. "They come through on the computer."

"And people who refused other offers were punished in some way?"

"It would seem that way," Minnie said, glaring at Julia. "You don't think—"

"That the ransom note is your punishment?" Julia cut in, shocked that Minnie hadn't connected those pieces of the jigsaw herself, considering her paranoid state. "Who has been offering to buy your hotel?"

Minnie thought about it for a moment, her brows tense, her eyes darting all over the valley.

"Lots of people," she said with a shrug. "I don't know. Lisa deals with it. She says the same person never gives more than three offers, and then the names change."

"Did you tell this to the police?"

"Like I said, I didn't think it was important." Minnie's shaky hands rested against her cheeks. "I'm sorry, I just—"

"Can't you see you're upsetting her?" Rodger pulled Minnie away from the railing and set her back down in the deckchair. "What she needs is a hot cup of tea or a stiff drink, not an interrogation."

Before Julia could retort that what *she* wanted was her gran back safe and sound and that no amount of tea would placate *her*, Minnie let out a tiny gasp.

"No, sweet Julia is right." Minnie's trembling fingers rested against her lips. "I've been so distracted, so selfish, that I didn't see the obvious. I thought it was random. I *hoped* it was random. But it can't be, can it? It's all my fault."

"Now, Minnie. You mustn't torture yourself this way." Rodger fired a sharp glance at Julia over his shoulder, so Julia glared right back. "Why don't I make you that cup of tea you so clearly need right now?"

"That would be lovely."

Rodger took himself to the dining room, where the tea-making station remained stocked despite the day's lack of breakfast.

Conspiracy theory or not, Maria's café had considered the break-ins threatening enough to install cameras. And Julia didn't forget the way Maria's father had immediately shut down any conversation on the subject.

"I'm sorry there's no breakfast for you this morning," Minnie said, changing the subject before Julia could press her further. "Let me fetch Lisa to make you something. She probably won't see me right now, but the hotel still needs running, and you are a paying guest."

"Maybe it's best to give her some space," Julia suggested, even as her stomach rumbled at the suggestion of food. "If you point me in the right direction, I'll happily make something for myself. After so many years running the café, I know my way around a kitchen."

"Dot was right," Minnie said with a melancholy smile, "you really are a good girl."

Julia followed Minnie's directions, pushing through the door behind desk, where she was met with an upward staircase to the living quarters and a downwards one. As she headed to the basement kitchen, Julia considered her great-aunt. On some level, deep down, Julia knew that Minnie cared. Obviously, she just wasn't in the right frame of mind to deal with reality. As entertaining as she had been on their first night at La Casa, she had seemed a little frantic even then.

Knowing what Julia knew now, they couldn't have arrived at a worse time for the hotel – which made Minnie's invitation out of the blue all the stranger. Julia hated to suspect her, but she wasn't ruling out anyone or anything until she had her gran back.

At the bottom of the dark staircase, Julia fumbled around for a light switch for a good minute until her fingers brushed against the plastic casing. The lights of the industrial kitchen flickered to life, revealing a kitchen so large she couldn't help but be jealous. It was at least four times bigger than her café's kitchen. Stainless-steel counters wrapped around the entire perimeter. There were two giant fridges and two sinks, and a large metal island filled the centre.

Even with all of her worries, she imagined how many cakes she could bake if she had this much space at her disposal. Although she wasn't sure how much baking she'd be able to do in this exact kitchen. Aside from the fridges and some pans and basic utensils, the kitchen was as good as empty. Not even a mixing bowl or a wooden spoon met her searching gaze.

She did, however, find a plate. She carried it to the fridge, where she found the usual contents of the breakfast buffet on plates under plastic wrap. Though the food was there, and it seemed fresh, it hadn't made its way up to the hotel. Strange. She filled her plate with enough sliced meat and cheese to tide her over until lunchtime.

A slice of ham already in her mouth, she closed the fridge and turned around. She gasped, and the plate slipped from her hands and smashed against the floor. She didn't spare it a glance. Her eyes were firmly locked on the puddle of blood on the other side of the island.

Already sensing what she'd find, Julia swallowed the ham and crept around the stainless-steel island. Lisa wasn't in bed, sulking. She was lying hidden behind the island in a pool of her own blood, a knife jutting out of her stomach.

A whimper escaped Julia's lips. She assumed Lisa was dead, but as she took a single step closer, a rattling, weak breath escaped her cousin, and her eyelids fluttered.

She was alive.

Julia looked around for a phone, but there wasn't one. She reached for her bag, but it was still upstairs behind the reception desk and not over her shoulder like usual. As the walls closed in around her, Julia doubled back to the door and screamed up the stairs, praying she wouldn't faint again. It felt like an age before Minnie and Rodger appeared at the top of the stairs, even though it was probably only a few seconds.

"Oh, dear God!" Minnie cried, tumbling back into the counter when she saw her daughter on the floor. "How can this be?"

Rodger steadied her with one hand while he dialled his mobile phone with the other. As he spoke quickly down the phone in Spanish, presumably calling for an ambulance, Julia went to Lisa's side. She clutched her cousin's hand, and though weak, Lisa squeezed back.

"Not like this," Julia whispered to the universe. "We didn't even get to know each other."

Looking away from poor Lisa, Julia's gaze landed on something shiny under the island: a watch.

12
DOT

"Ninety-nine," Dot called out, pausing to sip her tea. "One hundred. Ready or not, here I come."

She carefully placed her cup on the coffee table, in no rush to get up. Playing hide and seek, of course, hadn't been her idea, but as resistant as she had been to the juvenile game, at least it was passing the time until breakfast arrived. She rechecked her watch. It was already close to noon, and this time, it wasn't a mistake.

Even if this was the price they had to pay for Dot pushing too hard, she couldn't quite regret it. And she couldn't do much about it now. What she could do, however, was find her husband in one of the three hiding places he had picked for the previous seven games of hide and seek. She walked straight into the bedroom and opened the wardrobe doors.

"You found me again, Dorothy!" Percy chuckled as she helped him up out of the wardrobe. "You're far too good at this game."

"Well, you were either in here, under the bed, or behind the shower curtain," she said, with yet another glance at the time. "I'm not sure this game is for me."

"How about another game of cards?"

She exhaled loudly, the mere thought of trouncing him in another poker match somehow even more unpleasant than the prospect of spending the entire day finding Percy as he rotated through the same three hiding spaces.

"No more cards," she said. "No more hide and seek. I'm unbelievably bored. I thought only boring people could get bored, but when there is truly so little to do, the mind starts to rot. Another day locked in here and I'm going to be as batty as Evelyn. Can you imagine?"

"I think you'd look quite fetching in one of her turbans."

"Ghastly!" Dot dusted the front of her crinkled but clean white blouse, glad to be back in her own clothes. "I did enough experimenting with my look yesterday to last a lifetime. Aren't you bored, dear?"

Percy perched on the edge of his neatly made bed and considered his response for a moment. He patted the covers next to him, so Dot took a seat.

"With you, my love," he said, holding her hand in his, "I could never get bored."

"I'm afraid I can't say the same," she said, before quickly adding, "No offence, of course."

He laughed. "None taken. Perhaps it's that I'm a simple soul, and you've got so much more going on upstairs than I have. To be totally honest, when I forget that we're being held here against our will, I quite enjoy how uncomplicated it is."

"You're enjoying this?"

"Enjoyment might not be the correct word." He tapped his finger against his chin as he thought for the right one. "Content? Yes, I'm quite content. While I'd rather be on the honeymoon we imagined or even back home in our cottage, there's something refreshing about not having to think about anything other than how to keep ourselves entertained. Our meals are brought to us, and we've been given clothes. Not having to think about how I'm going to make my pension stretch for the week has been a relief in itself. This might be the first time since childhood that I haven't felt any responsibilities pressing on me."

"Other than keeping ourselves alive?"

"Even that is out of our hands," he said, patting her knee. "Like you said before, if they were going to kill us, surely they would have done it already?"

The question had played on Dot's mind heavily. Knowing that Rafa didn't want to kill them didn't mean they weren't going to be killed. She hadn't told Percy about the revelation that Rafa's step-grandfather was apparently the person giving the orders, and she wouldn't. Knowing of the man's existence did little to help them. In fact, Dot suspected it showed where Rafa's loyalties would lie if the order ever came.

"We still don't know *why* we're here," she pointed out. "They're treating us like pets, but why?"

"I hadn't given it much thought."

"I suppose it doesn't matter." Dot looked around the room, her gaze lingering in the window with the loose bars. "We have no idea how long we're going to be here. Days? Weeks? Months? Years, even? How long will this be our life?"

"It's best not to get worked up." He flashed her a wink and a smile. "Now, how about one last game of hide and seek? But this time, you hide and I seek. I'm sure you'll be much more inventive than I was at finding a hiding space."

"Fine." She rechecked her watch. "But only because we have little else to do."

While Percy counted to one hundred in the sitting room with his eyes closed, Dot took her time looking around the villa for somewhere unique to hide. By the time Percy was halfway through his count, she realised his three hiding spaces were perhaps the only three hiding spaces to be had. Knowing Percy would likely check his most recent space last, she opted for the wardrobe.

The old wooden wardrobe smelled exactly as she would have expected. It had a hint of musk that only came from aged wood and the lingering scent of mothballs. In the dark, a sense of stillness and privacy that she hadn't felt since before their chase through the market came over her. She crouched down, her eyes immediately heavy thanks to another night of agitation and sleeplessness. She closed her eyes to rest them.

She must have drifted off for a couple of minutes, but the wardrobe doors ripping open startled her awake, making her heart drop so quickly it reminded her of riding the rollercoasters at Blackpool in her youth.

"Oh!" She looked up at Rafa, her cheeks burning hot. "We were just—"

"You found her!" Percy clapped his hands as he walked into the bedroom. "I was saving the wardrobe for last. It felt too obvious! Very clever, my dear."

After Percy helped her out of the wardrobe, they followed Rafa back into the sitting room and their breakfast. No yoghurts today, she noticed, but perhaps they were reserved for dinner time?

Somehow, she didn't think the conversation yesterday had pushed him too far away, after all. In fact, she sensed ease and openness around him that she hadn't felt before.

"It gets quite boring in here," she explained, fully embarrassed. "I wouldn't usually resort to such childish games to fend off the boredom, but one finds oneself willing to try new things in situations as strange as this."

"You do not need to explain this," he said, offering another rare smile. "I understand this situation is not an ideal."

"You could say that," Percy called from the kitchen table, already dishing up to plates of food. "But we make do and carry on. Although, saying that, I don't think my Dorothy can take another day locked up in here. I can already feel her going stir-crazy."

"It's quite all right," Dot said, trying to laugh away Percy's suggestion; it didn't quite measure up with the sweet old lady image she had crafted for Rafa. "It's not your fault that we're here, is it?"

Rafa smiled again, this time more regretfully. He scratched the back of his head, drawing attention to the bandage wrapped around his right hand. A little blood had pushed through the bandage, hinting at a deep cut. Some even stained the hem of his white t-shirt.

"When I was slicing your bread, I cut this," he explained quickly when he seemed to notice Dot's lingering gaze.

"Hope you didn't get any on it!" Percy muttered, a buttered slice already in his mouth. "I must say, not as fresh today."

Rafa crammed his hands into his leather jacket, making Dot wonder if he wanted to hide the bandage to stop her from questioning him further. Her gut reaction told her that there was more to the cut, but she wasn't sure she wanted to find out.

"Perhaps a walk?" Rafa suggested, hooking his unharmed thumb over his shoulder. "Around the clearing only. Nobody will come until the afternoon."

"A walk?" Percy jumped up, knocking the table and clattering the plates. "Outside?"

"In a circle," he said quickly. "Separately. If you try anything—"

"We won't," Dot jumped in. "The fresh air would do us good."

He nodded that he understood, and Dot wondered if he'd come in intending to let them to stretch their legs outside, or if he was simply reacting to their pathetic antics. Either way, she certainly wasn't going to pass up the opportunity.

They followed him out into the empty clearing. Stepping out into the fresh air felt somewhat alien after so many days locked up. She closed her eyes and let the sun warm her skin for a moment. As uncomfortably hot as it was, she intended to savour every second.

"In a circle," he repeated as he stood slap bang in the middle of the clearing. "Around me."

Dot set off first, walking in the biggest circle she dared. His bandaged hand was still in his pocket, but the other one was hooked over his belt, inches from where the gun was hiding. When she was parallel to the villa, Percy set off, his strides comically wide as he followed the pattern she had set out on the dusty ground.

On her laps, Dot inhaled the warm air, her lungs enjoying the freshness. It wasn't that the air in the villa was stale, but not being able to open the windows and feel the natural breeze made the outdoors taste that little bit sweeter.

It wasn't until her fourth lap around the clearing that the abstract concept of escape even came to mind. While she wasn't foolish enough to make a run for it now, she still hadn't given up on the idea of getting them out of the situation. Initially, she'd wanted to do it to save Julia the chore of having to track them down, but as the days passed, her focus had shifted from wanting to escape for Julia's sake to needing to escape for their own.

The vague sound of a car engine registered in Dot's brain. It snagged her ear from the left side of the clearing. Distant at first, and then closer, and then distant again. Arriving at the villa under a veil of darkness was already a foggy memory, but she knew they'd arrived from the left, which meant the road was in the direction of the car she had heard.

She took in the rest of their surroundings, hoping for an indication of how high up they were. The thick, dense trees entirely closed them in – which was likely the precise reason the place had been chosen. She'd spent the last few days assuming they were miles and miles from any civilisation, as one would when being held captive, but she heard another car on her sixth lap, and then two, one after the other, on her ninth. By her twentieth lap, she'd counted twelve cars.

"Time's up," Rafa called. "Back inside."

Dot finished her final lap and followed Percy into the villa. Before she could thank Rafa for letting them out, he closed the door and locked them in. She watched him head back to the outbuilding. She almost expected him to look at the villa on his way, but he didn't. She couldn't help but wonder what conditions he was living in over there. While the villa left much to be desired, at least it was clean and tidy. The outbuilding looked much older and was in a much worse state of repair.

"Wasn't that marvellous?" Percy exclaimed as he resumed his seat at the table and continued eating his breakfast. "It's amazing what a little fresh air can do for the soul."

"It is." Dot turned on the television and sat at the sofa, the cogs in her mind spinning too quickly to allow room for eating just yet. "I don't suppose you noticed the cars?"

"What cars?"

"I'll take that as a no." She adjusted her brooch as her eyes glazed over, piecing together the first concrete plan she'd had since their arrival. "I heard at least twelve cars drive by."

"That many?"

"It means we're not as far away from civilisation as we thought."

Percy loaded up another slice of bread with ham and cheese. "I suppose we're not."

Dot hadn't expected Percy to pick up what she was dropping, so she took the following silent minutes while he ate his breakfast to solidify the plan forming in her mind. What she came up with was risky, but considering their limited options, some danger was expected.

"Now, why don't you tell me what's causing that look in your eyes?" Percy asked as he set down two fresh cups of tea and joined her on the sofa. "Does it have anything to do with those cars you mentioned?"

"It does." She sipped the hot tea, unable to bear the thought that she might die without having another decent, traditional British cuppa. "You'll remember the loose bars in the bedroom? We haven't acted on that because we feared we'd be dead out there in the wilderness or shot before we made it ten yards, but what if we didn't need to brave whatever was beyond those trees?"

"Are you suggesting we steal a car?" Percy asked. "I don't know if you recall, but neither of us can drive."

"We don't have to." She sipped more tea. "Say, for arguments' sake, we could get out to that road undetected. If cars regularly use that road, we don't need to steal a car, we just have to get someone to stop."

"You mean we hitchhike our way back?"

She nodded. "We'd just need one person to stop, and I don't think it would take long. Not many people would drive past a pair our age, especially since our faces were briefly plastered on the news."

"It sounds like you've . . ." Percy's voice drifted off as his eyes wandered to the television screen. "Isn't that—"

"Lisa." Dot hurried over to the television and cranked up the volume, not that it mattered since she still couldn't speak Spanish. "Why is my niece on the news?"

"Whatever it is, it can't be good." Percy chewed at his thumbnail. "I don't need to speak the language to know what that tone of voice means. What on earth could be going on down at La Casa?"

Dot couldn't respond, her imagination running away with her. Her eyes stayed trained on Lisa's face until the news reporter moved on to another story. She hadn't had a chance to get to know her niece much outside of Minnie's brief descriptions in her letters, but the mere thought that something had happened to her was enough to turn her stomach.

"It seems we're not the only ones in a tricky situation," Dot finally said as she returned to her seat next to Percy. "We can't rely on anyone coming to rescue us. We need to get out of here on our own."

"Do you really think we stand a chance?"

"I don't know," she admitted, "but as much as we want to pretend everything is okay, it's not. We can't sit around forever, waiting for our fates to be decided. We need to take matters into our own hands."

"And when do you propose we do that?" he asked, gulping hard.

"Tonight," Dot said firmly, without needing to think about it. "And I know exactly how we're going to do it. But first, that soap opera is on next, and I'd quite like to see what happened after yesterday's cliff-hanger."

13

JULIA

*S*itting on the terrace later that afternoon, Julia turned the pages of her gran's photo album. Once again, the four of them were in fancy dress, and it made her smile.

"Who are they supposed to be?" Jessie asked as she joined her, a cocktail in each hand. "They look like hippie soldiers."

"The Beatles." Julia smiled her thanks as Jessie set the drink on the small table next to the cup of peppermint tea she'd yet to touch. "Sergeant Pepper era."

"Does the existence of a Sergeant Pepper imply there's a more powerful Sergeant Salt somewhere?"

"I'm not entirely sure," Julia admitted. "Naturally, my gran is dressed up as John Lennon."

"Is he the one who married that Linda woman who makes the vegetarian sausages your sister raves about?"

"No, that was Paul. Minnie swears she went skiing with him once."

"Oh." Jessie took the album from her and stretched out on the next deck chair. "Was he the one who played the drums?"

"You're thinking of Ringo."

"So, which one was shot in the theatre?"

"Abraham Lincoln." Julia narrowed her eyes. "John was the one who was shot, but that was in the street. I think he was still alive when they did that fancy dress."

"You've lost me." Jessie flicked through the album, tilting her head at the images. "Looks like they threw a lot of fancy dress parties. It's weird to think of Dot having had a life like this so many years before I was born."

"Before I was born too."

"Yeah, but not *too* many years before." Jessie shot her a wink. "Did they even have colour TVs when you were a kid?"

"I *will* throw my drink over you." Julia picked up her cocktail, but she paused before taking a sip. "Virgin?"

"None of your business, Mother."

"I meant the cocktail."

"I know." Jessie slapped the album shut. "I just wanted to see if I could make you smile, and it worked. And of course it's virgin. It's basically fruit juice with a fancy straw and an umbrella. I'm not gonna push alcohol on a pregnant woman, am I?" She sipped her drink and winced. "Maybe vodka and tequila don't quite go together in these quantities."

"Jessie..."

"*What?*" She rolled her eyes and sipped again. "Legal drinking age, remember? I'm having enough for the both of us. It's five o'clock somewhere, and we're still sorta kinda on holiday."

"It doesn't feel like one." Julia checked her watch. "Do you think it's too soon to call the hospital again?"

"You called an hour ago."

"I know." Julia finally took a sip of her drink; the overwhelming sweetness was more biting than pleasant. "I feel so useless right now. Lisa is fighting for her life, Minnie is no doubt hysterical in the waiting room, my gran and Percy are God knows where, and I'm here—"

"Pregnant and not pushing yourself too hard," Jessie cut in as she slid her sunglasses down from her hair. "Nobody expects you to be running around this town with a magnifying glass and a notepad. Well, nobody *but* you."

While Julia heard the truth in Jessie's words, she couldn't seem to help herself. She pulled her phone from her bag, and Jessie quickly snatched it away.

"I just want to—"

"Check in on Lisa." Jessie slid the phone into her denim shorts. "I know. It's rubbish what happened to her. Stabbed in her kitchen by some psycho and left to bleed out isn't how anyone wants to start the day but calling again won't help her. It took you ten minutes to get through to someone who spoke English last time, all for them to tell you she was still in surgery, where she'll still likely be. You can't worry her better."

"But I can't sit here and do nothing."

"It's what you were doing when I turned up with the cocktails." She tucked her hands behind her head and positioned her face in the direction of the sun before adding, "There will be an answer, let it be."

"You just quoted a Beatles lyric."

"Oh, I know." A pleased grin spread from ear to ear. "I was pulling your leg. I'm nineteen, not stupid."

Julia opened her mouth to respond, but only a dry laugh emerged. Somehow, Jessie's sarcastic humour was the antidote to the continuously unfolding madness around her.

Still, as appealing as the proposition of sunbathing the afternoon away might be, she couldn't bring herself to keep at it. She'd only come out to the terrace on Barker's request, and she'd given him more than enough time to get somewhere with Inspector Hillard.

Leaving Jessie to slather herself in sun cream, Julia ventured back into the coolness of the hotel. Barker was by the reception desk where she'd left him, talking to the more agreeable Sub-Inspector Castro rather than the inspector. At least no one appeared poised to rip the other's head off.

"How is he even allowed to be an inspector here?" she overheard Barker say when she came into listening range. "I looked it up. You have to be Spanish and speak the language fluently to even join the force, let alone claw your way up to the rank of inspector."

"His mother, she is Spanish, I think," Castro replied. "He is far from fluent, but he knows enough to get by." The phone in his hand beeped. "Ah, that is him. He wants me in the kitchen. You cannot go down, you know this."

"I know the protocol," Barker replied with a huff. "Don't worry, I'll behave."

Castro patted Barker's arm and offered Julia a taut smile as he slid around the reception desk to venture down into the kitchen.

Julia joined Barker in leaning against the reception desk and asked, "Get anywhere?"

"If by 'anywhere' you mean even more frustrated, then yes, I definitely got somewhere." He sighed and rubbed at the faint wrinkles on his forehead. "It's not easy being on this side of the line. I wish I could go down there and look at the crime scene myself, but I know the rules. At least that Castro seems to have some sense. He's certainly the only one I'd want on my team, were I still on the force. He obviously dislikes Hillard as much as we do, but he's not going to openly question his superior. He's too much of a—"

The door behind the reception desk flew open, cutting Barker off. Hillard stormed out, a phone to his ear. Castro followed closely behind, hurrying to keep up.

"Inspector?" Julia stood in his way as he tried to walk straight for the door. "Any updates?"

He sighed and held the phone against his shoulder. "None. I'm a little—"

"Busy," she finished the line for him. "Yes, I imagine you are. But three members of my family have been the victims of crimes in your town, and I can't help but feel like you're not doing enough about it."

The inspector ended the phone call while glaring at Julia. He tucked the device into the inside of his jacket before folding his arms and nodding at Julia to talk.

"Are you any closer to finding my gran?" she asked, making sure to keep her tone firm. "It's been days, and you've told us nothing. We know *nothing*."

"We're following several lines of inquiry."

"Yeah, right," Barker scoffed, shaking his head. "That's police waffle for 'we have no clue what's going on.' You can't pull that trick on us, mate. I speak the language. It won't work." He gestured with his phone. "You wouldn't even look at the video footage I obtained *for you*. What exactly are you doing to find my wife's grandparents, Inspector Hillard?"

"That's confidential," he replied, not bothering to

look at Barker. "Now, if you'll excuse me, there's somewhere I need to be."

He attempted to step around Julia, but like their first meeting, she matched his step and blocked his path.

"Do you think Lisa's stabbing is connected?" she asked.

"Not at present."

"Oh, here we go." Barker exhaled, tossing his hands out. "How did I know you were going to say that?"

"Maybe you're psychic, Mr Brown," he replied dryly. "Or, perhaps not. If you were, you'd know I'm on my way to making an arrest connected to Lisa's attack based on fingerprints left at the scene of the crime. We've already found a match."

"The knife?" Barker asked.

"The watch." Hillard's phone rang in his pocket. "And before you ask whose prints, that is, quite frankly, none of your business. Now, if you'll excuse me and let me get on with my job, I have to take this call."

Evidently not wanting to risk another stand-off, Inspector Hillard clutched Julia's shoulders tightly and moved her to the side. He pulled out his phone, answered it, and marched for the door. The two officers smoking cigarettes and relaxing in front of the hotel momentarily snapped to attention as Hillard jumped into his car. He honked his horn, causing Castro to hurry after him.

"That Hillard is corrupt," Barker said as he watched the car drive off. "I'd bet my left leg on it."

"What are we betting our limbs on?" Jessie appeared between them, an arm around each of their necks. "Something good, I hope."

"Hillard being corrupt," said Julia.

"Oh, definitely. He's got shady written all over him." She plucked a complementary foil-wrapped chocolate from the bowl on the counter. "Forget him. We might be on the back foot, but there's a brain somewhere between the three of us. We can't just sit around and do nothing."

Julia arched a brow. "You've changed your tune."

"Sunbathing is more boring than I thought it would be." Jessie unwrapped the chocolate and tossed it into her mouth. "There's only so many times you can look out and be impressed by the view. It's not like it's changing. There must be something on your to-do list that we can tackle while we wait for Hillard to not find Dot?"

Julia followed Jessie's lead and plucked a chocolate out of the bowl. Chocolatería Valor sprang to mind. More importantly, Arlo's suggestion about who they should talk to.

"We still haven't spoken to Gabriel Caron," she suggested before biting into the chocolate; it was overly sweet and tasted cheap. "Minnie admitted to borrowing money from him and not paying it back."

"Minnie owes someone money and you haven't

spoken to him yet?" Jessie rolled her eyes and took a handful of the small chocolates. "I think that baby brain is getting to the both of you. Isn't that covered in Investigator 101? Lead the way."

The plaza was the quietest Julia had seen it. They walked around the fountain and straight to Eiffel restaurant, the grandest and most striking building by far. There were no diners outside, and from the looks of it, none inside either.

"Looks empty," Julia mused as they walked through the open doors. "Might be the perfect time to catch him."

"In a net?" Jessie replied, looking around the large, grand restaurant. "I thought French people were supposed to have style. This is *très tacky*."

"You can speak French?" Julia stopped dead in her tracks.

"No," she replied with a smirk, "but it sounded convincing, didn't it? Back to your plan about catching this French bloke in a net."

"Does she have an off button?" Barker whispered to Julia.

"I don't," Jessie responded with a broad, cheesy grin. "I think that cocktail has gone to my head already."

"You only had a sip."

"Who said that was my first?" Jessie leaned against the maître d' station and fanned herself with a menu. "Why is it always so hot here?"

"It's Spain," Barker replied, looking around the empty restaurant. "Where is everyone?"

"There's a guy behind the bar." Jessie pointed out before slapping the bell on the station until he set down the glass he was polishing. "Let me do the talking."

Julia and Barker exchanged unsure looks, but they stepped back and let Jessie take centre stage. The young barman drew near, slinging a towel over his shoulder and nodding for Jessie to talk.

"I want to speak with Gabriel Caron at *once!*" Jessie demanded in a voice that wasn't quite her own, looking around the restaurant with a slightly curled lip. "My parents and I dined here last night, and my poor father hasn't been off the toilet since. And, as you can clearly see, my mother's stomach has ballooned up to the size of a small house. Oh, you might *assume* she's pregnant, but she's not, she just has the opposite of my father's problem. I don't know what you're putting in the food here, but I'm sure Mr Caron would like to know what his chef is doing to his unsuspecting guests."

The barman stared at Jessie with an open mouth, obviously rendered as speechless as Julia felt.

"Go on then!" she called, ringing the bell again. "Fetch the man!"

He nodded and turned, knocking into a chair. He quickly straightened it, glanced back at Jessie with fear in his eyes, and hurried off to the back of the restaurant.

"Dare I ask?" said Barker.

"I improvised." Jessie circled her finger around the bell, clearly pleased with herself. "It's amazing what your mind comes up with on the spot."

"Yes. It's amazing what *your* mind comes up with."

"I could have said worse." She nodded across the restaurant. "Looks like it worked."

A fifty-something man with dark shaggy hair and a matching goatee marched across the restaurant, wearing a white t-shirt so short and tight it rose above the belt of his trousers and revealed his flat, tanned stomach. He was the same man they'd spotted zooming away from the restaurant in his red sports car only days earlier, although the current expression of rage was new.

"Which one of you *dares* insult the cooking of my restaurant?" he called in a thick, French accent, planting his hands on his hips. "Never in my life have I heard such *ridiculousness!*"

"Excuse my daughter," Julia said, glancing at Jessie before stepping forward to take the lead this time. "She has a very *specific* brand of humour that gets lost in translation sometimes."

"Are you insinuating the French do not have the sense of humour?" he retorted.

"Not at all."

"Good." He narrowed his eyes on Julia, his arms crossing tightly across his chest. "So, what is it you want from me then, if it is *not* insulting my food?"

"We're relatives of Minnie's," Julia explained,

deciding now wasn't the time for games. "We heard that you—"

"Is Lisa okay?" he interrupted, both his voice and his gaze softening. "Oh, the poor woman. We have all heard what happened this morning."

"Last I checked, she's still alive," Julia said, taken aback by the question and by Gabriel's obvious sincerity in asking it. "You know them well, then?"

"Of course!" he cried, planting his hands on his hips once more. "Twenty years I have been here. Minnie has been here also for twenty years. It is impossible to be strangers after so long. It is only that her bad luck has come through all at once, but she is not the only one who struggles, oh no."

"Is that why you let her borrow money?" Julia pushed. "Because you knew she was struggling?"

"Of course!" he replied, eyes narrowing slightly on Julia. "If this is about the money, please, you must tell Minnie to forget about it. The last thing she needs is money stress. The debt is cleared."

"Just like that?"

"Why, of course!" he said, as though it should have been obvious. Again, Julia was struck by his sincerity. "Like I said, we neighbours, we must look out for each other. So much has changed in our little town so quickly. I have been doing my part to help keep people's businesses open. Fortunately, I do not share in these struggles. They say I am crazy for opening a French restaurant in a sea of flamenco dancers and sangria, but the tourists, they adore the novelty."

"But to waive her debt so easily?" Julia continued, unable to let the subject go. "She'll be grateful, I'm sure, but don't you need the money you gave her?"

Gabriel forced back a laugh and looked around his restaurant, casting his arms out.

"Madame," he said, "I gave her only two thousand euros to cover bills. We make *double* this in a night. Like I said, the tourists *love* it! Don't let this quiet fool you. No table will be free tonight. Please come and dine with us. Then you will see how excellent the food is." He gestured back at the way he'd come. "But now, I must return to the accounts, yes?"

Gabriel nodded to each of them in turn before turning on his heels. Julia watched him walk away, the image of him as some benevolent loan shark melting away with each step he took. It took her a moment to snap out of her daze, but when she did, she chased after him.

"One more thing," she said quietly when she caught him up. "Does 'The Buyer' conspiracy theory mean anything to you?"

Gabriel stopped and stared down at Julia. "But of course, madame. This Buyer is not theory. This is truth."

"Do you know who it is?"

He shook his head. "Unfortunately, no. Does anyone? I am not so sure. The Buyer operates in the shadows, using others as his puppets, but you must not let this fool you. He exists, even if these people wish to pretend he does not."

"Do you have any proof?"

"Savega is proof." He turned and pointed through the open doors, sighing regretfully. "Unless you came before, you would not understand how much has changed. Minnie, she knows. Two years ago, the gang came. The business takeover, it starts within weeks. We used to have such variety in Savega, madame, and now it is all backstreet markets and clothes shops run by The Buyer's gang. Even I will not walk the streets alone at night. I am doing everything I can to, how do you say, protect things, but even with my wealth, I cannot match The Buyer. Eventually, the people, they stop asking for my help. They give up and move, and who can blame them? This Buyer plays dirty, and seems to have an endless supply of money and people to do this dirty work for him."

"Have you had offers?"

"Of course!" Gabriel's lips curved into a small smile. "But I will never accept this. The Buyer wants to own Savega, to run it like a private, lawless kingdom. They will not get their hands on my restaurant. They will never have the full takeover. If I was going to accept, I would have taken the money when I was offered double the value of my building six months ago!"

"Most people would have accepted that."

"Most people are not French," he said, puffing out his chest. "Now I sound like my mother, but it is true. As long as I have breath in my lungs and pride in my heart, this is where I stay." He reached out and patted her shoulder gently. "Now, I really must work." He set off, turning at the last moment to add, "Congratulations on the baby, madame."

Julia rested her hand on her bump as she walked back to the front of the restaurant, Gabriel's confirmation of The Buyer confirming the theory to be a fact. It wasn't that she hadn't believed her great aunt, but Minnie's delivery had been so frenzied it had been easy to doubt her. Gabriel's delivery, on the other hand, had been firm, honest, and quiet. She believed that he believed, and that was enough for her.

"Are we eating here tonight then?" Jessie asked, slotting the menu back. "I expected it to be all snails and frog's legs, but some of that stuff actually sounds decent."

"Maybe," Julia said, holding back to talk to Barker as Jessie headed for the door. "I think my aunt was—"

The sound of a scream from the plaza interrupted her. They glanced at each other and went outside. Everyone had stopped in their tracks to watch as a screaming man was dragged towards a police car. She immediately recognised the two officers dragging the cuffed man as the ones who had been smoking outside of La Casa when they'd left. They were closely followed by Inspector Hillard, who, as usual, had a phone to his ear.

Julia was so distracted by recognising their faces that she almost didn't see who they were arresting. She caught a brief glimpse of him seconds before he was shoved into the back of the car and out of view. She looked up at the restaurant they'd pulled him from: Chocolatería Valor.

"You know him," Jessie said, nodding at Julia. "I can tell."

"Arlo Garcia," she said, locking eyes with Inspector Hillard for a split second before he ducked into his car. "He was the chef at Minnie's hotel for a decade. He was fired, according to Minnie and Lisa, for stealing, something he denies doing."

"Looks like he was lying then," Jessie said, stuffing her hands into her pockets. "Oh, you can have this back now."

She passed over a phone. Julia had forgotten Jessie even had it.

"It must have been *his* watch," Barker said. "You don't think he'd stab Lisa over the firing, do you?"

"He seemed like an honest man when we spoke to him." Julia put her phone in her bag. "But I've been wrong before. Sometimes you can't tell. Maybe this is one of those times."

"But what does your gut say?" Jessie asked.

"That he wouldn't do something like that," she said

without needing to think about it. "Which is, of course, only based on the very little we know about him. He seemed more irked by being called a thief than about losing his job."

"That's the impression I got too," Barker said. "And it's not like he didn't get another job right away. The motive doesn't hold up."

Julia silently agreed as they watched the police cars drive away. Life in the plaza resumed within seconds, and everything carried on as though nothing had happened. Out of all the strange things to happen in the past week, it wasn't the oddest.

"Why didn't I notice it before?" Jessie said as she counted something around the plaza. "Eight. There's eight clothes shops around this tiny little bit, and I've seen loads more up those backstreets too."

"Yeah, I'd noticed that too," Barker said. "They're all selling the same stuff."

"It's not just the volume." Jessie walked over to the nearest one two doors down from the French restaurant. The display outside had hats on one side and bags and watches on the other. "These aren't just clothes. They're designer. And based on these price tags, I don't think they're real."

"Isn't counterfeit clothing common?" Julia asked, picking up a colourful cap with a logo she didn't recognise.

"Out in the open like this?" Jessie pointed at a male

and female officer patrolling the plaza, idly chatting between themselves. "Could you imagine this back home? The police would shut it down instantly."

"That's true," Barker confirmed. "I can't imagine this being allowed under Spanish law."

Jessie tried on a hat and looked in a mirror dangling on a string. "What kind of police officers walk past so many shops selling illegal crap like this and turn a blind eye?"

"Bribed ones," Barker said.

"Exactly." Jessie ripped off the hat and tossed it back. "It's all black market stuff, out in the open, right under the police's noses."

"It's the gang," Julia said without thinking about it. "The Buyer's gang. It's real. Gabriel just confirmed it. He said the clothes shops were part of it."

"Well, someone somewhere is making a fortune," Jessie said, pointing to another shop two doors down, packed out and selling the same clothes. "The tourists are eating this stuff up. They're probably buying all this tat to take home as souvenirs for people, not caring if it's 'real'."

"These shops have nearly a full monopoly on the plaza." Julia wondered how many used to be nice cafés and quaint gift shops run by locals who'd been chased out. "If all that profit is funnelling to one person, no wonder they can afford to throw so much money around, buying up all the buildings."

"Bribing the police wouldn't touch the sides." Barker ran his hands down his stubbly cheeks, blank eyes staring off to the ocean in the distance. "I owe your great-aunt an apology. I've been dismissing her as paranoid since we arrived."

"Me too." Julia turned back to the shop. "Where's Jessie?"

The shop door opened, and a tall man tossed Jessie out. He was wearing the same gaudy clothes as those sold in the shop. He yelled something in Spanish before slamming the door.

"Before you ask," she said, holding her hands up. "I didn't do anything. I simply asked if I could speak to his boss, The Buyer."

"And what did he say?" asked Barker.

"You saw his reaction." Jessie rubbed at her neck before purposefully knocking a row of the hats onto the floor and sticking her tongue out at the man, who was watching them through the window. "I think that confirms it. There really is an evil puppet master behind the scenes, and I'll join Barker in betting a left leg on them having Dot and Percy too."

"I think you're right," Julia said, feeling the shopkeeper's eyes burning holes into her skin. He held a phone to his ear, and she didn't want to be there to find out who he was calling. "C'mon. Let's get back to the hotel. I think it's time to call the hospital again."

14

DOT

The sun slid from the sky, bringing an end to another long, hot day in captivity. Alone in front of the television, Dot spun her wedding ring around her finger continuously. If anyone were to look through the window, they'd see the back of her head and assume she was transfixed on the programme. She occasionally glanced at the screen, but the mirror above the television provided a more interesting view.

Switching the picture above the TV with the mirror on the adjacent wall had been a simple but effective trick. The reflection gave her a perfect view of the clearing through the large window behind her, allowing her to keep watch without being caught. A stroke of genius, if she said so herself, and perhaps a trick she would employ if she ever made it home.

Dot's fellow villagers had been accused her of being

a 'nosey parker' and even a 'curtain twitcher' for her keen interest in the comings and goings of Peridale's residents. She wasn't arrogant enough to think there wasn't an element of truth in their accusations, even if she did refute the claims that her keen interest in village activity made her a gossip. She simply liked to keep her ear to the ground – an unofficial one-woman neighbourhood watch, of sorts.

Nobody had bestowed her with the responsibility, she'd voluntarily taken on the role. How could she not? Her peer group was ever-shrinking, with fewer of her fellow village elders surviving from one year to the next. Most died from age-related illness, some moved away for a last-minute change of scenery before curtain call, and the rest were cooped up in the Oakwood Nursing Home, spending their final days completing jigsaw puzzles of cats and taking slow walks around the gardens.

Dot wasn't sure which of these fates was the worst. She'd cling fiercely to her independence for as long as she could. Keeping her finger on the pulse of the village kept her as sharp as a knife, and until her mind left her, she'd put it to good use.

Using that experience now, she observed the two men in whacky clothes sitting in the white chairs on the opposite side of the clearing. They'd arrived a few hours earlier and handed additional plastic bags to Rafa. No doubt more bread, meat, and cheese to keep them fed.

If the men were there to keep watch, they were

taking a laid-back approach to the role. They occasionally glanced in the direction of the villa, but they seemed more interested in chatting and smoking what must have been a whole pack of cigarettes between them. They must have thought all their Christmases had come at once when they were tasked with keeping watch over two locked-up octogenarians.

Being so obviously underestimated would have irritated Dot under any other circumstances – but not this one. If they wanted to view her as a simple old lady more interested in watching television than attempting a bid for freedom, so be it.

The men lingered longer than they had on any other night, eventually standing and stretching out a little after nine. One of them knocked on the door of the outbuilding and called something through the door in Spanish as the other climbed into the car.

As soon as both men were in the vehicle, the engine roared to life and its headlights beamed directly at the villa. The light bounced off the mirror, blinding Dot. She held her breath, sure they'd notice. The car lingered for longer than felt necessary, forcing her to take a breath. Just when she was sure they were going to jump out and charge at the villa with their guns drawn, the car reversed and sped out of the clearing in the direction of the road.

Though she let out a relieved sigh, that relief was fleeting. Her stomach flipped, pushing her nerves further than they'd gone before. With shaking hands, she reached for her cup and quickly drank the last of the tea that had long since gone cold. It wasn't too late to turn back and try the plan another night, but the longer they stayed at the villa, the harder an escape would become.

"It's now or never," she whispered to herself, putting the empty cup back on the table. "One shot, Dorothy."

Five minutes passed before the second part of her plan kicked into action. The door to the outbuilding opened, and Rafa emerged with their evening tray of food. Somehow, Dot's nerves kicked into an even higher gear. She wasn't even sure if she'd be able to pull herself off the sofa to do what needed to be done. While she watched Rafa walk across the clearing, she remembered a piece of advice the director of the Christmas nativity play had given her during her brief stint in the amateur dramatics' society.

"Use your nerves!" Ross, the director, had insisted passionately during one of their early rehearsals. "It's your job as an actor to take all of that energy and emotion and funnel it into your performance."

Of course, Ross later attempted to frame Dot in front of the whole village for murdering his uncle for inheritance money by switching her prop gun with a real one during the debut. As unstable as he had been, his acting advice was still solid.

She took a steadying breath and closed her eyes as

she had done behind the curtain on opening night, paying attention to the silence while waiting for her cue.

The keys jangled.

In through the nose.

The first lock opened.

Out through the mouth.

The second and third followed.

In through the nose.

The deadbolt slid open.

Out through the mouth.

The door opened.

Action!

"Thank God you're finally here!" she cried, springing up and running to the door before Rafa could even get inside. "I've been trying to catch the attention of those men for hours, but I think they've been ignoring me. You have to help us."

"What has happened?" Rafa hurried inside and put the tray on the kitchen table. "Mrs Dorothy, are you okay?"

Dot glanced at the food, and an unexpected inclusion ripped her from the scene and fired her back into reality. The yoghurt pots, yesterday's new addition, had reappeared and something new had been added to the mix as well: a simple bar of milk chocolate.

"Dot?" he urged, panic clear in his voice. "What is it?"

But she couldn't stop staring. She had a sweet tooth,

but chocolate wasn't something she had craved while being locked up. More pressing issues had occupied her thoughts. Even if she had desired it, she would never have requested any. How silly would it have been to assume such a demand would be met in their current situation?

And yet there is was on the tray with the usual bread, meat, and cheese.

A simple gesture.

A kind gesture.

Rafa's gesture.

As she looked up at Rafa and then at the bedroom door, the unmistakable stone of guilt sank to the bottom of her stomach. Could she really go through with her plan? It wasn't too late to throw a spanner in the works. She could easily recover and improvise to cover her tracks. She blinked hard, reminding herself of the director's advice, and more importantly, the faces of her loved ones.

"It's Percy," she said after swallowing hard, unable to look Rafa in the eyes. "He's not well."

"What's wrong with him?"

"I-I don't know." The well-rehearsed script was slipping from her memory. "He . . . he collapsed. I put him in bed."

Dot dared a look at Rafa and immediately wished she hadn't. He stared at her with concerned eyes, his lips slightly parted. Of course, he'd bought it. He was a boy of nineteen in a sticky situation, with enough kindness to bring a bar of chocolate to an old woman he didn't know.

"Please," she pushed. "You have to help him."

Forcing the chocolate to the back of her mind, she pulled Rafa into the bedroom. Percy was where she had left him, the covers still tucked up to his chin.

"Is he ... dead?" Rafa whispered.

After they had first moved in together, Dot had wondered the same thing on more than one occasion. Many nights she had awoken and wondered if her husband had slipped off in his sleep. Without his glasses and dentures, his usually round and jolly face sank in on itself, an image not helped by his preference for sleeping on his back with his mouth wide open to catch flies.

Percy had promised to stay awake, but she knew him better than that. The man could fall asleep anywhere and during anything. She closed the bedroom door, slamming it just enough to stir him from his sleep. Before he reacted in a way that would betray them, she hurried over to his side and clutched his hand, her eyes firmly on his.

A couple of confused blinks later, Percy began moaning, his head lolling from side to side on his thin pillow. Dot squeezed his hand, hoping to convey that he didn't need to try so hard, but he hammed it up even further.

"I think he's had a heart attack," Dot explained, leaving Percy's side. "He needs to see a doctor."

"I-I—"

"Please, Rafa." She clutched his shoulders and turned him away from Percy. "I don't think he'll make it through the night if we don't get him to a hospital."

"I-I can't."

"I know." She nodded, sighing. "I know you're not in control of this, but I need you to help us. Please, Rafa, I know you're a good boy. You wouldn't let an old man die, would you?"

"No, but—"

"What if this was your grandmother?" she urged, tightening her grip on him. "Your abuela? You'd want someone to help her, wouldn't you?"

He nodded without missing a beat.

"Let us go," she whispered, no acting required to summon the tears that formed along her lashes. "Please, Rafael. I'm begging you. Let us go."

He closed his eyes and took a moment to think, like Dot had done with the chocolate. Before he opened them, Dot already knew what his response would be.

"No," he said firmly, his eyes locked on Dot's, brows tilted at the sides. "You don't know what *he'll* do to me. To my—" He swallowed what he was going to say before he could speak it. With new resolve, he shook his head. "I'm sorry, but I can't."

"I thought as much." Dot exhaled, her grip on his arms tightening. "I'd hoped differently. I'm sorry too."

"What for?"

Rafa's features softened. The penny seemed to drop, but seconds too late. The metal kettle struck the side of his head, sending his eyes rolling backwards. All the muscles in his body relaxed, and he became a dead weight in Dot's hands. She could have let him drop to the floor, but she guided his fall onto Percy's now-empty bed.

"Have I killed him?" Percy cried, letting the kettle fall from his hands onto the tiled floor. "Dorothy?"

"I don't even think you broke the skin," she said as she checked the back of Rafa's head for blood. "He won't be out for long. We need to move quickly."

Dot reached underneath his leather jacket and pulled the gun from his belt. Like the gun she'd fired during the play, assuming it was a prop, its weight surprised her. She tucked it into the back waistband of her skirt and pulled her blouse over it, hoping she wouldn't need to use it.

As discussed, Percy busied himself by tying Rafa's hands and legs with pre-ripped strips from a pair of hideous tracksuit bottoms. The boy moved like a ragdoll, looking younger still.

"Should we gag him?"

"Hmmm?"

"Dorothy?" Percy clicked his fingers in front of her

face when he'd finished. "The boy? Should we gag him so he can't scream for help."

But Dot didn't answer, so Percy took it upon himself to wrap another strip around Rafa's mouth. The fabric slipped between his teeth as Percy fastened it behind his head.

"We need to get a shake on," Percy said as she rushed past her to the window. "Like you said, it won't be long until the lad wakes up, and I wouldn't bet on either of us outrunning him if it came down to it."

Dot nodded, unable to look away from the boy.

"I wish we could help him."

"Help him?" Percy ripped the bars from the crumbling plaster with one firm tug. "He chased us through a market and locked us up. Working for someone else or not, he's one of the bad guys."

Dot nodded that she understood, but it wasn't that simple. Was this how Julia had felt when she'd caught Jessie stealing from her café as a wayward, homeless sixteen-year-old girl? Dot, and many others, had been critical of Julia for taking in a petty criminal, but Jessie's growth in the years since had proven everyone wrong. Rafa, like Jessie, was a victim of circumstance.

"Dorothy?"

Percy tugged the lamp from the wall and tossed it through the single-pane window. The glass shattered outwards on impact.

"Now or never, remember?"

"I know."

But she still couldn't move.

"Dorothy?"

Nothing.

"Your family need you."

Dot snapped back to reality, the reminder of her family all she'd needed to get her moving. Knocking Rafa out and escaping had always been Plan A. She'd offered him another option by presenting Plan B first. She'd desperately hoped he would take it.

"Get your teeth back in," she ordered, her spine stiffening. "You look gormless without them."

"Right you are, dear."

Dot hurried back into the living area. She shut the front door, which Rafa had left wide open. During their afternoon planning session, Percy had suggested that they flee through the front and save having to smash the window, but Dot had dismissed the idea. Just because she hadn't seen any cameras on their brief walk around the clearing didn't mean they weren't there. She didn't want to risk anyone or anything witnessing their flight. The less their captors knew, the more likely it was that she and Percy could make a clean escape.

"Dorothy?" Percy called from the bedroom. "I'm ready."

As she turned away from the door, the chocolate caught her eye once again. She scooped it up, guilt still writhing sickly in her stomach. Back in the bedroom, she placed the bar on Rafa's softly rising and falling chest.

"For when he wakes up," Dot explained to Percy, already waiting by the empty window. "To help with the shock."

Dot got a shock of her own when Rafa's mobile phone rang loudly in his jacket pocket. It vibrated its way out, sliding onto the mangled bedsheets. Rafa stirred, his neutral expression regaining some tension around the brows.

"Shut it up!" Percy hissed.

"I-I don't know how!" Dot picked up the phone, staring at the screen. "What does 'El Comprador' mean?"

Percy snatched the phone off the bed and dropped it onto the floor. He scooped up the kettle and smashed it down until the screen cracked and turned black. He kicked it under the bed.

"What did you do that for?" Dot slapped his arm. "We could have used it to call the police!"

"It's your plan, dear. I've caught the smashing bug." He yanked her over to the window. He'd knocked out as much of the glass as he could and laid the tracksuit's matching jacket along the bottom edge of the frame. "Let's not dilly or dally for a moment longer. Now, we need this bed by the window."

Snapping back into the plan, Dot helped Percy drag the bed she'd slept in up to the window. It hit just under the frame, making it easy for her to shuffle through. She landed on her feet, the glass shards and dried up dirt soft underfoot.

"He's really stirring now," Percy said as he crawled across the bed. "I don't trust my knotting skills enough to guarantee he won't get out of them, given enough time."

Unlike Dot, Percy chose to go through the frame head-first rather than feet-first. She scooped her arms under his and dragged him out like a mother would her child. As more of his body slid through the window, the heavier her short, plump husband felt.

Gravity took hold, and Percy's weight dragged Dot backwards. She yanked Percy through the window as she went. The jacket protecting them from the glass slid with him. Fabric tore as they tumbled into the dark forest. With both arms wrapped around Percy, Dot was unable to stop the momentum, and she landed with a soft thud on the forest floor, twigs poking her in her behind.

"Are you alright, dear?" Percy asked, rolling off her.

"A little winded." Dot sat upright, wincing through the sharp pain in the middle of her back. "Are you hurt?"

She used a nearby tree trunk to pull herself upright, immediately extending a hand to help Percy. Instead of reaching for her, his hand wandered down to his right shin, where a large rip had appeared in his cream trousers.

"Must have caught it on the glass." He pulled his

fingers out of the tear, and she could see blood on his fingertips even in the dark. "It's just a scratch."

"Percy?"

"It's just a scratch," he repeated, accepting Dot's helping hand after wiping the blood on his trousers; she tried not to stare at the stain. "Not to worry. Let's get moving."

Dot took one last look through the window into the bedroom. Rafa was still tied on the bed, but he'd started groaning, not too dissimilar from the noises Percy had been making when he'd feigned illness.

"I think you might have a touch of the Stockholm syndrome, dear," Percy whispered, pulling Dot away from the window.

"Don't be ridiculous," she snapped back, feeling her cheeks heat up. "Let's get to that road and get out of here."

Keeping to the safety of the forest's edge, they walked around the perimeter of the large clearing and found the opening exactly where Dot had expected to find it. It was a simple two-lane road, one side going further up the mountain and the other heading down.

"Would you look at that view," Percy said when they broke through the treeline and onto the road. "Not bad, eh?"

The road curved around at the bottom, the trees breaking to give a clear view all the way out to the coast.

The bright moon reflected in the sea, lighting up a strip of water in the dark.

"Not bad at all," she replied, allowing herself a single relieved sigh. "We're not too far."

"What now?"

"We wait for a car to pass." Dot walked to the edge of the road and looked in both silent directions. "One should be along soon."

Less than five minutes passed before Dot's theory was confirmed. A car appeared at the top of the road. They both jumped up and down, waving their arms, even pausing for a celebratory hug, but the car drove right past them.

"*Rude!*" Dot cried. "Didn't they see us on the news?"

"Perhaps not."

"I'm sure another will be along soon."

Once again, Dot was correct. Another car passed, and another, and another. None stopped. One even went as far as swerving into the opposite lane when Dot attempted to force them to stop.

"It's been ten minutes since the last one," Dot remarked after checking her watch. "How's your leg?"

"Oh, it's fine." Percy waved a dismissive hand. "Are you suggesting we walk?"

"I don't see what other option we have."

"Right you are, dear." Percy wrapped his hand around hers. "We've come this far. Might as well keep going. Who knows, there might be a little town around the corner where we can call for help."

"If only you hadn't smashed that phone."

Percy chuckled. "That was rather silly of me."

They walked for fifteen minutes, finding the downward incline kinder than the upward would have been. No little town appeared – just more twisting road and occasional breaks in the treeline to reveal the coast, which grew no closer. Dot could have walked faster alone, but Percy's glacial walking speed was even slower than usual.

"I hear another engine," Percy said, slowing to a halt. "Shall we give it another go?"

They turned towards the steep road they'd just walked down, but the sound grew closer from behind. A pickup truck turned the bend, its headlights blinding them. To Dot's absolute relief, the driver slowed down even before she had a chance to wave.

"It's going the wrong way," Percy whispered.

"Beggars can't be choosers."

The truck, with empty livestock cages filling the back, slowed to a halt right beside them. The passenger window rolled down, and a man in a cap ducked to look out at them.

"Everything okay?" he asked in a blessedly familiar accent.

"You're *British!*" Dot let out a sigh of relief. "Please,

sir, can you help us? We've found ourselves in a tricky situation. We were taken, and—"

"I know you two!" he cried. "Saw your faces on the news, I did!"

His accent was so neutral, Dot couldn't quite place it to a specific part of the UK

"You did?" Dot smiled from ear to ear. "Oh, thank God!"

"There's posters all over Savega too!" he said. "What are you doing up here in the mountains at this time of night?"

"It's a long story," she said. "We're trying to get back to Savega, and so far, you're the only person who has stopped. We were wondering if you could—"

"Get in," he said, nodding at the door to the back seats. "I've just come from Savega, and I'm heading back after this delivery. It's not a long round trip. Forty minutes, maximum."

Forty minutes or not, Dot didn't need asking twice. She climbed in, shuffling over to make space for Percy. He winced as he climbed in, sending Dot's eyes down to his leg. Blood had soaked through the cream fabric.

"Percy, your—"

"It's fine," he repeated, slamming the door. "We've been through worse these last few days. Let's just focus on getting home."

Percy was rarely short with her, so she didn't push him further. The driver set off, and they sat in silence for a few minutes against the backdrop of the noisy chickens.

Dot was too overwhelmed to speak.

For the first time in days, she felt safe.

"You two must have been through hell," the driver said, glancing at Dot in the rear-view mirror, only his eyes visible.

"You have no idea."

"Your family have been worried sick."

"They have?" Dot sat up straight. "You've seen them?"

"Oh, yes," he replied. "They've been handing out posters all over Savega. Pregnant woman?"

"That's Julia!" Dot patted Percy's knee. "Did you hear that? They've been looking for us."

"I didn't doubt it for a moment," he said, offering a weak smile.

"In fact," the driver said, reaching across to the glove compartment, "I think I have one here."

He passed back a sheet of paper that had been folded multiple times. Dot unravelled it, surprised to see the same picture from the news surrounded by both English and Spanish writing. She recognised Julia's mobile number as the contact information.

"Don't suppose they'll have to pay the ransom now," the driver said, looking through the mirror again. "That'll be a relief for them."

"Ransom?" Dot fired back. "We were being held ransom?"

"One hundred thousand euros."

"Bloody hell!" She looked back down at the missing poster. "How did you know about the ransom?"

"It's on the poster."

"No, it isn't." Dot scanned it again. "It just says we're missing. It doesn't say anything about a ransom on here."

"Must have heard it on the news then."

Dot glanced at the mirror again, but his eyes were firmly on the road ahead this time. Considering that Dot didn't speak Spanish, she had no way of knowing what the news report had been about, but she hadn't remembered seeing any numbers on the screen indicating the price on their heads.

"How far are we from the delivery drop off?" Dot asked, checking her watch; it was almost eleven.

"Oh, not much further." He glanced in the mirror again, the corners of his eyes crinkling. "In fact, it's just up here."

Dot's heart skipped several beats as they turned right into the trees onto an eerily familiar road. She nudged Percy, but he wasn't paying any attention. He was leaning as far forward as he could to clutch his shin.

"Lucky I found you when I did," the driver said as he turned into the all too familiar clearing. "Much longer, and somebody might actually have stopped to take you back."

Dot yanked on the handles, but the doors were locked.

"You won't get out," he said, looking through the mirror again; she felt his smirk even though she couldn't see it. "Child locks are a marvellous invention, don't you think?"

"Who are you?"

"That doesn't matter." The car stopped, and he killed the engine. "Now, time to make that delivery."

Knowing she was missing far too many pieces of the puzzle, Dot reacted instead of thinking. She pulled the gun from the back of her skirt and pointed it shakily at the driver.

"I'll shoot!" she cried.

"You won't."

"I've done it before!" She tried to steady the gun, but it was like trying to stiffen cooked spaghetti. "I'm warning you."

The driver laughed and tugged the keys from the ignition. Using the little experience gained from rehearsing with the prop gun and then firing the real one during the play, she cocked the hammer and tilted the gun up at the roof of the car. She pulled the trigger to fire a warning shot.

The gun clicked.

No recoil.

No bullet.

The driver laughed again, jumping out and slamming the car door. Dot tried the handle over and over, but like the gun, the door did nothing. She looked back at the gun, wondering if she'd done something wrong. She pushed on the side of the cylinder, and it fell open with ease.

Six empty chambers.

No bullets.

The door to the villa opened, and Rafa stumbled out, free of his restraints. He had one hand on his head, but both went up when he saw the driver marching towards him. His hands did little to protect his face from the punches.

"Percy?" she called, nudging him. "Percy, we need to get out of here."

"Right you are, dear," he said wearily, pulling his blood-soaked hand from his shin. "It's just, this might not be just a scratch, after all."

15

JULIA

*J*ulia sank her toes into the warm sand, leaned back on the wooden jetty, and closed her eyes. The hot morning sun caressed her cheeks in a way the sun back home never did. Cold ice cream dripped down her hand, continued to the point of the cone, and landed in small droplets on her foot.

"How's yours?" Jessie asked, already half-finished her four scoops of chocolate ice cream wedged into a large waffle cone. "Ice cream never tastes this good at home."

"I think it's the weather." Julia licked her more modest selection: one scoop of vanilla and another of butterscotch on a classic cone. "It's delicious."

At the edge of the golden sand on the cleanest beach Julia had ever seen in person, the turquoise Mediterranean Sea stretched out all the way to the northern tip of Africa. On a map, they appeared so close, yet the horizon offered no glimpse of the land beyond it.

Some small paddle boats and other larger liners, no doubt carrying tourists, dotted the water. People parasailed and surfed. One group was even being dragged behind a speedboat on a giant inflatable banana.

Julia licked more melting ice cream from her fingers, avoiding the scoops to prolong the pleasure. Until the final bite of the cone, she got to be on holiday like everyone else.

But Jessie finished before Julia had even reached the top of the cone, and the slower Julia ate, the more she felt Jessie's eagerness to get back to handing out posters. Reluctantly, Julia bit her way to the bottom of the cone.

"Should we go and put our feet in the water?" Jessie suggested, clearly sensing Julia's reluctance.

"No," Julia replied quickly, already dusting the sand from her toes. "The water will only make the sand stick. I've had my fill. I'm ready to get back."

Jessie helped Julia up off the jetty, and they put their sandals back on. Against the backdrop of the tree-dense mountains sprinkled with white buildings and terracotta roofs, they carried on handing out missing posters along the seafront.

If the posters hadn't led to Maria recognising Dot and Percy and giving Julia the photo album, she might have started to believe they were a waste of time. With each passing day, handing them out increasingly felt like a fool's errand. Half the people who might have seen something had probably already flown home, and the other half were too busy stocking up on cheap fake-designer clothes to notice anything else.

Julia handed her last poster to an old lady sat on a bench in the shade of a tree. Even being of a similar age to the people on the pamphlet wasn't enough to make her care. She barely glanced at it before shaking her head, and when Julia insisted she keep it, the woman screwed it up and tossed it into the metal bin next to the bench.

"I'm out too," Jessie said, joining Julia on the bench when the woman shuffled off, only to sit on the next along the row. "I know people can be rude, but tourists take it to a whole new level. You'd think we were trying to sell them something."

"They probably think that's what we're doing." Julia pointed out the men up and down the promenade, trying to get people into their restaurants and bars. "We'd probably get more attention if we were selling boat trips with every missing poster."

"I think I know a guy with enough money to make that happen," Jessie said, nudging Julia with her arm. "He made quite a bit of money selling a book, and I'm quite friendly with his wife. Might be able to twist their arms."

"You're funnier on holiday."

"It must be the vitamin D." Jessie showed off her arms, which were even more tanned than the Peridale summer could account for. "But seriously, have you . . ."

"Considered trying to pay the ransom?" Julia finished the sentence for her. "Believe me, if we had the money, we would, but we don't. Even with my savings and Barker's, we're nowhere near."

"I have twelve hundred saved up," Jessie offered. "I would happily—"

"A kind offer," Julia jumped in, resting her hand on Jessie's shoulder, "but we'd still be miles away. If I could sell the house that quickly, I would. Believe me, I'd do anything to get my gran back, and yet the only thing I *can* do isn't making any difference."

"It might." Jessie sighed and smiled up at the sun. "Should we go back? It's almost easier to ignore what we're missing when it's not being shoved in our faces. I'm sick of seeing happy people."

"Me too." Julia slapped her knees and pushed herself up, groaning involuntarily; for once, Jessie didn't point it out. "Thanks for suggesting the ice cream. It was nice to sit down."

"Someone had to suggest it, and I knew it was never going to be you." Jessie sprang up with the vigour that never failed to make Julia feel old. "I'll even let us get a taxi back. Taking the steps down almost killed you."

"Because I'm unbelievably old?"

"Because you're unbelievably pregnant." Jessie poked

her in the ribs as they set off to the taxi rank on the corner. "I don't always go for the lowest hanging fruit, you know. It's not my fault that sometimes the meanest thing to say is also the funniest."

"Sounds like my gran." Julia couldn't help but smile. "Her sharp tongue can leave you laughing or crying, but she never means any harm. I'd give anything to hear one of her icy put-downs right about now."

"And she'd finish it with a bounce of her curls."

"Or a fiddle of her brooch." Julia's smile turned to laughter. "And then she'd vanish as quickly as she arrived, leaving everyone to wonder if they should take offence."

They secured the nod of approval from the driver in the white taxi at the front of the row of six and climbed into the back.

"La Casa hotel, please."

The driver nodded and pulled away from the kerb. If the car had air conditioning, he didn't turn it on, so Julia wound the window down. Once they'd crawled away from the rush of the seafront, they whizzed up to Savega through the twisting, tight roads and the warm breeze whipped at Julia's hair.

"Look what Alfie sent me," Jessie called over the sound of the wind, handing her phone over. "Fresh off the press, by the looks of it."

Julia shielded her eyes from the sun and squinted at the screen. It was a picture of an issue of *The Peridale*

Post, with the headline 'COME HOME DOT AND PERCY' accompanied by individual pictures of them both. There was a third image, which Julia had to pinch the screen to zoom in to see. Eight Peridale residents were holding a sheet of paper with a single letter on it. Together, they spelt out 'COME HOME'. She had been away from home for so long, she didn't notice they were standing in her café right away.

Julia wasn't sure if she wanted to smile or cry, but she knew one thing for certain: she missed home.

"Everyone's probably worried sick," Julia said, handing the phone back. "I should call to thank them."

"I don't think anyone expects that." Jessie's fingers tapped away on the screen at a speed that still shocked Julia. "Besides, this morning I called everyone that matters to give them updates so you wouldn't have to. Katie's doing fine at the café, and she's keeping Mowgli alive. Might not have been the right thing to do, but I also convinced your dad and sister to stay put, at least for now."

"Definitely the right thing to do," Julia said without a second thought. "As much as they'd want to help, they'd only complicate things." She paused before reaching out and grabbing Jessie's hand, adding, "I'm glad you're here, though."

"Because I make you laugh?"

"Amongst other things."

"You'll get the invoice for my clown services when we

get back home." Jessie smiled wryly. "We *will* go home, and when we do, Dot and Percy will be with us. I can feel it."

Julia wished she shared Jessie's youthful optimism, but since she couldn't bring herself to agree, she turned to look through the window. Time and time again, life had proven that the worst-case scenario could happen. As much as she wanted to believe everything would work out, a nagging voice in her mind told her not to be so naïve.

Unless a bag of cash fell from the sky and into their laps in the next four days, they'd have no reason to advertise a tractor in the post office window like the ransom note had demanded. Julia hadn't allowed her imagination to consider what might happen when it came time for their flights home. She couldn't bear the possibility that she'd seen her gran for the last time.

The taxi pulled up outside La Casa, thankfully breaking her morose train of thought. The driver tapped the metre. Twenty-two euros. A special inflated price for the tourists, she assumed. The same length journey in Peridale would have cost five pounds, if that. But Julia didn't complain. She pulled twenty-five euros from her barely touched holiday money and told him to keep the change. Three euros wasn't going to make much difference when one hundred thousand were on the line.

As soon as they climbed out of it, the taxi sped off

towards the plaza. A police car pulled up almost as quickly, with Sub-Inspector Castro behind the wheel. Minnie climbed out of the backseat, looking more than a little the worse for wear. Castro smiled tightly at Julia before following the taxi down the lane.

Minnie stared up at the hotel, and then at Julia and Jessie. She looked dazed and very bewildered.

"We only just got back," Julia explained, wrapping her arm around her great-aunt's shoulders. "Why don't we go inside and get you a cup of tea?"

"Something stronger, I think," she replied with a shaky nod, letting Julia lead her inside.

"I'll make cocktails," said Jessie.

Julia didn't bother telling Jessie not to make Minnie's as potent as she'd made her own the day before. Her entire body vibrated under Julia's touch, no doubt from exhaustion. If she'd slept at all, the dark bags under her weary eyes were betraying how poor that rest had been.

"There's no change," Minnie announced as she settled into a wicker chair in the sunroom, her distant gaze fixed on something out in the valley. "They said the surgery went well, but she still isn't waking up."

Jessie retreated to the bar in the corner of the dining room, leaving them alone. Julia pulled up a chair next to her great-aunt. Minnie smiled at her, her tired eyes softening.

"Thank you, Julia," she said softly. "If you hadn't

found her when you did, she would have bled to death right there on the kitchen floor."

"I was lucky," she said. "I almost didn't see her."

"But you did." Minnie's eyes returned to the valley. "If it had been down to me to find her, she'd already be dead, that's for sure. After our tiff, I swore I wouldn't talk to her until she apologised. Can you believe that?"

"You weren't to know this would happen."

"It shouldn't have taken something like this for me to realise how wrong that is." Minnie smiled sadly, her pain clear. "I've been relying on that girl far too much since my Bill died. Instead of learning to do things myself, I let Lisa fill the hole Bill left behind. I never even *asked* her to take on so much, I just expected it. I knew she'd never say no. What kind of mother does that make me?"

Julia didn't know how to answer. She'd noticed as much with her own eyes, but now wasn't the time to add to Minnie's guilt. Thankfully, Jessie walked in with the tray of cocktails and Minnie perked up a little.

"I didn't want to come home," Minnie explained after a sip of her bright orange cocktail. "The doctors told me to get some rest and a change of clothes, and I don't think they were giving me much choice. I've probably been getting under their feet this whole time, just trying to be by her side." She took another sip. "Oh, you should see her, Julia! All those tubes and wires—"

"Best not to think about it."

"I didn't know how I was going to get back," she

continued, pausing for another gulp. "Money for a taxi was the last thing on my mind when I left. They offered to let me use the phone, but I had no one to call. I don't know any numbers. Not even the hotel's! Bill always dealt with the phones, and I..."

Minnie's voice trailed off, tears following in the wake of her words. She sniffed them back, plucked the straw and umbrella from the cocktail, and drank deeply from the rim.

"I don't deserve to be upset," she said after slamming the empty cup down on the table. "Not while my daughter is fighting for her life. Everything she said during our argument was the truth. I've been living my life like I'm on permanent holiday since long before Bill died. I should have thrown in the towel back then, but instead, I let my daughter sacrifice her life so her washed-up, has-been mother could keep the party going."

"Minnie, it's best not to get yourself worked up."

"Maybe that's what I need." Her blank stare drifted from the valley to the empty pool. "At least Arlo is behind bars. That lovely copper fella . . . What's his name? Caster?"

"Castro," Julia corrected. "Sub-Inspector Castro."

"That's it." She nodded. "I would have been stuck at the hospital if he hadn't come to take my statement. Nice man offered me a lift back, so I took it."

"What did you tell him?"

"Everything." She sighed. "About Lisa catching Arlo stealing and how I had to fire him because of it."

"And you're certain Arlo could have done it?"

"Castro asked me that same question." Minnie frowned at the floor. "If they hadn't found his watch at the scene, I wouldn't have believed it. He worked in that kitchen for a decade and we never had any issues with him. He'd get angry, certainly, but Bill said that was true of most chefs. Arlo claimed it was because he was passionate about his food." She paused and reached for her drink but stopped when she realised it was empty. "Castro said they were going to charge him, most likely. I guess you never really know a person."

Julia wanted to push, to find out more about Arlo, but she decided against it. The last thing Minnie needed was yet another interrogation about the man who had been arrested for attempting to murder her daughter.

"Sooner I get myself together, sooner I can get back to the hospital." Minnie rose slowly. "Julia, would you walk me back to my room?"

Minnie held out an arm for Julia to link with, so she accepted. They walked slowly and silently through the dining room, and then to the door behind the reception desk. They took the narrow staircase upwards, which brought them to a small landing with three doors.

"I want you to help me with something," Minnie said, opening the door to the right. "Wait in here. I won't be two minutes."

Julia ventured into the darkened room, which appeared to be a self-contained flat. When she pushed the curtains aside, a large window revealed yet another stunning view of the valley.

The room, clearly Minnie's quarters, was decorated unlike anything else in the hotel, with rich, red damask wallpaper, dark wood furniture, and an overwhelming number of framed pictures on the walls. The sofa, cushions, rugs, and throws were all different animal prints that clashed so completely it somehow worked.

Julia examined the wall with the most pictures, instantly recognising some of the modelling headshots as ones she'd received, autographed, in the post for so many years. Many were new to her. In her own way, Minnie was still beautiful, but there was no denying the camera had loved her during her prime.

Amongst the modelling pictures were shots of Minnie with other people. Minnie's age varied more in these candid shots. In most, she'd been photographed with instantly recognisable people. Every picture appeared to have been taken at a party or a function. To Julia's surprise, most of the famous faces from Minnie's wild stories were up on the wall, smiling down at her.

Minnie returned with a laptop jammed under her arm, but Julia didn't immediately move away from the wall.

"Oh, those were the days," Minnie said, longing in her voice. "I know it's hard to believe, but before I turned into this old woman, I was something. I was an *it* girl much longer than I had a right to be. Life and soul of the party, they'd call me, but as it turns out, even I had an expiration date. Even the most expensive cheese goes off eventually."

"I don't suppose any of them would be willing to donate one hundred thousand euros to a worthy cause?"

Minnie chuckled. "Most could probably do it and not notice the expense, but they're the kind of people who call *you*, not the other way around. And let me tell you, it's been a long time since anyone called."

"Your stories made it sound like you were quite close to some of them."

"Embellished, my dear." She sighed, eyes darting from picture to picture. "I was just another party girl. There to fill the room and keep things lively. Took me an embarrassingly long time to realise that. In the early days, I thought I was there to network, to further my career. People would introduce me as 'upcoming model and actress, Minnie Harlow'. Eventually, they dropped the tagline. I became 'You remember Minnie, don't you? Surely you've met?' I once overheard Simon Cowell say 'that woman would turn up to the opening of an envelope'. He was right. It should have upset me, but it didn't – I didn't care." She sat on the sofa, her back to the wall. "My showbiz career was never up or coming, no matter how many famous people I rubbed shoulders with. By the time the wrinkles started showing up, it was clear my career was never going to take off like I wanted it to. In the end, being close to the light was enough for me. Sad, isn't it? I'm a widow with three failed marriages, and my most prized possessions are a bunch of photographs in an empty, failing hotel. None of those people could remember me if their lives depended on it. I should have filled my walls with pictures of my daughter. Instead, I memorialized my delusions. If she ever wakes up, I wouldn't even blame her if she never wanted to talk to me again."

Julia left the gallery wall and sat next to her great-aunt.

"I'm sure that's not going to happen," she reassured her. "I might not know her, but I could tell she didn't hate you from the way she talked about you. Frustrated, yes, but hate? That's not the impression I got."

"That's kind of you to say." She patted Julia's leg. "There's no relationship more complicated than that between a mother and a daughter, as I'm sure you know."

"My mother died when I was twelve."

"Of course." Minnie exhaled and blinked tightly. "I was heartbroken when I heard about Pearl."

"You knew her?"

Minnie nodded. "She was about five years younger than me, but you know what Peridale is like. Everyone knows everyone in that village. I was at your parents' wedding. They were so young but so clearly in love." Her smile turned wistful. "Albert and I also grew up without a mother. She died when we were very young. Our father only waited eight months to remarry. We used to call her the 'wicked stepmother' – not to her face, of course. She'd give us a swift slap for so much as breathing too loudly at the dinner table. She was a headmistress without a single ounce of patience for children." Minnie's expression turned sad. "I was so proud of never laying a finger on Lisa. It was something I held onto. I wasn't like *that woman*. I probably inherited some of my aloofness from my stepmother, but I never hit the girl. And now I can't even say that."

Minnie lifted a shaky hand to her mouth, obviously holding back tears.

"The night before she was stabbed," Minnie continued, "she came in here. Rare in itself. She tried to tell me she couldn't keep running everything. I didn't want to hear it. I was too busy listening to my old records. She was killing my mood. I even said that to her. Can you imagine?" Minnie looked stricken as if she couldn't even recognise the woman she'd been only a short time earlier. "I saw the snap in her eyes. I pushed her too far, and she pushed back. She laid it all out for me, every one of my flaws, and boy oh boy, was she honest. She might as well have held a mirror up to my soul." Minnie's shaking hand closed at her side. "I slapped her right across the face, and she didn't say a word. She just walked out. Didn't even slam the door."

Her searching gaze went to Julia. "What if that's the last moment I ever get with her? What if—"

"Let's not play that game," Julia interrupted gently. "Like you said, there's no relationship more complicated than mother and daughter. My mother might have died before things between us got complicated, but my gran was as good as a mother to me. After my mum died, my dad mentally checked out, so my gran was left to raise my sister and me. Granted, I was the better behaved, but my sister nearly pushed my gran to hit her more than once." Julia paused, knowing her words weren't sinking in; Minnie was too lost in her grief and guilt to hear them. "What did you want me to help with?"

"This," she said, resting her hand on the laptop. "It's Lisa's. I don't know how to use these things. I want to get into her emails. I know The Buyer has been contacting her with offers, but I've never seen them for myself. Every time she printed them off, I ripped them up without even reading them."

Minnie passed the laptop across to Julia. It opened on a password page. As someone who constantly forgot her laptop password, Julia knew about the 'hint' button all too well. She hovered over it, and the hint was 'father'.

"What was Lisa's father's name?"

"Lawrence," Minnie replied with a roll of her eyes. "Second husband. He was a photographer. Short fella, but he was beautiful – and he knew it. Tight with money.

Counted every penny like it was trying to run away. We met on a photo shoot in Milan. Caught him in bed with another woman six months into our marriage." She sighed. "He promised to take my career to new heights. Instead, he left me with a bun in the oven. Never wanted anything to do with Lisa when she was growing up. Pancreatic cancer got him in '98."

Julia typed in 'lawrence', but it didn't work. She followed it with 'Lawrence', and the screen magically unlocked. The desktop background looked like any other beautiful view until Julia realised it was the same valley through the window.

"Who was your third husband?" Julia asked as she double-clicked the email icon. "I'm curious now."

"Dick Richards." This eye roll was even more pronounced. "Don't ask. I don't know what I was thinking either. Incredibly boring. Strange looking, too. He had huge eyes, a giant nose, barely a chin to speak of, and this squeaky nasally voice. I used to call him Owl. We met when I was doing some extras work for a film company to make ends meet. He was on the soundstage next door, directing a workout video." She gave a little self-deprecating head shake. "It was the age of the Jane Fonda VHS, and I thought I was going to become the next big thing in fitness. I could barely stand on one leg, but we gave it a good shot. We self-produced a tape after our honeymoon, but we struggled to sell it. Let me tell you, shifting five hundred VHS tapes isn't as easy as it sounds. I was giving them away in the end, just to get them out of the garage. I gave that one five years, but one night I cracked and realised I couldn't stand listening to his voice for one more day. I think he was relieved when I told him I wanted a divorce."

Julia found her way to Lisa's inbox. Five new emails appeared instantly. One was for a book newsletter she was subscribed to, another a reminder to update payment settings for something. The other three, like the majority of the emails, had similar subject lines: Purchase Offer, Purchase Offer – Updated, Purchase Offer – Final. Julia didn't even have to scroll down to see that identical emails had been coming through, regular as clockwork, all with the same subjects, all from different email addresses.

"Is that them?" Minnie asked, leaning against Julia's arm as she stared at the screen. "There's so many. How do we read them?"

Julia double-clicked on the email at the top, and a short, formal message popped up.

"Read it out, dear," Minnie prompted. "My eyes aren't what they were."

"'Dear La Casa owners'," Julia read after clearing her throat. "'We are upping our offer to buy your hotel by another two thousand euros, bringing our current offer to four hundred and fifteen thousand euros. This is our final offer. On acceptance, you will receive the funds promptly, in cash. We await your timely reply.'"

"How much did you say that offer was, dear?"

"Four hundred and fifteen thousand."

"Four hundred?"

"And fifteen thousand."

"Bloody hell!" Minnie collapsed back into the sofa. "I could have sworn Lisa said the offers were in the low two-hundred-thousands. We only paid ninety-eight for the place, but that was twenty years ago. If I'd wanted to sell, we would have got more than they were offering by going to market." She blinked. "But four hundred and fifteen thousand? They want to pay that much for my hotel, and in cash?"

"Are you considering it?"

"What choice do I have?" Minnie bit into her lip. "Lisa was right. I can't run this place without her, and she doesn't want the job. That money would pay for the ransom with three hundred and fifteen thousand left over. Heck, if I wanted to, I could buy a house in Peridale. I've always wanted to visit the old place."

"Minnie, I—"

"If you're going to say you can't accept the ransom money, I insist," she said, holding up a hand. "The note was addressed to La Casa. This wouldn't have happened if I hadn't invited you all here. I got carried away with the idea of reliving the old days with Dot. The days before I became that fake woman in all those pictures."

Julia hadn't intended on refusing the offer. How could she? No amount of money mattered more than her gran. Julia didn't care where that money came from. If that made her selfish, then she was happy to throw up her hands and admit her selfishness without hesitation.

"Thank you." Exactly what Julia had been about to say before Minnie interrupted her. "I know she's my gran, but she's the closest thing to a mother I've had for most of my life."

"I thought your father remarried?"

"He did," Julia said, pausing to figure out the quickest way to explain that her 'stepmother', Katie, was her age and more like a friend or a sister – even if she had given birth to Julia's almost two-year-old brother, Vinnie. Instead, she simply opted for, "It's complicated."

"Told you it's the most complicated relationship," Minnie said with a wink, her spirits seemingly lifted after the talk. "Now, how do we reply to an email?"

"With another email," she explained. "You can type it out."

"I could never get the hang of a typewriter."

"You could dictate?"

"Okay." Minnie nodded, tapping her finger on her chin. "Okay, write 'I will accept your offer. Please contact us at your earliest convenience.' How does that sound?"

"Like what they want to hear," Julia said as she quickly typed out the short message. "Are you sure you want me to send it? Something tells me there's no going back with these people."

Minnie looked around the room and smiled. Julia

half-expected her to shake her head and throw the laptop out the window, but instead, she gave one firm nod. Julia clicked 'send' without hesitation.

"Then it's done," Minnie said, standing up. "I'm going to shower, and then I'll get back to the hospital. Would you stay here and watch for a reply? And if nothing comes before I head back, would you mind keeping hold of it to keep checking?"

"Of course."

Minnie stumbled across her small flat, her steps clunky and stiff as though multiple joints hurt at once. She reached a white door in the sea of rich colours and patterns. She paused before opening it and turned back to Julia.

"You look just like your mother, you know," she said. "Just as beautiful."

"Thank you." Julia blushed. "Lisa is the spitting image of you, too."

"She is?" Minnie furrowed her brow and looked over at the wall of pictures. "Yes, I suppose she is."

Julia waited in the cluttered living room, listening to the shower. Minnie's room had no television or any other sign of technology aside from a record player. She could see the appeal of such a life, although it wasn't one she could cope with for long. As much as she disliked the beeping of her phone and the constant stream of information it provided, she already felt completely disconnected from the world in Savega. She couldn't imagine how that would feel after twenty years.

After thirty minutes of no email reply, and with the shower still running, Julia gently knocked on the door to the bedroom. When no response came, she opened the door and popped her head in. As she'd suspected, Minnie was fast asleep on the edge of a king-sized bed in the middle of the eclectically decorated bedroom. Still fully dressed, she hadn't even made it to the shower.

Julia turned off the water in the en suite bathroom – the only part of the self-contained flat that resembled her room in La Casa – and turned off the light. She pulled an ice-white fur throw from the back of an ornate armchair and covered Minnie with it.

Leaving her great-aunt softly snoring, Julia tucked the laptop under her arm and headed back to the main part of the hotel. She crept down the staircase and emerged into brightness, where the soothing calmness of the decorating was utterly at odds with the rooms where she'd just been. In a moment of luck, Barker walked through the front doors just as she came around the desk.

"Been snooping?" he asked.

"I was . . ." Julia paused and thought about her response before saying, " . . . getting to know my great-aunt. What about you?"

"Oh," he said, grinning ear to ear. "I have definitely

been snooping. I did what I've spent the last few months being good at for retired women with too much money."

"You tried to prove someone's unfaithfulness?"

"Close," Barker replied, pulling out his phone. "I followed a dodgy man around with a camera, and for once, actually found something other than a secret gambling addiction or sneaky smoking habit. Swipe through these."

Julia accepted Barker's phone and looked through the pictures. Inspector Hillard was in all of them. The sequence of the photographs acted like stop-motion animations, showing the inspector going in and out of the clothes shops, talking to men in cars, and in more than a handful of the pictures, accepting thick brown envelopes.

"I called DI Christie and asked him to do something he *could* actually do," Barker said as Julia continued swiping. "Couldn't find much on Inspector Hillard myself, but Christie knows a guy who knows a guy who was able to dig up that Hillard has been working in Savega for two years. How long did Gabriel say the gang had been here?"

"Two years."

"Coincidence?" Barker whispered, looking around the empty hotel foyer. "Or have we just found The Buyer?"

Julia swiped one too many, landing on a picture of her asleep, mouth wide open, sprawled out on a lounger on the terrace with a book resting between her chest and bump. Hardly any time had passed since that first morning, and yet it felt like it had happened in a different lifetime.

"Good work," she said, swiping back one before returning the phone. "I have some news too. If the gang and The Buyer are connected, and Inspector Hillard is The Buyer, he's about to be four hundred and fifteen thousand euros short. Minnie's accepted an offer to buy the hotel."

"Seriously?"

"She's going to pay the ransom." Julia gulped, and for the first time allowed herself to feel excited. "This could be it, Barker. This could be how we get them back."

16

DOT

"I spy with my little eye," Percy said, dragging out each syllable as he looked around the small outbuilding, "something beginning with ... S."

Like with his ear-tugging poker giveaway, Percy's habit of staring at the thing he was picking made it easy for Dot to figure it out. Still, she looked around the room, pausing to glance at her watch. It was already six in the evening, and no food had been brought to them – if any was coming at all.

"Sink," she said.

"How do you get them so quickly?" Percy said, sighing heavily. "You're far too clever for me, my dear."

"You were staring right at the sink again." Dot dabbed at his forehead with the yellow pocket square he'd had in his shirt pocket when they were first taken. "I'd give anything for that fan right now."

"You never know what you've got until it's gone."

Dot had never heard a truer statement. She looked around the cramped space. It was as rundown as she'd assumed based on its exterior. The small room contained a single bed with no sheets, a sink on one wall with a small window above it, and a toilet with only a short half-wall for privacy. The walls were exposed plaster with huge chunks missing to show the old bricks between, and the single window was so dusty and streaky that it barely let in any natural light.

It was also far too small to crawl through, even if they could get up that high.

A prison cell, essentially, although Dot had seen prisoners on documentaries with better-kept rooms. The villa was a palace in comparison, but they were never setting foot back inside there, not after their failed break-out.

"It's your turn, Dorothy."

"Hmmm?"

"I spy."

Dot sighed. She wasn't in the mood to play another game of anything, especially since they'd long since run out of objects to spy.

She glanced down at Percy's leg.

She had to keep him distracted.

"I spy with my little eye," she said reluctantly, looking around the room for something neither of them had used yet, "something between with . . . L B."

"Oh, a two-letter game!" Percy shifted his weight, looking wearily around the room, a fresh layer of sweat already covering his face. "I might have to think about this one."

While he did, Dot looked at the makeshift bandage wrapped around the cut on his shin. After being thrown into the outbuilding last night and realising her cries for medical attention were going to be ignored, she gave nursing her best shot.

Dot had torn the trouser leg off at the knee, using the rip as a natural tearing point. Washing away the blood had revealed a chunk of glass from the window, around the size of a fifty pence piece, lodged in his shin. Percy cried when she pulled it out, but the relief that followed seemed worth it. With nothing to stitch him up, she did the only thing she could. She wrapped it as tightly as she could and prayed the bleeding would stop.

Somehow, they fell asleep side by side on the tiny bed, although Dot woke more than once to watch Percy's breathing.

In the morning, she cleaned the cut and changed the dressing with another strip of the trouser fabric. She noticed the darkening skin around the wound but didn't comment on it. She didn't need to be a real nurse to know what an infection looked like.

"Is it . . . long beam?" Percy asked, nodding up at the ceiling as she dabbed at his shiny face.

"Not quite."

"You might have me stumped here, my—"

Percy stopped as they heard jangling keys. They sat up straight, backs against the wall, legs stretched out in front of them on the bare mattress. Unlike the villa, this door had only one lock to keep them in. Not that more were needed. Dot hadn't braved looking through the window for a few hours, but the six men in the clearing with their guns pointed at the outbuilding were enough to stop any thought of attempting freedom.

The door opened. Dot was relieved to see Rafa. One eye was swollen entirely shut, the skin around it a similar hue to Percy's cut. His bottom lip jutted out, thick and split down the middle. Having taken a kettle to the back of his head seemed like the least of his worries.

"I won't insult you with an apology," Dot said, no longer attempting to push forward her sweeter voice. "In our position, anyone would have done the same."

Rafa didn't say a word. He dumped a loaf of bread in the sink under the window before turning to them. They flinched as his body blocked the light. Rafa glanced down at Percy's leg before diving forward to snatch his glasses.

"Goodness me," Percy muttered, blinking hard as he pushed himself against Dot. "I can't see a thing without them."

"I don't think he cares, dear."

Rafa pocketed the glasses and reached out for Dot. For a split second, she thought he was going to wrap his hands around her neck. Instead, he went for her brooch; she would have preferred the neck.

"No," she said firmly, snatching the brooch before he could yank it from its place at her collar. "It's very precious to me."

But Rafa didn't care. He grabbed her wrist and pried open her fingers until she had no choice but to release her grip. He grabbed the brooch and let go of her. His swollen features remained eerily expressionless the entire time. Dot had lived long enough to recognise the look of a broken man.

"You can only be controlled if you let people control you," she called as he walked back to the door with their things. "If that man last night is your grandmother's husband and the person in charge of all this, I can see why you're scared of him, but you still have a choice. You're young enough to have a life of your own. A real life."

Rafa paused at the door, and to Dot's surprise, he turned.

"You do not know me," he said, his tone as blank as his face.

"I know you didn't put bullets in your gun," she replied. "That's enough for me right now, Rafael."

Rafa's one good eye drifted up to her, only lingering for a moment – just long enough for Dot to see a line of tears forming along the lashes.

And then he left, slamming the door and locking it behind him.

"Was that part of your new plan, dear?" Percy asked, his voice breathier than she was used to.

"No plan this time," she admitted, not seeing the point in keeping up the façade. "We're truly at their mercy now."

Dot pulled the poster from her breast pocket and unfolded it. Knowing that Julia was looking for them had to be enough. Pregnant or not, she was their only way out.

"I think I've figured out L B," Percy said out of the blue. "Was it light bulb?"

"It was."

"Very clever, my love."

Dot folded the poster and tucked it back into her pocket.

"Another game?" Dot asked.

"I don't think I'm quite in the mood anymore. And I can't spy anything without my specs." Percy edged away from the wall and curled on his side, facing away from her. "Tell me about your life, dear."

"My life?"

"I want to hear it all."

"What about the bread?"

"For once," he said, pausing to sigh, "I don't think I'm all that hungry."

"Okay." Dot shimmied down behind her husband

and wrapped her arm around his middle; he looped his fingers through hers. "Where do I start?"

"I'd say at the beginning," he said, squeezing tight. "Day Dot. And don't skimp on the details. I want to hear everything."

And so Dot talked. She went as far back as she could remember, starting with the dreaded ballet lessons her snooty mother had pushed upon her when she was four years old.

She got all the way up to her mid-twenties and raising Brian with Albert before she realised Percy had fallen asleep. She carried on telling the story of her life anyway.

It beat sitting in silence.

17

JULIA

For the fourth time during the video call, Sue's face froze and turned to tiny, fuzzy squares on Julia's phone screen. She left the bedroom and walked out onto the balcony, spinning around until Sue unfroze.

"*Wow!*" Sue squinted at the screen, her focus so firm that her nose scrunched, bringing up her top lip, exposing her teeth. "Can you move out of the way? I want to get a look at that view!"

"I can do you one better," Julia said, scanning the symbols on the screen, trying to remember Jessie's exact words about the camera flip icon being 'stupidly obvious' since there were only four to choose from. Sun in her eyes, she pulled the phone up closer, tapped one, and while the camera didn't flip, the volume vanished, cutting off Katie's singing in the background. "Hang on."

"Nice double chin," Sue said when Julia pressed that same button again. "I just screenshotted that, so you're welcome."

"Here." Julia pressed the 'obvious flip' button and turned to face the valley. "Not a bad view, eh?"

"Not a bad view at all," she replied, still squinting. "Why didn't I get an invite?"

"On our honeymoon?"

"To our great-aunt's hotel."

"Last I heard you still hadn't remembered who she was."

"And I still haven't." Sue shrugged and bit into something flaky, pastry crumbs sticking around her lips. "You got cheques and signed headshots, and I didn't get diddly squat."

"She'd stopped sending them by the time you were old enough to remember." It was Julia's turn to squint at the screen. "What are you eating?"

"Oh." Sue flipped the camera this time, the view changing to one of the tables in Julia's café. "Shilpa's samosas. We've been selling them in the café. Evelyn's been baking too, although we're not sure about her cakes. Amy Clark swears she started seeing pink dragons in the sky after eating one yesterday. Might give one a try when the twins are in bed." She took another bite and flipped the camera back to her face. "Even dad's been chipping in when he's not flogging antiques. Alfie, too. It's a real village effort. Jessie is like a mini version of you these days, and even she just about manages when you're gone. Without the both of you, it's taking a village effort to make just one Julia."

"I miss the place," was all Julia could think, so she said it aloud.

"It misses you too." Sue's gaze drifted over the top of the screen and into the direction of what Julia knew was the kitchen. "Would you look at her go? How did we end up with an idiot like this for our stepmother?"

The camera flipped, and Sue graciously zoomed in on Katie dancing around the kitchen using a wooden spoon as a microphone, whipping her blonde curls from side to side.

Julia couldn't help but laugh.

"There's no music."

"I made her put headphones in," Sue groaned. "She was doing my head in with the singing. I swear to God she thinks she's a forty-year-old Britney Spears." Sue slowly zoomed in further, this time on the sequins spelling out 'DIVA' on the backside of Katie's pink tracksuit bottoms. "Bless her, though. She's trying her best. She's only almost burnt the place down twice."

"Be nice," Julia said, "I thought you two were friends now."

"Oh, we are," Sue replied, flipping the camera back to her face. "And I love how you assumed I was joking about her nearly burning the place down. Twice. Let's just say we had a very firm talk about why we don't leave tea towels next to the hob when we're trying to make scrambled eggs. And I do mean *eggs.* Including more shells than most people are comfortable with eating."

"What are you even doing there?"

"I've just finished a shift at the hospital," she said before taking another bite. "I've been coming as often as I can to pitch in."

"You really don't have to," Julia said, sitting at the table still set for the dinner they never had on the night the ransom note turned up. "You could just close it."

"You still need money coming in." Sue joined her in sitting, taking the table nearest the counter. "And it's the least we can do. You're out there doing whatever you can for Gran. I could still come over. There are flights three times a day. Just say the word and—"

"I think we're paying the ransom," Julia cut in, getting to the point of why she'd called Sue in the first place. "Well, not us but Minnie. She's selling the hotel, and there's going to be enough to pay off the ransom."

"Are you serious? She's actually going to do that?"

"They go back a long time." Julia shrugged, looking out over the valley. "She's been putting off selling for years, and Lisa's stabbing has made her realise a few things. In any other situation, I'd tell her to slow down and think about it, especially with Lisa being in hospital still, but what choice do I have? The ransom note was clear about giving us a week. Time's running out and we've barely made any progress."

She paused, looking into the bedroom. Barker was at the dressing table on Lisa's laptop. He caught her eyes and shook his head.

"It's just," she continued, exhaling heavily, "the buyers haven't replied yet."

"Will a sale go through so fast?"

"With these people, I'd say so."

"Is there something you're not telling me?" Sue whispered. "Have you figured something out?"

Julia considered telling Sue everything they'd discovered so far about The Buyer and Barker's theory that it had to be Inspector Hillard. Dot was, after all, Sue's grandmother too. She had a right to know what was going on. But Julia knew her sister well enough to anticipate a barrage of repetitive questions, and Julia didn't have enough answers yet.

"I need to get going."

"Okay." Sue pouted. "But don't think I don't know what thought process went on in your head because I do. Just promise you'll tell me if there's any big developments?"

"Of course."

"Then I'll let you go." Sue stood up, and flipped the screen, this time to the front door of the café, as Neil, her husband, walked in with Pearl and Dottie, Julia's nieces. "My lift home is here, anyway."

After a quick moment with the twins and Neil, Julia hung up and re-joined Barker in the bedroom. She sat on the edge of the bed and looked up at the sheets of paper Barker had stuck up over the dressing table.

He double-clicked the laptop trackpad, and another sheet of paper spat out of the printer they'd stolen from reception. He stuck the paper on the wall with tape and stepped back.

"It's going around in circles," he said, sitting next to Julia. "Every email address from the offer emails leads to a company, which leads to a holding company, which leads to a parent company. It just goes on and on in those loops. They're all crossed over, but the trail never seems to end. It's one giant cover-up. Whoever is sending those emails knows what they're doing. They've made it impossible to follow the paper trail to a single source."

The laptop had been in their possession for almost a full twenty-four hours, and Barker had spent most of them trying to find the source of the emails. She'd finally had to slap the laptop shut at three in the morning and drag him to bed because she couldn't stand jolting awake to the sound of the printer any longer.

"The emails have been coming in for eighteen months, all nearly identical," Barker said, picking up a notepad. "Three emails, one a day, always at the same time. Every three emails, the address and company name changes. I've only gone back eight months, and it seems like the stream of changes is never-ending." He paused to read over his notes. "As frustrating as it is, it's given me enough data to notice a pattern. All of the companies reach a dead-end eventually, with thirteen becoming dead-ends at this one."

"*Lo Que Viene Primero,*" Julia read aloud, knowing she was butchering the pronunciation. "Which means?"

"It loosely translates as 'What Comes First'," he said, underlining the words on his pad. "It could be one of those things that's lost in translation because the name alone tells me nothing. The minute I start digging into who owns it, I'm sent on another wild goose chase. To make it worse, it's all in Spanish, so who knows what I'm missing."

Julia wasn't sure it mattered anymore, even though she was impressed with her husband's determination. If The Buyer was as desperate to buy this hotel as he was every other business in town, the money would come through soon, even without another email. As long as they had the money, they could start the process of getting her gran and Percy home. Maybe then her interest in the 'who' would reignite. But for now, she only cared about getting them back. If that meant playing their game, then so be it.

"Maybe it doesn't—"

The door opened and Jessie walked in, giving Julia the perfect excuse to swallow the suggestion that Barker stop chasing the trail for a while. Jessie kicked the door closed behind her, hands filled with plastic bags. She plonked herself on the edge of the bed, dropped the bags, and collapsed backwards. Her face was bright red and glistening.

"Shopping is *exhausting*," she whined, propping herself up on her elbows. "Turns out not everything in those shops is disgusting. Alfie's never going to believe I have all of these designer clothes, especially since I didn't even spend a hundred euros."

"So, we're openly donating money to gangs now?" Barker asked, arching both brows at Jessie as he glanced into one of the bags. "These are the people who might have Dot and Percy."

"I wasn't *just* shopping." Jessie rolled her eyes and stood up, ripping the bags away from Barker. "I was questioning people. Thought I'd get further if I was buying stuff. People love money."

"And what did you find out?"

"That these people really don't like talking about their boss." Jessie pulled a t-shirt from her bag and held it up against herself while looking in the mirror. "This looked less hideous in the shop."

"So you learned nothing?"

"One guy told me he didn't even know who The Buyer was and that he dealt with other people." She screwed up the t-shirt and stuffed it back in its bag. "Oh, and there's a guy sat in reception. Said he's waiting for Minnie. Told him she was probably going to be at the hospital for hours, but he said he wasn't moving."

"What guy?" Julia asked, already standing.

"Didn't ask." Jessie shrugged and pulled out another t-shirt, even crazier than the first. "I'm all questioned out. I think I was too distracted with the questions that I didn't pay enough attention to what I was buying. These are crap."

Leaving Jessie to continue digging through her illegal clothes, Julia took the lift down to the ground floor to try and get rid of the newcomer. Minnie had yet to return after rushing back to the hospital a little before eleven the previous night.

The lift doors slid open. The 'guy' wasn't just a random person, it was Arlo Garcia. For a moment, Julia wondered why Jessie hadn't recognised him. Then she remembered she'd only caught a brief glimpse of him as he was pushed, screaming, into a police car. Arlo glanced in her direction with a flicker of recognition in his eyes.

"I came to see you at the café," Julia explained as she walked towards him. "My husband's the private investigator."

"Ahh, yes, I remember." He stood and walked over to the desk, so Julia assumed the position on the other side. "Where is Minnie? I would like to speak to her."

"She's at the hospital," Julia explained, "with Lisa."

"How is Lisa?"

"She's stable," she said. "Showing good signs, according to Minnie's last phone call. They think she'll pull through."

"Good." He nodded, almost to himself. "This makes me glad."

"You didn't do it, did you?" Julia asked. "Stab Lisa, I mean."

"No." He shook his head, his brows furrowing tightly. "I cannot believe Minnie would think this of me. The inspector told me she gave a statement against me."

"And the watch?"

"I was attacked." He lifted up his t-shirt to show his bruised ribs. "Night before Lisa was stabbed, two men, they beat me and took all my stuff. I did not even think about my watch, not that it mattered. These police did not believe me until someone anonymously handed in the security camera footage of the mugging happening outside their shop."

"Did you know the men?"

Arlo shook his head. "It was dark. I remember only their clothes."

"Same clothes sold in the plaza?"

"So, you have noticed the gang?" He seemed to relax. "Glad I am not the only one. Yes, it was them. I do not know why they would want to frame me, but they did."

Julia had a few ideas. A car engine drew Julia's attention to the door, and a taxi pulled up.

"Are you still adamant you didn't steal from La Casa?" she asked. The passenger window was blocked by the menu board in front of the hotel.

"Absolutely." The accusation seemed to upset more

than offend him. "Between us, I think Lisa wanted my job. Please, if you see Minnie, tell her I am leaving Savega. This place, it does not feel like the home it once was."

"Tell her yourself," Julia said, nodding towards the doors as Minnie walked slowly down the steps in front of the hotel.

Arlo met Minnie halfway across the small courtyard. She stopped in her tracks but softened just as quickly. She pulled him into a hug, and after minutes of crying and hushed conversation, Arlo kissed Minnie on the cheek and left.

"How's Lisa?" Julia asked when Minnie finally came inside.

"She's doing better," she replied, clearly distracted by what had just happened. "The police told me they were releasing him. They said he was framed. I feel for the man, I really do. I feel awful."

"You weren't to know."

"Who would want to kill Lisa and frame Arlo for it?" Minnie scratched at her grey hair, which was rattier than ever. "It seems absurd!"

"Someone who knew about Arlo's alleged theft from the hotel," Julia said, pieces of her theory still falling into place. "You said Lisa was the one who caught Arlo?"

Minnie nodded. "And I'm not sure I believe that anymore."

"I don't think I ever did," Julia said, almost to herself.

"Arlo seems to think Lisa wanted his job, but I think it might be the opposite. She didn't want to take on his role. I think she hoped—"

"That having no chef would push me to sell," Minnie finished. "Instead, I just dumped the work on her and expected her to fill yet another role. I've been so blind. I. . ." Her voice trailed off as she walked over to the desk. "Where did these come from?"

Julia hadn't looked down while she was speaking with Arlo. If she had, she would have recognised the handwriting on the two white envelopes instantly. They were perfectly laid out side by side, each addressed to 'La Casa' in careful, neat handwriting.

"Don't suppose you have cameras in here?"

"Couldn't afford to." Minnie gulped, reaching out with a shaky hand. "I-I don't want to look."

Without hesitating, Julia picked up the first envelope and ripped it open. She pulled out a thick stack of papers clipped at the corner. A note had been tucked in front of the first sheet, it's message written in the same handwriting as the ransom note. Once again, an English section followed the Spanish.

"'Take to Designer Fabrics when signed,'" Julia read aloud. "'If correct, you will find an unmarked duffle bag on your doorstep when you wake tomorrow. Do not attempt to intercept delivery. You are being watched. If we sense anything untoward, the deal will be off. If you find the money tomorrow, we are satisfied with your co-operation, and you will have twenty-four hours to vacate the property.'"

"Is that everything?"

"Looks like it," Julia replied, flicking through the weighty document. "Contracts to hand over the deeds to the hotel. Do you trust them?"

"No," Minnie replied with a gulp, "but everyone else got their money, so why should I be any different?"

"Seems they've had the paperwork ready to go for a while."

"And the other?" Minnie nodded at the second envelope, apparently identical to the first. "What else could they have to say?"

Julia picked it up, surprised when something heavy dropped to the corner. She ripped open the top and tipped the contents out onto the desk.

She gasped and jumped back.

The envelope fluttered from her hands, and her fingers went up to her mouth. She inhaled shakily, and her tears came with the exhale.

"That's my gran's brooch," she managed to say, extending a trembling finger, "and Percy's glasses."

This time, Minnie picked up the note. Instead of reading it out, she passed it to Julia. The message was short but clear.

You have two days. You keep up your end of the bargain, and we will keep ours.

"No time like the present." Minnie sat at the desk and plucked a pen from the pot before Julia could take a moment to digest the note. "Would you help me see where I need to sign, sweet Julia? My eyes aren't what they were, and I never found a pair of specs that weren't sunglasses that suited my face."

18
DOT

"I don't think he's coming back," Dot said as she looked out the window and into the night. "I can't see him."

"They're leaving us here to starve."

Considering it had been over twenty-four hours since Rafa had thrown in the loaf of bread, she was inclined to agree, but she didn't want to add to Percy's worries.

Any day with nothing to eat but stale bread would have been enough to tip Percy over the edge. He was a foodie in a way Dot wasn't, and as much as she enjoyed good food, Percy ate like every meal was his last.

"What's happening out there?" he asked. "Are they still pointing guns?"

"Not right now."

The once-dark clearing had been lit up with small

lamps dotted around the ground. They gave off a creamy glow, and the six men standing guard cast long shadows every time they moved.

At least they hadn't been stood in a row in front of the outbuilding with their guns trained at them for the last few hours. White deck chairs had appeared again, and like before, they were sat around talking, smoking, and laughing.

Three men were playing a game of poker, and from the looks of the box, using the same cards Dot and Percy had used in the villa. Two more patrolled the perimeter, while the last read a paperback with the spine bent all the way back.

"There's still a slice of bread left," Percy said. His voice was growing weaker by the hour. "We could split it. I know we said we'd save it for breakfast, just in case, but surely someone should feed us before then?"

"You have it," she said, turning away from the window to offer him the biggest smile she could muster. "I'm sure you're right. We'll probably get a fresh loaf slung at us tomorrow. I can wait."

"We can split it," he offered again.

"I'm not hungry," she lied. "Besides, it's a crust piece. Who likes them?"

"A stale crust piece, at that." Percy tipped the bag upside down, and the final piece of bread fell into his lap. He picked it up and inhaled, eyes closed. "I'm going to pretend this is one of Julia's scones, filled with cream and jam, and served with a cup of hot sweet tea."

Dot's mouth watered. Percy ripped the slice in two and offered one half to her before taking a bite. She shook her head and turned away. As hungry as she was, she wouldn't take the bread from Percy. They'd agreed to have two slices per meal, but Dot had been living off one, giving her extra slice to her husband.

Dot glanced down at his leg again. The purple had spread past the latest bandage, which she'd ripped from the other leg of his trousers. She'd only cleaned the wound and dressing an hour ago, but fresh blood had already spotted through. Dot didn't know how much damage leaving a wound like that could do in two days, but combined with the lack of his blood pressure pills, she was worried enough to go hungry in the hopes the extra bread would keep Percy's strength up.

"Did it work?" she asked when he finished the slice.

"Not remotely." He sighed and picked the crumbs off his belly. "But it fills a corner. A small one."

They sat in silence for a couple of minutes, staring at the high window above the sink as though it were a television. It was a position they had defaulted to numerous times, but since they'd run out of things to spy – not that Percy could spy much at all without his glasses – it was all they had.

"Tell me a joke," she said, resting her head on his shoulder.

"Two dragons walked into a bar," he said without missing a beat. "One says, 'It's hot in here', and the other says, 'Close your bloody mouth.'"

Dot continued to stare at the window.

"It's because dragons breathe fire, you see, and he had his—"

"I got it," she said. "Maybe try another?"

"A man walks into a bar," he said. "Ouch."

Dot laughed. Not because it was funny, but because it was awful, and she knew Percy was trying his best. She laughed until he laughed, and they carried on laughing until Dot couldn't remember what she was laughing at anymore and the laughter was coming awfully close to crying.

"We're going mad," she said, wiping the tears from the corners of her eyes. "Well, I suppose you were always mad, but I'm joining you."

"Best way to be, love."

"If we ever get out of here, they'll put us in a nuthouse," she said.

"If that's not where we are already." He paused and looked around the room. "I don't suppose we would know. This could be a padded cell. We could be figments of each other's imaginations."

Dot laughed again, this time sure she was actually going insane. She was only brought back down to reality when she heard something ping outside. She'd been hearing the noises on and off for most of the night and had assumed it was someone's mobile phone.

Another ping followed close behind, and another. They continued until there were six, one for each of the men. Shouts came in Spanish, feet crunched against gravel, glass smashed, and more shouting followed. A car door slammed, and another, and another. Once again, Dot counted six slams.

She stood up just in time to see the first car speed off towards the opening of the road, headlights illuminating the way – enough for Dot to see them turn upwards. The other two cars went downwards, zooming off at lightning speed.

From the pings to the clearing emptying, barely sixty seconds must have passed. Dot couldn't imagine why they were suddenly on their own, however. Out of the corner of her eye, an orange blaze confirmed the source of the smashing glass during the panic to escape.

"Remember that story you told me about setting fire to your curtains because you knocked over an oil lamp?"

"1984," he replied with a raspy chuckle, followed by a cough. "Went up in flames before I even realised what was going on."

"Well," she said, pausing to swallow the lump in her throat, "I think the same thing is happening here."

She dared to look back at Percy before returning her attention to the small fire taking hold on the edge of the forest.

"How dry did that forest floor feel to you when we fell over?"

"Incredibly."

Dot tore herself away from the window and sat back down next to Percy, her eyes immediately going to his shin.

"Somehow, starving to death is no longer at the top of my worry list," she said as she clenched his hand. "Pray for a miracle, Percy, because I fear we're going to need one."

19

JULIA

After over an hour of being unable to add anything to the conversation, Julia retreated to the terrace, leaving Barker and Minnie to continue poring over the contract in the dining room. Every page had been signed, and it would already have been delivered if Barker hadn't insisted that they comb over every detail to make sure no trickery was buried between the lines.

A sensible idea, of course. Julia was glad Barker was more tuned into understanding the legal mumbo jumbo than she was. If it had been left solely to her to decipher, she would have concluded that the whole contract was a trick simply because she couldn't comprehend most of it. Understanding paperwork had never been part of her skill set, and she wasn't too proud to admit it.

Sensing her presence, soft, motion-activated lights

illuminated the terrace. She perched on the edge of a sunbed. Glad to give her mind a break from complicated legal phrasing, she inhaled the night air and unclenched her fist, revealing the brooch. She rolled it face up with her thumb, and the silver trim around the emerald centre caught the light.

Dot had worn the antique jewellery at her collar for as long as Julia could remember, and yet Julia couldn't recall ever holding it in her hands. The weight of the brooch surprised her, as did its beauty. The piece was so permanently attached to her gran, she noticed it as infrequently as she would a mole or a birthmark. Now, up close, it was like she was looking at it for the first time.

"Penny for your thoughts?" Barker asked as he joined her. "Felt like as good a time as any to take a break."

Barker nodded back into the dining room. Rodger had joined them, and he was at the bar pouring two large glasses of sangria. He fiddled with something under the counter, and soft Spanish guitar music played through the hidden speakers. He carried the drinks over to the table and took Barker's seat.

"I was just thinking about how wrong it is that I have this," Julia said, shuffling over on the sunbed to make room for Barker. "My gran wouldn't have given this up without a fight."

"Better than an ear or a finger."

Julia arched a brow at her husband. "Is that supposed to make me feel better?"

"It makes *me* feel better," he replied, wrapping his arm around her shoulders. "I've heard of much worse being sent to scare people into paying."

"And you think that's a reason to trust whoever sent them?" She clenched her fist around the brooch again, the sight of it too much to bear. "We're no closer to finding out who has them, and in the meantime, we're pinning all our hopes on a master manipulator keeping up their end of a shady bargain and that's only if Minnie gets the money in time or still wants to sell after all this."

Julia glanced into the dining room again. Rodger appeared to have picked up reading the contract where Barker left off.

"It all seems legit to me." Barker gently turned her face away from the dining room. "I was dubious at first, but it appears to be a straightforward transferal of ownership."

"Nothing with these people has been straightforward."

"You're right." He squeezed her shoulder and pulled her in tighter. "This entire situation has been a mess from start to finish, but we have no reason to believe they won't keep up their end of the bargain. If The Buyer has taken them to force Minnie to sell, this is exactly what they want. Why would they want to hurt Dot or Percy?"

She shook her head. Lisa's stabbing threw a spanner in the works. A confession of guilt from Arlo would have separated the attempt on Lisa's life from the ransom situation, but his innocence did the opposite. The lengths the attacker had gone to in order to frame Arlo stank of the same manipulative tactics she'd been hearing about since learning of The Buyer's existence. No matter what the notes said, she didn't trust them, and yet . . . and yet, she had no choice but to put her faith in them.

"Go up to our room and have a lie-down," Barker said, squeezing her arm again. "I'll go to the kitchen and dig up something for dinner."

"There wasn't much left at lunchtime," she said, "except for a few of Rodger's eggs."

"An omelette it is." He stood and pulled her up with him. "There's nothing else for you to do tonight."

The urge to object bubbled up, but Julia forced it down. Barker was right. Unless she suddenly learned the language of contracts or dared to go out alone in the dark to hand out more posters, she was done for the day.

Leaving Barker to venture down to the kitchen, Julia took the lift up to her bedroom. As she hadn't wanted to carry a bag and the maxi dress had no pockets, she retrieved the key card from her bra, a trick her gran had taught her.

After swiping the key, she walked into the dark bedroom and collapsed on the soft bed without bothering to turn on the lights. She placed the brooch on her bedside table and rolled away from the view of the valley through the open curtains. Mind and body equally exhausted, her eyes closed easily.

Knuckles rapidly knocking on the door jolted her awake. She had no idea how long she'd been asleep, but it had been long enough for her to drool onto the pillow. Wiping her cheek, she forced herself up and out of bed.

"Alright, alright," she called as she walked to the door. "I'm coming, Barker."

But when she opened the door, it wasn't to Barker with an omelette. Jessie stood on the other side, holding Lisa's open laptop.

"I need to show you something," Jessie said as she marched into the room, eyes trained on the screen. "Why are you sat in the dark, you weirdo?"

"I was napping." Julia stifled a yawn as she closed the door. "How did you get Lisa's laptop? I could have sworn it was in here."

"It was." Jessie dumped the laptop on the dressing table. "I borrowed it."

Too tired for the ceiling light, Julia flicked on the softer lamps on either side of the bed.

"Wait," she said, "how did you even get in here?"

"Lifted Barker's key card." She shrugged as she looked around. "Would have used it then, but I heard you come back ten minutes ago. Do you have a charger for this thing? Battery's down to five percent."

"Minnie didn't give me one."

"Then I need to show you this quickly." She sat Julia down in front of the laptop at the dressing table. "I'm going to assume you and Barker didn't check Lisa's sent emails?"

"You can do that?"

Jessie rolled her eyes skyward. "Give me strength." She jabbed the screen. "It's right *there*. If you had checked, you'd have known the reply you sent on Minnie's behalf wasn't the first."

"Lisa replied?"

"Oh, she did more than reply." Jessie forced a laugh, crossed over to the window, and stared out into the valley. "I suggest you start at the top and read what your ninth-cousin, six times removed, or whatever she is on the family tree, has been up to."

First cousin, once removed, but Julia didn't bother with the correction. As instructed, she scrolled to the top of the page. She wasn't the most proficient when it came to technology, but she could recognise an email thread when it was in front of her.

July 29 08:31 pm (*11 days ago*)
From: lisa@lacasahotel97.es
URGENT!!!!!

Circumstances have changed. You need to delay the plan until at least the last week of the month!

July 30 07:45 am (*10 days ago*)
From: polloohuevo@savegaSA.es
Re: *URGENT!!!!!*
Is there a problem with the insurance?

July 30 07:53 am (*10 days ago*)
From: lisa@lacasahotel97.es
Re: Re: *URGENT!!!!!*
No, my mother has guests coming. She sprang it on me last night, and they're getting here on Sunday. Old family she hasn't seen for years. They go home on the 16th. Please don't do anything until after then.

July 31 07:45 pm (*9 days ago*)
From: lisa@lacasahotel97.es
Re: Re: *URGENT!!!!!*
Hello??

August 1 04:34 pm (*8 days ago*)
From: lisa@lacasahotel97.es
Re: Re: *URGENT!!!!!*
Please reply. They arrive on Sunday. It can't happen while they're here. My mum needs this. It will make it easier to get her to agree, I promise.

August 3 09:23 am (*6 days ago*)
From: polloohuevo@savegaSA.es
Re: Re: Re: *URGENT!!!!!*
Okay. The plan has changed. Thank you for cooperating. We will be in touch.

"I think something is on fire out there," Jessie said, breaking Julia's concentration. "Halfway up that mountain, in the trees."

"Is it bad?"

"Can't tell," she said. "Can only see the smoke."

Julia glanced through the window, but she couldn't even see that much. Like her ability to read legal contracts, her long-distance vision was a weakness. She turned back to the laptop.

August 5 09:23 pm (*4 days ago*)
From: lisa@lacasahotel97.es
Re: Re: Re: *URGENT!!!!!*
Are you doing this?

August 5 11:45 pm (*4 days ago*)
From: lisa@lacasahotel97.es
Re: Re: Re: *URGENT!!!!!*
This can't be a coincidence. This was you. I know it. This wasn't the plan. I agreed to a break-in and robbery, not a ransom!! They are my family.

August 6 08:12 am (*3 days ago*)
From: lisa@lacasahotel97.es
Re: Re: Re: *URGENT!!!!!*
You can't just ignore me.

August 7 01:03 am (*2 days ago*)
From: lisa@lacasahotel97.es
Re: Re: Re: *URGENT!!!!!*
I know who you are.

Julia scrolled, but the page ended.

She sat back in the chair and stared at Lisa's final email. The time and date put it in the early hours of the same morning she was stabbed in the kitchen.

"Have you finished?" Jessie asked, still at the window.

"I have." Julia sighed and continued to stare at the screen. "I knew Lisa was desperate for her mother to sell, but I would never have guessed she was trying to work with The Buyer."

"Lisa handed them Dot and Percy on a silver platter."

"I don't think she realised that until it was too late."

"She could have said something, though." Jessie finally turned from the window. "You saw the emails with your own two eyes. She emailed them the night the first ransom note showed up. And she reckons *she* knows who The Buyer is? Why didn't she say anything?"

"I don't think she got the chance." Julia rubbed the bridge of her nose. "How did she figure out The Buyer's identity when no one else has?"

"I don't know." Jessie shrugged. "Did you look at the picture?"

There was another knock at the door, timid enough to belong to Barker, who probably thought she was asleep.

"I'll get it," Jessie said as she went for the door, pointing at the laptop. "Double-click that 'attachment' button under the last email and it'll load the picture. It's so random."

Julia double-clicked the image, and a picture of a chicken popped up for a split second before the screen turned black. Julia stared at the dark screen, her confusion reflected back at her.

"I bring you a glorious omelette," Barker announced as he walked in carrying a tray with two plates. "Threw some chips into the deep fat fryer too, although I might have overdone them a little."

"Even I know how to not burn chips," Jessie said, plucking one from the plate before closing the door. "How kind of you to bring me food."

"It's not for you." He put the tray onto the dressing table, pushing the dead laptop away from Julia. "I thought you were going to lie down?"

"I was," Julia said, staring down at the messy

omelette Barker had cobbled together. "Jessie came in with Lisa's laptop. Did you check her sent emails?"

"It didn't occur to me. Why?"

"Old people." Jessie rolled her eyes and pulled a key card from the pocket of her denim shorts. She tossed it to Barker. "You might want to watch your pockets more carefully. It wasn't even difficult."

"I was looking everywhere for this!" He caught it and scowled at Jessie. "That's why the chips are burnt."

"Yeah, yeah. Likely story." Jessie playfully punched him in the arm. "Did you see the picture, Mum?"

"A chicken."

"Random, right?" Jessie leaned across and snatched a handful of chips off the plate. "I didn't really get it either. I translated the email address too, and it came out as 'chicken or egg' – which makes just as much sense as the picture. None."

Chickens.

Eggs.

Julia looked up at the investigation wall above the dressing table, her eyes landing on the translated business name around which Barker had drawn a giant circle and several question marks.

"What Came First," she said, eyes still trained on the wall. "Chicken or egg?"

"I'm far too tired and far too sober for this kind of debate," Jessie muttered through a mouthful of chips.

"But I think the egg. Has to be. How else did a chicken hatch?"

"But what laid the egg?" Barker asked, sitting next to her on the edge of the bed. "A chicken."

Julia stood and ripped the paper off the wall. She stared down at it, her hands shaking as her mind raced and missing pieces fell into place.

"It wasn't a question," she said, turning to show them the paper. "What Came First. It's the name of the company you traced thirteen of those email addresses to."

"Twenty-eight now," he corrected, accepting the paper. "I can't get any deeper into who owns it, though."

"It doesn't matter." Julia sat down and stared at the omelette. "Lisa figured out who The Buyer was and she paid the price. Instead of an email, they delivered the message via a knife in the stomach."

"Wait, what message?" Barker frowned. "What emails?"

"Miss a minute, miss a lot." Jessie patted him on the shoulder. "I'm keeping up, Mum. Keep going. You have that look in your eyes."

"What look?"

"Same crazy look Dot gets when she thinks she's about to get one over on someone." Jessie reached out and scooped up the last of the chips. "If you're about to tell me you've figured out who The Buyer is over a bunch of chicken stuff, I have to hear it."

"You weren't here when he brought the eggs," Julia said, glancing at the omelette. "If you had been, you might have made the connection yourself."

"Who?"

"Rodger."

"That posh old bloke?" Jessie laughed as she licked the salt from her fingers. "You think he's The Buyer? He's as loopy as Minnie."

After feeling so out of her element for so much of the investigation, Julia wasn't prepared to dismiss the first genuine lightbulb moment she'd felt since her gran and Percy vanished into thin air. Chickens were too bizarre to be a coincidence.

"I think it's worth a conversation at least." Julia glanced at the omelette one last time. "The worst-case scenario is we look like idiots for making such a tenuous link. Barker?"

"Worth a shot." He stood and checked his watch. "He was still downstairs when I came up. You two stay here and—"

"Fat chance!" Jessie jumped up and headed straight for the door. "You two never would have found those emails or made any chicken-related assumptions without me. I was the one who found the eggs, and I want to be there when you make the chicken cluck!"

Before Barker could go through his usual routine of insisting Julia stay behind for pregnancy-related reasons, she followed Jessie through the bedroom door, glad to piggyback on her daughter's gutsy nature.

They took the lift to the ground floor, where they found Minnie alone in the dining room, swaying to the increased volume of the plucky music. Her eyes were closed, and she clutched a full glass of sangria to her chest.

"I'll get the music," Jessie said, already cutting across to the bar.

Rather than turning it down, she turned it off entirely. Minnie's eyes opened wearily, and an easy smile filled her face when she saw Julia.

"Sweet Julia," she said, holding out her arms for a hug. Sangria sloshed out of the glass, but Minnie didn't seem to notice. "Come and dance with your auntie. It's my last night here, after all."

Julia gave Minnie a quick hug but stepped away again before the dancing could begin. "Where's Rodger gone?"

"Just left." She clamped a hand against Julia's hips and rocked her side to side while she slurped sangria with the other. "Loosen up! The world will still be ending tomorrow. Pour yourself a glass of sangria and have fun with me."

"I'm pregnant," Julia reminded her as she pulled away. "Please, Minnie. Focus. Do you know where Rodger went?"

Minnie looked Julia up and down and frowned. She

stumbled back on her heels, catching herself on the edge of the table they'd been sat at for most of the night.

"Where's the contract?" Barker asked just as Julia was opening her mouth to ask the same thing.

"Rodger took it," she called, wafting her hand in the direction of the door as she sloppily dragged out a chair. "He said he'd drop it off for me. He's good like that. Knows I don't like going out." Her expression crumpled into an exaggerated pout. "Hoped he'd stay longer, but it seems it's his turn for trouble."

"What trouble?" Julia asked.

"Smashed window at his hotel," she said as she topped her glass up from the bottle of sangria Rodger had left on the table. "That's what the inspector man said."

"Inspector Hillard was here?"

"You just missed them." She waved in the general direction of the door again. "The inspector ran in all huffing and puffing and said he needed to talk to Rodger about something urgent. Said he'd been trying to call him, but Rodger couldn't find his phone. Rodger said some kids had smashed a window at his hotel, and nothing gets fixed if you don't report it, does—"

"Did you say we *just* missed him?" Barker interjected.

"That's what I said." She slammed the bottle on the table. "Is someone going to turn the music back on, or do I have to do it myself?"

The three of them ran for the front door, and the

music turned on behind them, even louder than before. They broke out into the night and up the steps into the dark alley.

"Which way is Rodger's hotel?" Barker asked as he looked in each direction.

"I don't know," Julia admitted, joining him in looking. "Minnie just said he had the hotel next door."

"You two really are blind, aren't you?" Jessie nudged Julia and pointed into the blurry darkness. "They're walking in that direction. I don't know what you would do without me, honestly." She looked Julia's bright yellow maxi dress up and down. "Couldn't have worn a more inconspicuous colour, could you? You're practically glowing in the dark." She turned her gaze to Barker. "And tropical shorts? Really? Are you twelve?"

"We'll talk fashion later," he said, already crossing the street. "We'll follow behind this row of cars. They shouldn't see us if we stay down."

With Barker leading the charge, Julia took the rear, behind Jessie, ducking as low as she could – though the bump hindered her attempt. Unless their long-distance vision was as bad as hers, if Rodger or Inspector Hillard so much as glanced over their shoulders, they'd spot her. She hoped Rodger's glasses were for reading only.

Since hiding was out of the question, Julia decided to use it to her advantage. She watched the two men hurry down the tight lane until they stopped outside a building almost identical to Minnie's hotel. Unlike

Minnie's, however, the front doors were entirely frosted, as were all the other windows. There didn't even appear to be a sign, and the only writing Julia could see was a 'NO VACANIES' notice written in Spanish and English stuck in the window next to the door.

"This is Rodger's hotel?" Jessie whispered as they slowed to a halt. "Looks more like an office block."

Julia peeked over the top of the car and watched as Rodger punched a code into a keypad in the door. He looked over his shoulder, and Julia ducked down so quickly she nearly landed flat on her bottom. Barker put out a steadying hand. She held her breath and waited, but nothing happened.

"They've gone inside," she whispered as she dared to peek over the top again. "Lights are on. What now?"

"We go and listen at the door?" Jessie suggested. "Admittedly not my best plan, but—"

"*Shhh!*" Barker held his finger up to his mouth as something further down the street seemed to catch his attention. "I don't think we're the only ones here."

Julia peeked over the top of the car just in time to see a figure dressed in black from head to toe pop up from behind a car on the other side of the street and slip down an alley between the hotel and the next building over.

"Stay here!" Barker ordered, pointing at them both. "I mean it this time."

Before either of them could argue, Barker darted

across the road in a crouch and disappeared down the same alley the stranger had just vanished into. Julia and Jessie glanced at each other, nodding decisively at one another. They hurried across the road, only straightening up when they reached the alley.

Jessie bumped right into Barker, who hadn't gone any further than the opening. He and the mystery figure stood across from each other, each looking as perplexed as the other. Even with the black hat and the change in outfit, Julia recognised the man at once.

"Sub-Inspector Castro?" she whispered.

The sub-inspector held a finger to lips, and his gaze was steely enough to tell Julia not to speak again until prompted. The officer pulled a small device from his pocket and plugged it into his phone. It was fluffy and grey, and looked like a recording device of some kind. After a few taps on the screen, he held it up to an air vent above their heads.

His finger went back to his lips.

Seconds seemed to drag out into hours before Julia heard a series of doors open inside the hotel. The sound of opening doors grew closer and closer until the one leading to the room on the other side of the vent opened and closed.

"Are you *stupid?*" Rodger's voice cried. "Did you think about how *any* of that would look to Minnie? She was already having second thoughts! I practically had to snatch the contract from her."

"It was *urgent*," Hillard replied. "Did you send this text message?"

Silence.

"Well?"

"No." Rodger's voice was firm. "Obviously I would never send out a message like that. Where did it come from?"

"Your phone."

"I told you," said Rodger, pausing to exhale in irritation, "I've lost my phone."

"Lost? Or was it stolen?" Hillard paused and laughed. "It's him, isn't it? Your little pet project?"

"Rafa wouldn't do this."

"Rafa let them *escape!*" Hillard cried. "You put too much trust in the boy. I'm his uncle, I should know. He's never been cut out for this—"

Hillard's voice cut off abruptly, and Julia didn't need to see through the wall to know what happened next. She was well aware of what it sounded like when a man was punched in the face.

"Remember your place, Inspector," Rodger snapped. "Everything is under control. I have six armed men up there making sure those old idiots don't get another chance to mess this up. I've commanded them to shoot on sight, which will save me a job."

Jessie's hand tightened around Julia's.

"You're going to kill them?"

She squeezed tightly.

"They've seen my face," said Rodger. "It's not worth the risk. They might give a description that makes a connection. I wanted to keep them alive until I at least had the contract incase the old idiot next door needed more proof, but she never bothered asking."

"And how do I explain their deaths at the station?" Hillard replied. "The British authorities are already starting to sniff around. That idiot PI has been making calls. Do you really want this to go to Interpol? To become an international incident?" Hillard sighed noisily; Julia could picture him rolling his eyes. "You keep complicating things! Setting some fires and smashing some windows to scare people into selling was one thing, but ransom? Attempted murder? This situation has gone *too far!*"

"*I* say when things have gone too far!" Rodger cried, followed by the sound of another punch. "Minnie was always going to be the hardest to convince. She thinks her dead husband is fused into the walls! Putting her family at risk was the only way to get through to her."

"And Lisa?" Hillard's words were becoming more slurred. "Was that part of the plan?"

"She figured it out!" Another punch. "Of course I had to sort her out. Now that I have the paperwork, I'll send some men to finish what I started. Nothing can go wrong now."

"Unless," slurred Hillard, sounding like he was further away now, "the men you're going to send to the hospital got the same text I did. And what about those six keeping watch at the villa? Text came through nearly an hour ago. How d'you know they're not all long gone?"

"An *hour*?"

"How many more times must I explain? I looked everywhere for you before I went to La Casa." Hillard made a sound somewhere between laughter and a gurgle. Julia's stomach twisted as she imagined the blood in Hillard's mouth. "Not one of your men knows your face. You've trained them to obey first and ask questions never. I imagine one text from The Buyer sent half running for the harbour and the rest to the airport." Hillard laughed again, hard and bitter. "There you go, Rodger. All the power you ever wanted, undone by a teenaged boy. Isn't this when you pack up, run away, change your name, and start this whole game over? Think you'll live long enough to win, this time?" Hillard coughed wetly and spat. "Whatever you do, I'm done doing your dirty work. And I'll do everything I can to convince my mother not to follow you, either."

"Let her stay," said Rodger, scoffing. "I only married her because of her easily corruptible son in the police. You're all useless. Worthless."

The silence dragged out.

"Is this the part where you kill me, too?"

Rodger uttered a bark of sharp, cruel laughter. "You're not worth the bullet. Do it yourself."

A door slammed, and after a series of other doors

deep in the building followed, the front door of the hotel opened. Moments later, Rodger jumped into a rundown pickup truck full of empty cages. He sped off without looking in their direction. Through the air vent, Hillard's maniacal laughter turned to sobs, and then the unmistakable sound of a man smashing up the contents of a room.

"You have heard far too much," Castro whispered as he unplugged the device from his phone and pocketed both. "Speak of this to no one, or you will blow the whole case."

"How did you know to come here?" Julia asked.

"They always go there," he replied, holding back a pleased smile. "I stumbled upon it by an accident. Rodger thinks he cannot be heard from his office."

"You're undercover, aren't you?" Barker whispered back. "I knew it! Well, I didn't know it *exactly,* but I knew you were one of the good—"

"Yes, Mr Brown," he replied, holding up his hand for silence. "I am undercover. I have been building this corruption case for over one year now. Hillard led me down a much darker path. My superiors, they need hard evidence, and I have just recorded everything I need to prove this is no conspiracy theory. I have been following Hillard since he received that text message and bolted out of the station. I had a feeling he would run to Rodger." He checked his watch. "We need to move quickly. We have not very much time to find your missing relatives."

"And how do we do that?" Jessie hissed. "Rodger has already bolted and—"

A door on the other side of the vent slammed, and seconds later, Hillard burst through the hotel's front door. His face was as beaten and bloody as the sounds of punches and slurring words had led Julia to imagine. He climbed into his car and sped off in the same direction Rodger had gone.

"We've lost another one!" Jessie cried. After all the hushed whispering, Jessie at full volume made Julia jump. "Now we'll never—" Jessie stopped mid-sentence when Castro held up his phone screen. "Oh, a tracker. Nice. See, you're good at this. No yellow maxi dresses and tropical shorts for you."

"We must move quickly," Castro said as he slipped past them and through the opening of the tight alley. "Mr Brown, are you coming?"

"Me?"

"You are a former detective?" Castro clicked a key and the car they'd hidden behind across the street lit up with a reassuring beep. "I could spend the next half hour trying to convince my superiors to act, or I can act immediately. But I need back up, and you are—"

"Of course, I'll do it!" Barker said before Castro could finish, already heading towards the car. Turning to Julia, he said, "Stay here. I'll sort this out. I'll bring them home, I promise."

The men jumped into the car, but Castro took his time settling in instead of tearing off down the street like Hillard and Rodger had done.

"Is that it?" Jessie asked, hands planted on her hips. "We're meant to sit tight and wait here until they get back?"

"We should," Julia said, biting her lip and looking back towards Minnie's hotel. She rested both hands on the curve of her bump. "But . . . my gran and Percy are still out there, and Rodger and Hillard are about to lead the way."

"Well, whatever you're thinking," Jessie said, nodding at Castro's car as he struggled to reverse out of the tight space, "you better do it quickly, or we'll lose them."

20
DOT

The crackling flames of the fire were an orange blur through the thick smoke on the other side of the outbuilding window. Dot attempted to pull herself up as high as she could, desperate to force the window open. The cracked sink wobbled under her weight, and the screws tugged away from the crumbling brick just like the bars in the bedroom's villa. This time, the disrepair was nothing to celebrate.

"You wouldn't fit, dear," Percy said, quickly adding, "Not that you're not slim enough, but the window looks tiny from here."

"I know." Dot gave up and cycled around to the door again, rattling the handle for all she was worth. "I simply can't believe it. After getting so close to freedom, we're going to be barbecued to death?"

"Smoked I should think, my love."

"Even more pathetic!" Dot threw as much of her weight at the door as she could. "Why couldn't this have happened twenty years ago? Even ten? But no! I have to be trapped in a tiny building with a fire creeping towards it at eighty-*bloody*-five."

"You're spritelier than most."

"But my bones are still as fragile as wafer biscuits!" she cried, pushing her shoulder into the door. "I can't give it enough weight."

"I do think it opens inwards anyway."

"Then why am I wasting my time?" She slapped the door, wanting to start kicking and screaming though she knew a tantrum wouldn't help anything. "This can't be it, Percy. Can it?"

Percy looked thoughtful, his blinks slow and shaky. He patted the bare mattress next to him and opened his arm for Dot. She slid up next to him, close as could be. Her eyes went straight to the bandage on his shin, somewhat in disbelief that the infection that had consumed her every waking thought was no longer even a priority concern.

"If this is it," he said, running his fingers up and down her arm, "we had a good run, and we gave our escape a fair shot. Not many our age would have been brave enough to do what we did. We got one over on a *teenager*. Not bad for two old codgers, don't you think?"

She huffed an almost-laugh. "Not bad at all."

They sat in silence for a few minutes. The popping and sizzling of the fire was almost soothing, as if they were sat at home in front of the fireplace. Dorothy could almost imagine her perfect cup of tea in hand and an overflowing plate of biscuits between them.

"I wish we'd met when we were younger, Dorothy."

"Percy, don't."

"I need to get it out, dear," he said, clinging to her arm. "Meeting you gave me another slice of life, and as much as I wish we'd had longer, we had fun, didn't we?"

"We did."

"We had a *Wizard of Oz* themed wedding," he said, chuckling softly, "and then we burnt to death on our honeymoon after being held hostage for ransom money. They'll make a film about this one day."

"They'll probably cast us younger. I expect Helen Mirren will play me."

"I see myself as Michael Caine."

"Michael Caine?" Dot pursed her lips. "I think he's older than both of us and far too tall. And he has too much hair for that matter. Danny DeVito springs to mind for you."

"Who's that?"

"He was in a film with that Austrian chap," she said. "And no, not Hitler. The *Terminator* fella, but not that film, another film. I think they were twins. It's another one Jessie made me watch."

"Twins with the muscular robot chap?"

"*Fraternal* twins," she replied flatly. "Imagine a short, egg-looking man."

"Oh." Percy sighed. "I think I preferred Michael Caine."

Grey smoke began curling through the gap at the bottom of the door. Dot decided against calling Percy's attention to it. She grabbed his hand in hers and clung tightly.

"Michael Caine it is then," she said, pushing forward the biggest smile she could. "Because I'll say this for you, Percival Cropper, you've certainly the soul of a Michael Caine. In fact, Michael Caine should be so lucky as to play you!"

They said no more as the smoke poured in. Hands clasped and fingers woven together, they stared silently ahead, an unspoken promise that they'd meet their end with as much dignity as they could muster hanging in the air between them. Dot wasn't ready to go, but then, she doubted she ever would be.

"I love you, Percy."

He lifted her hand to his lips and kissed her fingers.

"I love you too, my Do—"

A loud bang at the door cut him off. They both cried out and jumped, clinging even more tightly to each other. Bang after bang reverberated through the door, each like a small bomb going off. Finally, the door burst open, its hinges popping out of the frame with the sheer force. It flew across the room, missing the bed by inches.

A figure stumbled through the smoke.

"*Rafa?*" Dot cried, jumping off the bed. "Is that really you?"

"It is!" He coughed into his elbow as he held out his hand. "Out, now!"

"Are we dead, Dorothy?"

"Not quite." She scooped her arm under Percy's right side and nodded for Rafa to do the same on the other. "I think you're going to have to put up with me a little while longer. We're getting out of here."

They dragged Percy through the thick smoke, finally emerging into fresh air on the other side of the clearing. They took him to the dark villa and settled him against the front door. Dot clutched her side and caught her breath, eyes trained on the fire. It had taken over all the trees around the opening to the road, blocking the escape.

"You were right, Mrs Dorothy," Rafa said between deep, shuddering inhales. "I was letting Rodger control me. Only I could change this."

"That's his name?" Dot asked, leaning against the wall with one hand. "Rodger? Who's ever been scared of a Rodger?"

"You do not know this Rodger." Rafa straightened, hands on his hips as he continued to wheeze. "He is a man with many faces, and I believed the face he wanted me to see. It is the same face my abuela sees. He makes people feel safe, but he is an evil man. I see this now. I wanted to be like him, to have power, to not be weak, but I never thought people would get hurt. He told me this ransom plot was for show only, but he... he tried to kill her."

"Kill who?"

"The hotel lady's daughter." He unravelled the bandage around his hand and showed Dot the deep cut in his palm. "He did this. I did not cut my hand on the bread. I refused to kill her when she figured out who he was. I failed his test, so he taught me a lesson."

"Lisa?" Dot's hand drifted to her mouth. "Is she—"

"Not yet," he said, his eyes wide and focused, "but he does not like the loose ends." He blinked and looked at the fire. "We must go."

"Where's your car?"

"No car," he said. "I ran. I expected Rodger's men to be here still. I did not think my trick would work."

"That was you?"

Rafa nodded. "I stole Rodger's phone and told everyone the police had uncovered everything and that they should all run. Every man for himself. And it worked."

"They were in such a rush," Dot said, nodding at the inferno, "they did that."

"We must walk." Rafa bent to help Percy. "We cannot wait here. He will figure this out."

"We can't walk." Dot rushed to grab Percy's other side. "His leg is bad. He can't put weight on it."

"I'm quite alright, dear," Percy said in his weakest voice yet. "It's just a flesh wound."

"An *infected* flesh wound," she reminded him, her shoulder caving under his weight. "And as much as I don't want to admit it, I don't have the strength to carry you, dear. I've been surviving off scraps of stale bread for days."

"Right you are."

"Use your phone," Dot ordered as they settled Percy back onto the ground. "Call someone."

"You smashed it."

"Use the one you stole!"

"I smashed that one."

"Why did you do that?"

"Because he would use it to track me." Rafa looked around the clearing. "Someone will see the smoke and call for help."

"It's the middle of the night!" Dot looked up and squinted at the smoke. "It blends into the dark."

"Then we get to the road." Rafa looked down at Percy, scratching the side of his head. "The old man will have to get on my back."

"Less with the old, if you please," Percy grunted, coughing heavily. "I bested a teenager, I'll have you know."

Dot helped get Percy up onto Rafa's back, but Rafa let him slide back down when bright lights broke through the smoke. Dot steadied Percy against the wall of the villa and squinted as headlights emerged. She prayed for a fire engine but got something more hauntingly familiar, instead: the pickup truck with the cages.

"I. . ." Rafa said, stepping in front of Dot. "I am sorry. I tried."

"I know you did." She clenched his shoulder. "I'm proud of you."

The truck skidded to a halt, and Rodger jumped out, a gun already in his hand. Rather than the dark outfit with a cap he'd worn the night he'd picked up Dot and Percy during their great escape, he wore a beige linen suit and a pair of round silver spectacles. Subtle changes, but a quite a transformation. Remembering what Rafa had said about Rodger being a man with many faces, she wondered which version was the costume.

"Nobody move an inch!" he cried, firing two warning shots into the air as he walked towards them. "Oh, Rafa. I gave you a second chance after you let them escape, and this is how you repay me? You steal my phone, scatter my men, release my hostages, and set fire to my villa?"

Dot cleared her throat and said, "Technically, your men set fire to your villa in their rush to—"

He fired another warning shot.

Rafa spread his arms out, but Dot didn't shrink

behind him. She held her ground, keeping her eyes trained on the man who had masterminded the mess they were in. She'd imagined someone tall and handsome with an air of authority, but he was nothing of the sort. Rodger was as short as Percy, skinny as a rake, and perhaps only a decade their junior. And yet, Dot found herself scared of him – or scared of the crazed look in his beady little eyes and the pricked-up corners of his mouth, at least. Was he excited?

"You couldn't just play along, could you?" He sighed and pointed the gun directly at Dot over Rafa's shoulder. "If you'd just sat and watched television, you'd have got out of this alive. The plan worked better than a break-in ever could! When Minnie signed over the hotel, she was going to get her money, she'd give one hundred thousand of it back to me for the convenience, and I'd continue my plan to own Savega."

"But why?" Dot stared down the barrel of the gun, the threat of being shot barely an inconvenience after the week she'd had. "What's the point?"

"The point?" Rodger laughed. "Power. Control. Why else?"

She frowned. "And why do you want power so badly?"

"Who doesn't want the power I have?" he cried, shaking the gun. "I was raised in the East End of London – and not the East End of today where nobody can afford to live. It was the East End where you could never make enough to escape. You had to claw your way out with your fingernails. In my family, the criminal life wasn't a choice, it was an expectation. We were good old-fashioned East End gangsters. There's a reason they didn't survive into the new century. I watched my brothers, my father, my uncles all go to court and beg for their lives, and then get sent to prison anyway. I had to do things differently. I had to speak differently. Dress differently. Operate from the shadows. I had to survive. Every test in my life has led to this moment, to being truly in control. Only a few more businesses stand in the way of my total domination, but they'll fall. Everyone has a price. Everyone has something they're not willing to lose."

His posh accent had slipped completely.

"Frankly, my dear," Dot said, "I don't know how you can be bothered at your age."

Rodger fired two more warning shots, this time at the ground. Dot jumped backwards as the noise rang in her ears and the bullets burst the dry ground open. She looked back at Percy. He was struggling to keep his eyes open. Ignoring the gun, she went to Percy's side and held him tight. When she glanced up to see what Rodger was doing, her gaze drifted to Rafa, instead. Very, very slowly, he was moving his arm behind his back and under his leather jacket.

The gun shimmered in the light of the fires. The

revolver was identical to the empty one she'd tried to fire at Rodger. She recalled the empty chambers of the cylinder. Enough room for six bullets. She looked at Rodger's gun, and even through the smoke, creeping ever closer to them as the breeze shifted, she could tell they were the same.

How many warning shots had he fired?

Two.

Then one.

Then another two.

Rafa pulled out the gun and pointed it at Rodger.

"Touché," Rodger said, tipping his head at Rafa. "Maybe I taught you well, after all? But you're weak, Rafa. You're too scared to carry a loaded gun. That much we have already established."

"Do you think I would make the same mistake twice?" Rafa steadied the gun and parted his feet in a shooting stance.

The final shot left Rodger's barrel without a moment's hesitation. Rafa dropped as though he'd anticipated it. The bullet shot through the large sitting room window in the villa, shattering the glass – and then the mirror Dot had moved above the television, too, by the sounds of it.

"He doesn't have any bullets left!" Dot cried.

Instead of shooting his step-grandfather, Rafa jumped up and punched him squarely in the middle of the face. The old man stumbled back, dropping his gun and keys to clutch at the nose now gushing blood down the front of his suit. He stumbled into the smoke, tumbling back against the bonnet of his car. Steadying himself, his eyes darted down to the fallen keys. They both went for them, but the nimbleness of youth won. Rafa scooped them up and tossed them overhand into the fire.

Rodger staggered back again. His gaze lingered on his step-grandson. Dot could see the disappointment all over his face, but she felt nothing but pride. Rodger turned and fled into the smoke, his hands still clutching his bleeding nose.

Rafa exhaled as though he'd been holding his breath the whole time. He dropped both guns and fell to his knees.

Distant sirens began to sing in Dot's ears. She let out a laugh and looked up at the sky. Fire engine, ambulance, or police, she couldn't tell, but all were more than welcome. She picked up Rafa's gun and popped open the cylinder. Just like in the truck, the gun held no bullets.

"You could learn a thing or two about a poker face from that boy," Dot whispered to Percy as she gave his earlobe a little tug. "We'll have you in a hospital before you know it."

She turned and stared at the blaze. One of the trees buckled under the heat of the flames and snapped halfway up. It landed on the roof of the outbuilding. The wood under the terracotta tiles caught fire in seconds.

"Let's get to the road," Dot urged Rafa softly as she helped him up out of the shallow smoke. "We've had quite enough near-death experiences in this clearing, thank you very much."

21

JULIA

The old car trundled up the hill, every bump and pothole shuddering through a frame that had long since lost its suspension. The dim headlights still reflected off of Castro's unmarked police car. If they had any idea who was following them, they were too rushed to stop and insist they go back. Julia imagined her phone vibrating all over the bedside table at the hotel the second Barker spotted them.

Through the rear-view mirror, she watched as Minnie was tossed from side to side in the backseat. Just as Julia was about to tell her great-aunt to put her seatbelt on, she remembered there hadn't been any when Lisa picked them up from the airport. Somehow, Minnie didn't spill a drop from the bottle of sangria clutched in her fist.

"You have to wiggle the gearstick, Jessie!" she cried,

using the headrest to pull herself forward. "To the left. Go on, *ram* it!"

"I'm *trying*," Jessie grumbled through gritted teeth, attempting to shift the car down a gear as the road steepened. "The stupid thing won't budge! I can see why they don't make cars like this anymore."

Minnie reached forward and hauled the gearstick to the left and down into the second gear. The car bolted forward before Jessie eased off the acceleration. A pothole sent Minnie bouncing right back into her seat.

"Why did she have to come?" Jessie whispered to Julia as they used the rear-view mirror to watch her chug sangria.

"She insisted."

"Haven't you had enough?" Jessie called into the backseat. "You're gonna throw up."

"It's to settle my nerves, sweet child." She rubbed the spillage from her chin, but it left a faint stain. "I still can't believe it! My dear neighbour, Rodger, *The Buyer*? Under my nose this whole time! Lies upon lies once again. I stupidly thought Rodger might be the one to replace my dear departed Bill, but he was playing me like a fiddle!"

Minnie paused to glug more sangria. Julia bit her tongue, wanting to point out that Minnie had freely admitted that at least two of her marriages were shams to further her career.

"And my poor Lisa," she continued, wiping her lips with the sleeve of her leopard-print silk dressing gown.

"She never trusted him! Never liked him. I could tell. I thought she was jealous that I had someone else in my life, but as usual, my daughter was right. Despite her rotten mother, she was always a bright one. None of this would have happened if I'd listened to her."

"How could you not tell he was dodgy?" Jessie asked, speeding up when Castro's car vanished around a bend in the mountain road. "He was giving off major weirdo vibes."

"Maybe I'm not as tuned-in as I thought."

"Or maybe you're always drunk," Jessie said, this time under her breath just loudly enough for Julia to catch it.

"He always seemed so charming." Minnie hugged the sangria bottle and sank into the corner. "So kind and generous. Always listened. I thought he cared about me."

"He manipulated you," Julia said, locking eyes with her great-aunt through the mirror. "I wouldn't be surprised if he tailored that personality especially for you."

"Well, it worked!" she cried. "I fell for it hook, line, and sinker! Silly old Minnie. I should have let the party end a long time ago."

Julia leaned forward and looked up the mountain. Smoke billowed from the trees in the distance, and dancing flames bathed a small section of forest in an amber glow.

"Why do I have a horrible feeling that's where we're heading?" Julia said, sitting back in her seat. "Please be okay, Gran. Please be—"

"And *Hillard!*" Minnie exclaimed out of nowhere, sitting bolt upright before rolling into the opposite corner. "The inspector! Cut from the same cloth! Just as charming... and he was in on it too? All this time? And Rodger, his stepfather? No wonder he was in no rush to find dear Dorothy and Percival! Rodger's little lapdog. I bet he was in on the cover-up of my daughter's attempted murder, too. Oh, poor Arlo. We didn't stand a chance."

Minnie paused, tipping yet more sangria into her waiting mouth. Julia had to wonder when the bottle would finally be empty. In the silence, distant sirens caught Julia's attention.

"Do you hear that?" Jessie asked. "I think they're coming from the opposite direction."

Castro sped up so Jessie followed, closing the gap between them to less than a car's distance. Through the rear-view of the car ahead, Julia saw the moment Barker's eyes popped open in recognition. He ripped himself around in his seat and squinted past his headrest, both eyebrows angled upwards as he shouted something she was grateful she didn't have to hear.

"I think he might be angry," Jessie said, leaning on the horn. "Yeah, yeah! We can't hear you, mate. Too late to turn back now!"

"He's only thinking of the baby," Julia said, her hands guiltily going to the bump.

"And I'm not?" Jessie shot her a sideways glance. "Like I'm going to let anything happen to you two. You're not even getting out of this car. You can stay here and look after Amy Winehouse back there."

A helicopter appeared over the tip of the mountain, training its spotlight on the forest below. A second appeared, and they flew down to the fire, lighting up the trees like a stadium concert. In the white light, the smoke was even thicker.

Jessie sighed as the road curved up in the direction of the fire. "Well, that's definitely where we're heading."

The dense trees closed around the road, blocking off the views from both sides. As the trees whizzed by, Julia caught sight of Inspector Hillard's car for the first time. Castro sped up and Jessie tailed him, jamming the gearstick back into third as the road levelled out.

Julia ducked to take in the helicopters hovering above them like spaceships. The light of one whooshed past, blinding her. Jessie swerved, sending Minnie tumbling all over again.

"Flipping heck!" Jessie cried. "Are they trying to beam us up? A little warning next . . ."

Jessie's voice trailed away, all the muscles in her face tightening as she slammed her foot down on the break. They skidded to a halt behind Castro's car, which was also screeching to an abrupt stop. The seatbelt caught

Julia, but Minnie tumbled forward, hitting her head on the gearstick. They rocked to sudden stillness, flopping back in their chairs.

"I'm fine!" Minnie cried out, one hand on her head, the other still clutching the sangria.

Julia brushed her hair from her face and squinted ahead. She wished she hadn't been putting off that trip to the opticians for so many years. The blurry lines of the fire were a little further up on the right, through the trees. All the cars had stopped, with Castro's having skidded into the opposite lane. Inspector Hillard's car, at the front, was the only one pointing straight ahead, and its headlights illuminated a figure standing like a statue in the middle of the road. Blood dripped from the statue's nose and all down the front of his beige linen suit.

"That's Rodger!" Minnie cried.

Castro and Barker jumped out of their car, both holding up their hands in gestures that begged Julia and Jessie to stay where they were. Castro pulled a pair of handcuffs from his belt and set off up the road, but Inspector Hillard had different ideas. The back wheels of his car spun. Dirt kicked backwards at Castro and Barker, obscuring Julia's view of them.

But as the rest of the scene unfolded, she had a ringside seat. Inspector Hillard raced at Rodger. Julia expected the man to run, but he simply stood, wide-eyed as the proverbial deer, as the headlights got closer. The car struck him, and he rolled up the bonnet and over the roof as Hillard continued his mad push forward. Rodger landed on the ground, rolling until he settled flat on his back.

Hillard slammed on his brakes and performed one of the quickest three-point turns Julia had ever witnessed. Once again, his headlights illuminated Rodger. Somehow, the man wasn't dead. He was trying and failing to prop himself up with his elbows. Inspector Hillard revved his engine, but Castro sprinted up to the inspector's car and dragged him out before he could finish what he'd started.

Julia and Jessie jumped out of the car as Barker hurried to Rodger's side. He forced the man back down to the ground and clutched his hands together in front of him. Blue lights flashed at the top of the road, the sirens growing deafeningly close. Two fire engines came into view, large and red and almost identical to the ones Julia was used to seeing back at home. Instead of stopping behind Inspector Hillard's abandoned car, they turned into the trees.

Julia hadn't noticed the little slip road until the lights of the fire engines lit it up. They drove deeper into the forest, until their lights were indistinguishable from the glow of the fire. She could make out the blurry outlines of two buildings. One of them was ferociously ablaze.

"*Mum!*" Jessie pointed over the car into the forest. "Look!"

The lights of the helicopter swept through the forest, dancing from side to side as the aircraft danced around the edges of the fire. The light flashed past figures one way, and then seconds later, another. Julia squinted, sure the flash of white she saw belonged to a familiar blouse.

"It's *them!*" Jessie cried, slapping the roof of the car. "It's them!"

Julia's hands clamped to her mouth.

She'd given up hope.

She hated to admit it, but she had.

And now, after everything, her gran was walking towards her through the forest, her clothes filthy and torn and her curls flattened to her head. Percy's arm was wrapped around her shoulders, and the other was slung around the neck of a young man in a leather jacket who Julia didn't recognise.

"*Julia?*" Dot cried, squinting through the forest. "Tell me this isn't another cruel trick!"

Jessie rushed over and took over from Dot, using her strength to prop Percy up, but Julia couldn't move. She stared at her gran and blinked through her tears, frozen to the spot.

Leaving her limping husband in good hands, Dot rushed at Julia with arm opens. Julia's shocked stillness broke, and she wrapped her arms around her gran, clinging to her tightly and staring in open-mouthed awe at the fire in the distance as she tried to find her voice.

"I was beginning to think you'd never show up," Dot

said with a smile, wiping Julia's tears as she leaned back from their tight embrace. "It really is you." She turned and looked back at Percy, her smile vanishing. "I know you'll have a lot of questions, but they have to wait. We need to get Percy to a hospital. Right now."

Minnie stumbled out of the car, the sangria bottle still in hand. She went to sloppily hug Dot, but Dot dodged the embrace and snatched the bottle from Minnie's grip, downing the contents in seconds. After throwing the bottle into the forest, Dot let out a small burp and yanked open the door so that Jessie and the young stranger could load Percy into the back of the car.

"I can drive!" Minnie announced raising a finger in the air. She swayed on her feet. "I know the way."

"Fat chance." Jessie pushed her out of the way. "In fact, looks like you'll have to catch a different ride. No room in this one."

Jessie jumped behind the wheel and slammed the door, and Julia did the same on the passenger side. She yanked her seatbelt across and looked into the backseat. With Percy propped up in the middle, attempting to meekly smile at her, Dot climbed in on one side, and the stranger on the other. As soon as their doors were closed, Jessie set off. To Minnie, left standing on the side of the road, Jessie offered a jaunty and unapologetic wave.

"Barker will take care of you," Julia called through the window as they drove away.

Through the rear-view mirror, she watched Minnie shuffle towards Barker and Rodger. It shouldn't have pleased Julia when Minnie booted Rodger between the legs as she passed him, but it did.

"Okay, but does anyone actually know the way to the hospital?" Jessie called out when they reached a turning in the road.

"Take a right," the young man said, leaning forward. "I will lead."

Julia looked back at the stranger and wondered where he slotted into the picture. Was this the 'Rafa' Rodger and Hillard had spoken of? He looked about Jessie's age, and of all of them, he somehow seemed the most shaken up.

"Put your foot down, kiddo," Percy said, his voice croaky and barely above a whisper. "I'd quite like to see at least one more sunrise."

Julia reached through the gap and clutched her gran's hands. In the split second before Dot noticed she was watching her in the rear-view mirror, Julia saw how wracked with worry her gran was. Still, she mustered a smile and a wink for Julia, and Julia believed it enough to smile back.

She had her gran back.

22

DOT

"Another win!" Dot said, slapping her cards down on the table. "You're not such a bad poker player, after all."

"Was I really tugging at my ear the whole time?" Percy asked as he claimed the chocolate buttons Dot had procured from the vending machine down the corridor.

"Every time."

"I never noticed." He began to shuffle the deck for a new game. "Still, I'm sure you're letting me win."

She was, but she'd never own up to it. While Percy dealt the cards for their next match, she looked through the hospital window. Seeing people going about their business on the other side with no bars or locks to stop them coming and going made her smile. The beeps and buzzes of hospitals had always unsettled her, but today they provided a much-needed sense of protection.

The doctor who had been treating Percy all night passed the window, eyes trained to a clipboard. He doubled back and knocked on the door before entering.

"Mr Percy!" The young, handsome doctor clung to the bottom of the bed and smiled at them both, his Spanish accent thick and silky. "How are you feeling today?"

"Much better." Percy ripped back the blue hospital covers to show his fresh bandage. "That lovely nurse lady came by and changed the dressing five minutes ago."

"You will need to watch him." The doctor winked at Dot. "He has a little crush, I think."

"Don't worry." Dot reached up to fiddle with her brooch, but her fingers met nothing but fabric. "I've got my eyes on him. He's not leaving my sight again."

"I only have eyes for you, my dear." Percy sent a loving glance her way before looking down at his bandages and rolling his leg from side to side. "You're not going to amputate, are you, doc?"

"Not this time." He laughed and checked the clipboard. "The antibiotics are working already on the infection. You keep this wound clean, and you will have only a big scar and a good story."

"It adds character." Percy tossed back the covers further. "Does this mean I can go?"

"Yes, Mr Percy." The doctor pulled the wheelchair from the bottom of the bed and rolled it up to Percy's bedside. "You must rest a few days more, still. Do not put on it any weight. I do not want to put more stitches in."

"Don't worry, doc." Percy shuffled into the chair with Dot's help. "I intend to remain positively horizontal for the rest of the week."

"I am not sure I know what this means," the doctor replied, cheeks turning pink.

"It means he won't be getting up for anything other than trips to the loo, and I'll be waiting on him hand and foot." Dot kissed the top of Percy's head. "But I'm very glad to do it."

Like her white lie that Percy was winning every third poker game, she'd vowed never to tell him how scared she'd been to lose him. About how close to death he'd been. With injuries no more severe than a bruised shoulder and some light smoke inhalation, Dot could have left the hospital at any time. Though Julia and Barker had begged her to return to the hotel for some proper rest, Dot chose to sleep upright in the chair by Percy's bed.

Somehow, it wasn't the worst sleep she'd had in the last week.

With no clean clothes to change into, Dot decided they would steal the hospital dressing gown. They wheeled to the pharmacy to pick up the prescription for the rest of Percy's antibiotics and painkillers. Afterwards, they ventured deeper into the hospital, following the way Dot remembered from her late-night visit with Minnie.

"It's just up here," Dot whispered as they pushed through the doors into the much quieter intensive care unit.

"Your sense of direction never fails you."

She guided him through the intertwining corridors. She heard the chaos even before she turned the corner. Doctors and nurses rushed in and out of Lisa's room. Dot stopped so abruptly she almost tipped Percy out of the chair.

She had feared the worst, but thankfully that was not the scene she saw unfolding through the room's window. Lisa was half-sat up in bed, and from the looks of her swollen eyes, she hadn't been awake for long. Minnie was by her side, clutching her daughter's hand and wearing an enormous smile on her face. Through the lines and changes left by decades of ageing, Dot saw a glimpse of the young Minnie still there, still a part of her sister-in-law. Despite their late-night walk through the hospital, they still didn't really know these new versions of each other. But now, they had time ahead of them. Minnie noticed them, and after kissing Lisa on the forehead, joined them in the corridor.

"She woke up ten minutes ago," Minnie whispered, eyes trained on her daughter through the window. "She's still a bit confused, but she confirmed that Rodger was the one who stabbed her. The psychopath was waiting for her when she went down to start breakfast. Lord knows how long he was crouched there in the dark. It doesn't bear thinking about."

"Did she say how she figured it out?" Dot asked.

"Inspector Hillard gave the game away," Minnie replied, pausing when two nurses rushed down the corridor behind them, speaking quickly in Spanish. "He left his phone on the reception desk. Lisa just happened to be there. She said she saw 'The Buyer' on the screen, but in Spanish. 'El Comprador', she said it was."

"That's what we saw on Rafa's phone!" Percy pointed out. "We should have picked it up and given him what for!"

"Well, Lisa *did* answer it," Minnie continued. "She didn't say anything, but she recognised Rodger's voice and hung up. She sent her emails, and he stabbed her the next morning." She drew a deep, shuddering breath. "I could have lost her."

"But you haven't." Dot wiped a stray tear from Minnie's cheek. "You know, she's almost the age Albert was when we lost him. Looking at her now, it seems a lot younger than it felt at the time."

"It really does."

"We thought we had it all figured out." Dot smiled and waved at Lisa, and even though she didn't seem to have the strength to wave back, her mouth turned up a little at the corners. "We're going back to the hotel now."

"Please, make yourselves at home. As much as you

can," Minnie said, pulling Dot into another hug. "I'm so sorry this happened."

"Just another story to tell the great-grandkids," Dot said, pulling away. "Get yourself home soon. You stink like a brewery."

"You don't smell too fresh yourself." Minnie fought back a smile and lost. "You know, I forgot how mean you could be. I missed it, Dot."

"And I missed you too, Mins," Dot said, her old nickname for her sister-in-law pushing to the front of her mind for the first time in decades. "See you back at the hotel. I really do mean it about the shower, though. You're absolutely ripe."

Leaving Minnie to sniff at the armpits of her wrinkled dressing gown, Dot and Percy headed for the exit. She caught sight of herself in various shiny stainless-steel reflections as they walked, but she was determined not to look in a mirror until she'd had a shower, at the very least. She refused to admit how unlike herself she must look.

They took a taxi back to the hotel, which Dot paid for with the money still tucked in the strap of her bra. Instead of going straight inside, Dot pushed Percy down the uneven cobbled street to where Jessie stood outside an unmarked building with frosted windows, taking pictures with her phone of the police carting out clear plastic box after clear plastic box, each filled with clothes.

"What's going on?" Dot asked, startling Jessie enough that she dropped her phone.

"Turns out Rodger's hotel wasn't a hotel at all." Jessie scooped up the phone and tucked it into her denim shorts, which were revealing quite a lot more of her legs than Dot would have done at that age; how things had changed. "It was a factory for his shady fake-clothes shops. Proper sweatshop style. They've been carting this stuff out all morning."

"They're the same clothes we were wearing, Dorothy!" Percy pointed to a box stuffed with the same bright fabric used to make the graffiti tracksuit Dot had so briefly been forced to wear.

"Rodger owned all those clothes shops?" Dot asked.

Jessie nodded. "All part of that weirdo's grand scheme. Must have been bringing in a fortune. I wouldn't be surprised if that's how he made the money he needed to snap up every business in town. Those shops were packed out. *Were* being the operative word. Funnily enough, none of them opened this morning. All the shutters are down, and the tourists are spending their euros in the few businesses that resisted The Buyer's offers and threats." She paused and glanced sideways at Dot. "That kid is awake, by the way. I took him breakfast. Didn't say much, so I left him to it."

"Does anyone else know?"

"What do you take me for?" Jessie rolled her eyes. "An amateur?"

"Not for a second, kiddo."

They walked back to La Casa. Barker rushed out and, with Jessie's help, carried Percy down the stairs in the chair to save him having to test the strength of his painkillers. When they were safely inside, Barker returned to the terrace again, where Julia was talking with the officer who had taken Dot's statement at the hospital. Julia spotted them and hurried over, her pink maxi dress fluttering around her and making her bump look gigantic.

Even in less than a week, it seemed to have grown.

"Lisa's awake," Dot announced.

Julia let out a giant sigh as she wrapped Dot in what had to be the hundredth hug since she stumbled out of the trees and into her granddaughter's arms the night before.

"Did you say Lisa was awake?" the police officer asked, joining them in the reception foyer. "If this is the case, I must get to the hospital to take her statement."

"She confirmed everything we already knew," Dot said. "Rodger was waiting for her in the kitchen that morning, and he attacked her for daring to figure out who he was – which she did by answering the phone Hillard left lying around."

"Never the brightest bulb," the officer said before checking his watch. "I'll leave you to settle in. I have a meeting with my superiors in an hour, and all of this will make a lot more sense with a statement from Lisa."

The officer left, and the four of them sat around a table in the dining room while Jessie perched on the edge of the pool, feet submerged in the water and her mind submerged in whatever was happening on her mobile phone.

For the first time all week, things felt normal, and Dot couldn't have loved it more.

"That was Sub-Inspector Castro," Julia explained when they were all settled in with cups of tea. "He's been secretly building a case against Hillard for over a year, and desperately trying to get people to take him seriously. Nobody would."

"Turns out Hillard wasn't the only corrupt officer on the force," Barker added. "Hillard's singing like a canary and revealing the names of everyone who accepted a hefty bribe from Rodger to ignore his dodgy dealings. His confession alone is enough to send Rodger down for a very long time, even without all the other insane stuff. He'll go from his hospital bed to a jail cell, where he'll hopefully stay until his last breath."

"He'll be running the place within a week," Dot said after a sip of tea, still longing for her usual teabags. "Although I'm sure his bribes will be downgraded to chocolate bars and soap, and his market will go from clothes to cigarettes and wine made in toilets."

They kept the conversation light as they finished their tea, and the serious questions Dot knew were on the tips of Julia and Barker's tongues never came up.

Barker wheeled Percy out to the terrace on Dot's request, leaving her alone with her granddaughter. They left the dining area and walked back into the foyer, and Julia retrieved something from behind the desk.

"I think these belong to you," she said as she pushed the photo album into Dot's hands. Her emerald brooch wobbled precariously on top of it. "Your little trick with the bin and the note at the café was quite clever."

"How did you find it?"

"Maria, the waitress." Julia pulled one of the missing posters from the pile on the desk. "Never stopped handing these to people. Must have given out hundreds, all over Savega." Julia paused and looked down, her brows dropping. "I gave up hope."

Dot clipped her brooch back onto her blouse and immediately felt much more like herself. She fiddled with it, her posture stiffening. She reached across the desk and lifted Julia's chin.

"Gran's home now," she whispered, pinching Julia's cheeks. "You weren't going to get rid of me that easily."

Julia nodded, her frown turning into a smile. She had a great deal on her mind, Dot could see that much, but she didn't ask. Not yet, at least. When the dust settled and the time finally came, Dot was sure she'd be ready for honesty, but for now, she was glad not to go into the details.

Ready to finally have the long soak in the bath she'd been looking forward to, Dot crammed herself and the

Cocktails and Cowardice

wheelchair in the tiny lift. When the doors slid open, she wheeled Percy down the corridor. The sights and sounds were almost brand new, given how brief their stay before their capture had been. At least she remembered which room they'd been in. She didn't have a key, but she didn't need one. She knocked, and Rafa opened the door immediately.

"How did you sleep?" Dot asked, noticing that he'd had a shower and used one of the single beds. "Beds are too soft if I recall."

"Fine." Rafa closed the door behind them. "What is going on? There is police crawling all over Savega."

"Don't worry." Dot gestured for Rafa to help her get Percy into the made bed. "I didn't give them your name."

"Neither of us did," Percy insisted.

"Why are you protecting me?" Rafa scooped Percy up and plopped him in the middle of the bed, leaving Dot to straighten out his legs. "I do not deserve this."

"You saved us, lad," Percy patted him on the cheek. "You showed up when it mattered the most."

Dot pulled the covers up to Percy's chin and fluffed up the pillow behind him. Knowing he needed a nap, she closed the curtains. The painkillers made him sleepy, and he hadn't stopped yawning since leaving the hospital. Adrenaline mixed with the mild caffeine hit from the cup of tea was enough to keep Dot going. She'd fall asleep the second her head hit the pillow, but she had things to do before that could happen. Leaving

Percy to drift off, she took Rafa out onto the balcony and closed the door.

She looked out into the valley, and even though she'd spent the worst week of her life somewhere out there, the view was still as breath-taking as it had been upon arrival. She inhaled the air, its freshness what she'd missed most. The air really had been thinner up in the mountains. And the smoke had, quite literally, added injury to insult.

"Inspector Hillard has confessed everything," Dot said, motioning for Rafa to join her at the small patio table. "While we didn't give your name, there's no guarantee he won't. He's your uncle?"

"Yes." Rafa sat down, his demeanour the shyest Dot had seen so far. "He was born . . . how do you say this? Out of the marriage? My abuela visited England many times, and one time, she came home with a half-English surprise in her tummy. My grandfather was furious. The child was banished to England as soon as he was born."

"But Hillard eventually moved to Spain?"

"Ten years ago," Rafa explained. "I was a boy only. My parents were dead. He never met his brother. But my abuela, his mother, he got to know. We have never been close. My English was not good enough, and his Spanish was worse."

"And your gran – your abuela – she married Rodger?"

"Five years ago." Rafa's gaze drifted off into the

valley, no doubt to the clearing Dot wouldn't go searching for. "He bought businesses in our village. My abuela always joked that she liked English men. We came to Savega two years ago. Rodger said it was for a business opportunity. Everything unravelled from there."

"How long have you worked for him?"

"Since I am eighteen." He sighed. "Fetching and carrying. Then things were more complicated. He is good at convincing people to do things for him. Good at explaining things away. Like the kidnapping. He made it sound like this was a play only to put pressure on Minnie. I did not think you were in real danger until he stabbed Lisa. My uncle had warned me of this man. Behind the mask lived this monster."

"That cut must have hurt." Dot wished she had a cup of tea to busy her hands. "Where is your abuela now?"

"Hidden away in another of his properties." He looked back out into the valley again. "She will have no idea what is going on. When Rodger does not come home, she will realise. I do not think she understood how her husband made his money. She did not want to understand, I think. But she enjoyed the results. She is probably lounging by the pool right now."

"Will you go to her?"

Rafa looked down and shook his head.

"She will think I betrayed the family," he said, his voice small. "Her son and husband are in prison, and not me. She will know." He slouched into the chair. "I should be there for what I did to you."

"Have you ever killed anyone, Rafael?"

"Never."

The answer didn't surprise her. He was a scared boy trapped in a world he should never have known about. The innocence of youth was complicated, and Rafa had lost that innocence too soon. Dot wouldn't take any amount of money to go back to that time, not for all the tight skin and pain-free joints in the world.

"I want you to have this," she said, pulling the cash from her bra strap. "Might be a bit warm, but there's nearly five hundred euros there." She put it on the table and pushed it across to him. "I'm not intending on leaving this hotel much until it's time to go home, so I have no use for it."

"I cannot accept this."

"You can." She pushed it closer. "And you will."

"But, Mrs Dorothy, I—"

She held up her hand. "When you followed us through the market, I thought you meant to mug us. That's when I hid the money there. I did everything in my power to stop you getting your hands on it, but it turns out you didn't even want it." She pushed it towards him as far as she could. "So now, I offer it freely. I have enough saved-up pension money stuffed under the rugs around my cottage to keep me going. Take it and get as far as way from this place as you can. Please, Rafa."

Rafa scooped up the money and slowly rolled it up before putting it in his pocket.

She turned her head up to the sun and closed her eyes. "Now get out of here, Rafael. Have a nice life and be good. There are plenty of honest ways to make a living."

Dot kept her eyes closed and listened as Rafa's chair scraped back against the balcony floor. His figure blocked the sun before a soft kiss landed on her cheek, and when she opened her eyes, Rafa had already gone. The bedroom door was closed, and she knew she'd likely never see the boy again. In the end, he'd proved he was better than blindly following orders. Dot had faith he would follow the right path from now on. She was glad to be the one to have help course correct his future.

After basking in the sun for a couple of minutes, Dot stood and stretched. The longest yawn of her life caught her off-guard. She scratched at her deflated curls. It was beyond time for that long, hot bubble bath.

"Dorothy?" Percy whispered as Dot crept in. "Shall we stay the extra week? I'd quite like to have some sort of honeymoon before we go home."

She smiled even though his eyes were closed and he couldn't see it. "You know, my love, I'd quite like that too."

23

JULIA

The second week of the holiday was exactly what Julia had hoped her honeymoon would be. Most of the remaining days were spent lounging lazily around the pool, glancing at the clock only to remind them when to eat meals.

On the penultimate day, they ventured down to the beach and spent time sunbathing like everyone else, with a constant flow of cold drinks and ice creams in between dips in the sea. Jessie and Barker even braved an adventurous round of paragliding, although a closer zoom in on the pictures Julia snapped on her phone showed Jessie enjoying it a lot more than her husband.

Minnie spent most of the week claiming she wasn't ready to venture into Savega, too embarrassed to face her neighbours after almost falling for Rodger's tricks. On the final morning of the honeymoon, Julia and

Barker finally coaxed Minnie out of La Casa and into the plaza.

"This is more like I remember it," Minnie announced as she took shaky steps into the plaza, Julia and Barker looping arms with her on either side. "I can feel the difference in the air."

Despite its delectable window displays, Julia had avoided sampling the treats at Chocolatería Valor until now. She'd wanted to end the honeymoon on a high – and there was no high better than the one from a café dedicated to chocolate creations.

"Just a tea, please," Minnie said to the waitress when she offered her the wine menu. "Need to keep a clear head for Lisa's homecoming tonight."

Nobody had mentioned it, but everyone had noticed that Minnie hadn't reached for the bar all week, opting for cups of tea, instead. Two days earlier, Julia had educated her great-aunt on the caffeine content of tea when she found her anxiously pacing the terrace at one in the morning, unable to sleep one night after going through twelve cups of the stuff in one day.

Julia also ordered tea, although she chose her favourite peppermint leaves, and Barker opted for a double espresso. The menu for the chocolate creations was entirely in Spanish, and twenty years sheltered in her hotel hadn't made Minnie as fluent in the language as a few short years had done for her daughter. She knew enough to point out the key words, but the pictures were so gorgeously shot, they hardly needed descriptions. It wasn't so much that Julia struggled to pick something – it was limiting herself to picking only *one*.

When put on the spot by the waitress, Julia stabbed her finger at one of the two options she'd dithered between after Barker and Minnie placed their orders. Minutes later, a chocolate cheesecake encased in an interwoven dome of chocolate lattice was presented to her. Each of the curved lines forming the lattice was a different kind of chocolate. After admiring its beauty, Julia smashed it open with her spoon and tasted each colour at once. White, milk, and dark, and they all blended together magnificently against her tongue.

The cheesecake itself was perfect, even by Julia's exacting standards. She'd often found chocolate cheesecakes could stray too far into the sickly sweet territory. The flavours at Chocolatería Valor, however, were so balanced and well thought out, Julia was jealous of the inventor. She scribbled down notes as she ate, shooting in the dark at the ingredients, hoping to take something new home to experiment with.

"How's yours?" Julia asked Barker, who had ordered the same silky chocolate cake as Minnie.

"Amazing," he muttered through a mouthful. "Not a patch on your double chocolate fudge cake, which you know I love so much, but it's close. Really close."

"I'll second that," said Minnie, sucking her fork with

her eyes closed. "Although I can't compare. It's a shame I never got to try any of your famous baking, sweet Julia. The reviews I've heard are nothing short of perfection."

"You'll have to come to the café one day," she offered, meaning it. "Unless you're still thinking of moving back to Peridale?"

Minnie stared at the cake and smiled as she forked off another chunk. She took her time and ate it slowly, her cogs no doubt churning up an answer.

"Not just yet," she said finally, still smiling. "The pull of the old place has never left me, but I think we're going to stay here. For a little while, at least. Lisa and I have had some very serious and honest discussions, and we've decided we're going to give the hotel another go."

Julia and Barker shared a look.

"Yes, I know what you're thinking." Minnie laughed before dabbing at the corners of her mouth with a napkin. "It was Lisa's idea, don't worry. It turns out I'm not the only one who has realised a lot during this ordeal. She sends her apologies again, Julia."

Julia wafted her hand. "Lisa doesn't need to apologise. She was a victim in all of this too."

"She just feels so terrible for not telling you as soon as she figured out what was going on." Minnie sighed as she traced her fork around the cake on the plate. "I think she's embarrassed she let herself get sucked into The Buyer's games. She's not a malicious woman. Far from it, actually."

"And she's happy to get back to work when she can?" Barker asked.

"On the condition that I give her an official managerial position," Minnie said with a nod. "She wants to see if she can revive the old place. She has a lot of ideas. Good ideas. Reminds me of Bill, actually, but she's more tech-savvy than either of us ever were. Holidays were booked in travel agents last time I checked, but it all seems to be done over the internet these days." She cut off another piece. "She can do her own hiring and firing, and I'll step in to help where I can. I'm not exactly going to be slaving away in the kitchen or flipping mattresses at my age, but I think there's a hosting position somewhere in there for me. And I don't mean the kind where I sit around drinking sangria and telling those same stories over and over every night. They might be new to the guests, but if I'm honest, I'm sick of hearing them."

"And the money situation?" Barker pushed.

"I have an idea." She sighed and looked down at her wedding finger, on which she still wore a ring. "I collected enough gold and diamonds over four marriages to buy a jeweller a second home. I'd just never considered parting ways with them. I'd call them my memories, the stories of my life – but there's hardly a lot of good memories in three divorces." She tilted the ring, and the modest diamond twinkled in the light. "No, it's time to live in the present and stop rehashing the past.

I'll keep Bill's ring, ironically the smallest of them, and yet the longest and happiest marriage of them all. I should be able to raise enough money to stay afloat while Lisa recovers, giving us enough time to come up with an action plan for the winter season. It's Lisa's time now. I'm ready to step out of her way so she can fly."

If not for the transfer pick-up time growing ever closer, Julia would have stayed in Chocolatería Valor and sampled the menu until she popped or they closed. With only fifteen minutes to spare until the taxi was meant to arrive, they settled the bill, leaving the last of their coins as a decent tip.

Minnie promised to meet them outside, so Julia and Barker left the café and sat on the benches around the water fountain for the first and last time. Tiny cold water droplets splashed at the back of her neck, bringing relief from the hot sun as she looked around the calmer plaza.

Julia didn't have the same connection to Savega that Minnie did, but even she could feel the difference the week without a gang calling all the shots had made. Without Rodger's counterfeit-clothes shops cluttering the place, the true beauty of the traditional buildings shone. Tourists still flocked to the space, but now they were filling the small independent local trinket shops, cafés, bars, and restaurants that had been buried behind the garish exteriors of The Buyer's empire.

"Your gran really is a changed woman." Barker nudged Julia and nodded across the square to another of the cafés. "She'll be volunteering on peace missions soon."

Julia craned her neck and observed as her gran and Percy took turns hugging Maria, the young waitress who had kept the photo album safe. Dot appeared to give her another tip before heading in the direction of the alley that would take them back to La Casa. Hands full of shopping bags, they cut across when they spotted Julia and Percy.

"How's the cane treating you?" Julia asked as Percy settled down next to her on the bench.

"It's peachy." He held it up, the stainless-steel twinkling in the light. "Doc said I shouldn't need it for too long at the final check-up this morning, but it'll come in handy when I need to nudge Dorothy on the sofa after she falls asleep in front of the ten o'clock news."

"I think you'll find that's usually *you*, dear," Dot called from Barker's other side as she dug through her bags. "I think I fit all the shopping in. I got t-shirts for the great-grandkids, some trinkets for the house, and fridge magnets for everyone else. Do you think that'll be enough?"

"People will be happy just to see you," Julia said.

"Can't go home empty-handed." Dot pushed up her curls, which she'd had freshly set and blow-dried at the local salon that morning in preparation for her grand return to Peridale. "I still have standards, dear."

While they waited for Minnie to exit Chocolatería Valor, a familiar red sportscar zoomed around the plaza. Gabriel whizzed past their bench, slammed on his brakes, and reversed back to them. He pulled off his sunglasses, already grinning.

"Ahh, the South-Brown-Croppers!" he exclaimed, their blend of surnames still amusing him as much as it had done all week. "Will I be seeing you tonight at the restaurant?"

They'd eaten in Gabriel's busy French restaurant almost every night, minus Minnie, who spent the evenings at the hospital by Lisa's bedside. Gabriel was the type of host who somehow felt like a family friend by the end of a single sitting in his restaurant. Even after only four visits, Julia knew about his childhood growing on up a vineyard in the south of France with eccentric parents, his young adult years working in the finest kitchens in Paris, his work as a holiday rep in the more tourist-driven parts of Spain, and finally how he came to own Eiffel. Barker had admitted to finding his flamboyant personality and loud voice grating by the end of the week, but Julia had warmed to Gabriel much more than she would have expected. Behind the showman was someone who truly cared not only about this place, but also the people who inhabited it.

"I'm afraid it's our last day," she said, shielding her eyes from the sun. "We fly home in a couple of hours."

"No!" he cried. "Really? You have only just arrived!"

He sighed dramatically. "But alas, this is how we are used to things. Savega has certainly felt your influence for the better, South-Brown-Croppers!"

"I'm sure Sub-Inspector Castro played a bigger part in that," she said, feeling her cheeks blush. "He seemed to be close to cracking things before we turned up. We just helped push him over the finish line."

"You mean *we* helped push him over the finish line," Dot corrected, fiddling with her brooch as she pursed her lips. "The ransom was on *our* heads, remember."

"I will miss your fiery spirit the most, ma belle Dorothy." Gabriel winked at Dot before slipping on his glasses. "Now, I must bid you farewell. Have a safe flight, and we will see you in Savega soon, oui?"

Julia waved him off as he sped out of the plaza. Over the past week, Julia had concluded that the plaza, and the rest of Savega, would have fallen into The Buyer's hands much sooner if Gabriel hadn't put up such a fight. As long as he was there, Savega had a goateed guardian angel to man the defences, and she knew he wouldn't let the darkness fall so quickly if another opportunist turned up one day.

After a few minutes of last-minute sunbathing by the fountain, Minnie finally left Chocolatería Valor. They met her on the other side of the road.

"I wanted to try and get Arlo's new address," she explained as they walked back to the hotel, "to write to him. To apologise. To maybe even offer his job back. But the waitress said he never left Savega after all. Gabriel has given him a job in the kitchen at Eiffel."

"Without The Buyer looming, it's not such a bad place to live," Dot said as they trundled down the tight, cobbled alley. "Although, saying that, we won't be in a rush to return, if it's all the same to you, Mins."

"I think I owe you a visit next time."

"You could still ask Arlo to come back," Barker pointed out when they reached the steps down to La Casa. "For old time's sake?"

"No." Minnie shook her head, her mind clearly made up. "He's where he belongs. He was always too good a chef for us. Arlo was loyal, and we didn't repay that loyalty. Gabriel will take care of him."

Jessie rushed at them the second they walked through the doors into the cool air-conditioned foyer.

"About *bloody* time!" she cried, glancing at the clock on the wall. "Transfer will be here in five minutes."

"Then we're back just in time," Barker said, ruffling her hair before she could duck.

"Not quite." Jessie hooked her thumb into the dining room, where Sub-Inspector Castro sat alone at one of the dining tables, his suit replaced with casual jeans and a t-shirt. "Undercover spy dude has been waiting for you for nearly half an hour."

As it turned out, Castro wanted to speak with Minnie. The pair sat at the table and talked in hushed tones for a couple of minutes before he handed over a white envelope and stood. On his way out, he lingered by Julia and Barker with a tight smile.

"I guess this is goodbye," he said, holding his hand out to Barker, "not just for you, but for me as well."

"You're leaving Savega?"

"I am being moved on," he said with a gentle shrug. "There is little glory for the whistle-blower. The confession of Hillard has already led to the arrests of three of my superiors, and there will be more by the time this is over. Hillard was a rotten branch on the tree, but the roots? They are just as infected."

"Hardly seems fair," Julia said, offering him a smile.

"All of this, it is not for the glory," he replied, his soft smile convincing. "Seeing Savega without the influence of The Buyer is enough. Now, perhaps, I will finally get to spend more time at home." He nodded at Julia's bump. "My wife, she is the same size as you right now. Our little girl, she comes in the winter, so perhaps the timing is a blessing in disguise." He gave Julia a quick kiss on either cheek and shook Barker's hand firmly. "For now, it is goodbye, and if our paths cross again, I hope it is under better circumstances."

Castro left just as the two transfer taxis slowed to a halt outside. While Jessie and Barker loaded all their cases into the boots, Minnie ushered Julia out onto the terrace. She tore open the envelope and pulled out The Buyer's contract.

"Castro said Rodger could fight for ownership from

behind bars if he wanted to," she said as she ripped the contract in two, and then three, and then four. "I did sign them, after all. Luckily for me, Rodger never got time to make copies, and *somehow* this contract was never catalogued as evidence."

Minnie tossed the shredded paper over the edge of the balcony and down to the valley below. The white fragments caught the breeze, fluttering in all directions like confetti – the celebration of a new start. Minnie looped her arm through Julia's, and they walked through to the foyer before the paper touched the ground.

"Take care of yourself, Julia." Minnie hugged her, one hand resting on the bump. "Promise you'll send pictures of the little one when they're here?"

"I promise."

"You look after her." Minnie pulled Barker down into a hug before moving onto Jessie. "And it was so lovely to meet you, Jessie. You remind me so much of myself at your age. It's nice to know the youth aren't as bad as you hear about these days."

"We are," Jessie replied as she squirmed away from the hug. "In fact, we're worse."

Julia, Barker, and Jessie climbed into the first taxi, giving Dot and Percy their own time to say goodbye. Percy went first, giving Minnie a one-armed hug before climbing into the backseat of the second taxi. Minnie and Dot hugged the longest, only separating when the driver pipped his horn. The taxi meter was already at five euros.

"This is goodbye *for now*," Minnie said as she opened the taxi door for Dot. "We don't have another forty years left to waste, so let's keep in touch this time."

"I'll hold you to visiting Peridale," Dot said, kissing Minnie one last time before climbing in. "You can stay with us, of course, but there's also a local bed and breakfast. You and the owner would get on. She's a fellow fan of kaftans."

"Then I shall see you there." Minnie slammed the door behind Dot and stepped back. "Have a safe flight!"

Julia wrapped her hand around Barker's and rested her head on his shoulder as they drove down the narrow lane. They emerged into the plaza and headed down the road they'd taken into Savega two long weeks ago. It wasn't long before they were zooming to the airport. Julia spotted a plane taking off in the distance, and more than ever, she was glad to be on her way home.

∾

The morning after their quiet return to the village and a much-needed night in their own beds, all five of them made their way to the café, huddled under umbrellas, for Dot and Percy's official 'Welcome Home' party.

Most of the village had crammed themselves into the café, which had been transformed with banners, balloons, and bunting, all bright pink. Katie's choice, no doubt.

"You could have brought the sun with you," Sue said, nodding past the crowded café as the rain lashed outside. "So much for a hot summer!"

"It feels like home," Julia replied, smiling.

From behind the counter, they watched silently as Dot held court in the centre of the café. The villagers had been hanging off her every word since the start of the party. Only Julia knew the edges of Dot's wild ransom stories had been softened.

Dot had told Julia everything, and in such detail, she knew she was the only one who would ever hear it. Dot forced her to promise she'd never tell the full account, and Julia had been happy to oblige.

Not that the omissions mattered. Dot had never seemed more in her element. As usual, she relished being the centre of attention and having more wild stories to tell than ever before. She'd be dining out on the Savega stories for years to come.

"Where did Barker sneak off to?" Julia asked Jessie once she'd joined her in the kitchen. Jessie looked up from the mountain of washing up the guests had already created, and which she and Katie were diligently trying to work through.

"Went out the back." Jessie nodded at the kitchen door. "Probably hiding away in his cave."

Julia pulled on the heavy fire door and slipped out

into the small yard. The humid rain drenched her as she yanked on the wooden doors set into the ground. She crept down the wooden staircase into the basement, which had been Barker's private investigator's office for the last few months.

Barker was at his mahogany desk in the centre of the room, focused on his laptop. Once a bare, empty basement, Barker had transformed the room into a comfortable office space. Rugs covered the concrete floor, and bookcases and pictures disguised the old walls. Softly lit lamps, tall potted plants, and a dark red Chesterfield sofa completed the look.

"Sorry," he said, typing away without looking up. "I wanted to get a start on these emails. More keep flooding in. That I wasn't the one to solve the case doesn't seem to matter to any of these people. Barker Brown, PI is officially in business."

"Anything catching your eye?"

"A woman up in Lancashire with a missing sister," he said, closing his laptop slightly. "Another suspects her husband of bigamy – not something you see every day. I'm going to have a busy few months ahead of me."

"Well, I'm glad I was the one who *technically* hired you for the Savega case." Julia winked as she sat down in the chair on the other side of the desk. "Does all this mean you're going to be too busy for Mrs Morton?"

"She fired me." Barker grinned from ear to ear. "I'm free! It turns out she was the one cheating on her husband, and she was so consumed with guilt, she wanted to get even by proving he was doing the same to her. Still, I was right about something. He has a little issue with gambling. But he's denying any extracurricular activity and he's already called the divorce lawyers."

"Poor Mrs Morton."

"I think she's as relieved that it's over as I am." He leaned back in his chair and looked around the office. "It's good to be home, isn't it?"

"It really is." She smiled when she looked at his desk and saw their wedding picture next to the first scan of their unborn child. "Now that we have the honeymoon ticked off the list, let's stay in Peridale for a while."

"You don't have to tell me twice." Barker held his hands up. "Turns out, you were right. A holiday isn't a holiday when you're living in one all the time."

"Changed your mind about buying that holiday home, then?"

"For now." He closed his laptop fully and leaned across the desk to kiss her. "Never say never, though. I need to spend all the money I'll make from all these new cases on something."

"Let's not count your chickens before they've hatched."

"A chicken pun?" Barker arched a brow. "Really?"

Julia went to laugh, but instead she jolted in her seat, something twinging in her stomach. She squirmed, doubling over slightly, immediately pressing her hands on the bump. It happened again, this time fluttering like butterflies. She rested her hand on the spot where she felt the sensation and was rewarded with another twinge – but this time, it prodded lightly against her hand.

"What is it?" he asked, hurrying to her side. "Is something wrong?"

"I think I just felt the first kick."

Julia grabbed Barker's hand and pressed it firmly against the spot. There was another gentle thud, and Barker's eyes lit up. Neither of them moved for the next ten minutes, and the baby kicked twice more.

"He's going to be a footballer," Barker said after the baby finally settled. "I can feel it."

"Or she." Julia followed him up the stairs, glad to see the rain had eased off a little. "And while we're on the subject, don't you go thinking these cases will get you out of putting up that flatpack. The baby will be here, kicking and screaming in front of us, in no time, and I'd quite like to have a nursery before that happens."

"Plenty of time yet." Barker held open the kitchen door and ushered her inside, his hand resting gently on the small of her back. "But for now, I want to try one of those cakes Evelyn made. People can't seem to get enough of them."

The party continued on late into the evening, the villagers dropping off one by one until only family remained. While Jessie and Barker helped Sue and Katie clean up, and Percy and Brian played a game of poker, Julia followed Dot around the waterlogged village green and into her cottage.

When they were settled in the sitting room with cups of tea, Dot handed over a rectangular object concealed in Christmas wrapping paper.

"It's all I had in," she explained, waving at the red and green paper.

Julia ripped back the paper to reveal a small book with 'MEMORIES' embossed in gold on the black leather cover. On the first page, Dot's familiar handwriting greeted her:

You never know when you might need to look back at the good times.

Julia flicked through the album, surprised and touched to see a photograph taken while on the second week of the holiday on every page. She remembered posing for a handful of Dot's shots, but the rest were candid pictures taken of Julia, Barker, and Jessie. They were smiling or laughing in most of them, seemingly unaware of the camera.

"How did you do this so quickly?"

"Jessie helped me send the pictures ahead of time," Dot said after sipping her tea. "Alfie put the book together for me. I wanted you to have it as thanks for what you did."

"I didn't solve this one on my own," she replied, "but thank you."

"But even when you gave up hope, you still kept plodding along, and that's all that matters." Dot looked down into her cup as she swirled the tea in it. "Life can be a long slog, Julia. Everything will change when that baby gets here. You're going to have good days and bad days, but if you're anything like me, those pictures will get you through and remind you what's important."

"Family."

"Exactly." Dot smiled. "You get it."

Julia held the album tight to her chest. She'd treasure it for the rest of her life – not just because of the pictures it contained, but because of everything they'd gone through to have enough happy moments to fill the pages. The two of them had been tested in very different ways, but the experience had created even closer bonds – something Julia hadn't thought possible until Savega.

"What now?" Julia asked, glancing through the rain as the twilight settled in. "Should we go help them clear up the mess your honoured guests made in my café?"

"We should." Dot lifted her teacup in a salute. "But first, I intend on savouring every last drop of this miraculous brew. Oh, how I missed thee."

Rain pattered softly against the windowpane as they sipped their tea, and the comfortable silence between them was a sign that their lives were well on their way back to normal – or as normal, Julia supposed with a smile, as things ever truly were in Peridale.

~

Julia and the gang will be back for a *BRAND NEW* cozy adventure in Peridale later in the year! **Sign-up to Agatha Frost's newsletter** to be the first to find out details!

In the meantime, have you tried Agatha's **NEW** series, Claire's Candles? The first book, **Vanilla Bean Vengeance** is *OUT NOW* and only 0.99/FREE on Kindle Unlimited, and the second, **Black Cherry Betrayal**, is coming May 26th 2020. *PRE-ORDER NOW*!

Thank you for reading!

DON'T FORGET TO RATE AND REVIEW ON AMAZON

Reviews are more important than ever, so show your support for the series by rating and reviewing the book on Amazon! Reviews are **CRUCIAL** for the longevity of any series, and they're the best way to let authors know you want more! They help us reach more people! I appreciate any feedback, no matter how long or short. It's a great way of letting other cozy mystery fans know what you thought about the book.

Being an independent author means this is my livelihood, and *every review* really does make a **huge difference**. Reviews are the best way to support me so I can continue doing what I love, which is bringing you, the readers, more fun cozy adventures!

WANT TO BE KEPT UP TO DATE WITH AGATHA FROST RELEASES? *SIGN UP THE FREE NEWSLETTER!*

www.AgathaFrost.com

You can also follow **Agatha Frost** across social media. Search 'Agatha Frost' on:

Facebook
Twitter
Goodreads
Instagram

ALSO BY AGATHA FROST

Claire's Candles
1. Vanilla Bean Vengeance
2. Black Cherry Betrayal
3. Coconut Milk Casualty

Peridale Cafe
1. Pancakes and Corpses
2. Lemonade and Lies
3. Doughnuts and Deception
4. Chocolate Cake and Chaos
5. Shortbread and Sorrow
6. Espresso and Evil
7. Macarons and Mayhem
8. Fruit Cake and Fear
9. Birthday Cake and Bodies
10. Gingerbread and Ghosts
11. Cupcakes and Casualties
12. Blueberry Muffins and Misfortune
13. Ice Cream and Incidents
14. Champagne and Catastrophes

15. Wedding Cake and Woes
16. Red Velvet and Revenge
17. Vegetables and Vengeance
18. Cheesecake and Confusion
19. Brownies and Bloodshed
20. Cocktails and Cowardice

Printed in Great Britain
by Amazon